The Way U Look Tonight

The Way U Look Tonight

Dianne Castell

BRAVA

KENSINGTON PUBLISHING CORP.
http://www.kensingtonbooks.com

BRAVA BOOKS are published by

Kensington Publishing Corp.
850 Third Avenue
New York, NY 10022

All Kensington titles, imprints and distributed lines are available at special quantity discounts for bulk purchases for sales promotion, premiums, fund-raising, educational or institutional use.

Special book excerpts or customized printings can also be created to fit specific needs. For details, write or phone the office of the Kensington Special Sales Manager: Kensington Publishing Corp., 850 Third Avenue, New York, NY 10022. Attn. Special Sales Department. Phone: 1-800-221-2647.

Brava and the B logo Reg. U.S. Pat. & TM Off.

ISBN 0-7582-1006-X

First Kensington Trade Paperback Printing: April 2006
10 9 8 7 6 5 4 3 2 1

Printed in the United States of America

The Way U Look Tonight

Chapter 1

How could such a little thing make so much noise! Keefe felt every cell of his body tingle as baby Bonnie scrunched up her face framed with soft brown curls and let out another bellow that rattled windowpanes in every corner of O'Fallon's Landing, Tennessee. His stomach knotted, and his brain split with a migraine. He was used to working long hours, being under pressure, performing under hot lights . . . but caring for a baby? How the hell did he get into this?

He came home to help search for Bonnie's mother, that's how!

"Shh, shh," he cooed as he paced the totally pink nursery and held the baby close like he'd seen others do on the set of *Sins and Secrets*. "The sitter's going to be here any minute. She speaks your language; she'll know what to do . . . Least I hope to hell she does." He sang, "Hush little baby don't you cry, brother's going to cook you a big fat . . . pie."

Bonnie yowled louder.

"You're right, you're right, that sucks. I'm no good at this big brother thing. I need Big-Brother 101."

Outside, Max, the four-legged alarm system, went on a

barking spree that wasn't hampered one bit by the wound in his side. The doorbell bonged and Keefe went weak with relief. "The sitter. Bless the sitter." He kissed Bonnie. "We're saved."

He tucked Bonnie in the crook of his arm like a football and sprinted down the stairs to the front door. He yanked it open, then grabbed the sitter's hand, hauling her inside. "Thank God, you're here!" He thrust Bonnie into her arms. "I think I broke this kid. All she does is cry. I was in the shower and she started to holler and I ran out and got my jeans and picked her up, and for the last three hours I've walked and sang and bribed and . . . and . . ."

He cut his gaze from the sitter to Bonnie. "And she's not crying now. How'd you do that? She's smiling." And considering the woman who held her, Keefe understood why. Curly blond hair pulled back into a clip, big brown eyes, petite, familiar . . . except it wasn't a good familiar. Why was that? This gal was way hot. "Is there an off switch on babies I don't know about?"

"No switches, but I should tell you—"

"Never mind." He held up his hands in surrender. "I don't care. All I know is whatever you did worked." He pointed to the silver duct tape holding the diaper together. "And everything I tried didn't work." He let out a long sigh. "Everyone had to go out today, and I got to baby-sit Bonnie, and that's okay except sitting wasn't involved, just a lot of howling. I need a beer; would you like a beer? Iced tea? Tea's good for baby-sitters, right?" He went to shake her hand, but it was full of contented baby. "Damn, I'm glad you're here, I really mean that. Well done, Ms. . . ."

"Cahill. Callie Cahill. I take it you're not the father. Babies can sense if you're not at ease with them. You'll get the hang of it soon enough but—"

"Listen."

Callie held Bonnie over her shoulder, and the baby

looked around as if she were queen of the world . . . which she was. Callie said, "I don't hear anything but a far-off boat horn somewhere and the grandfather clock."

Keefe stroked Bonnie's soft cheek. "And that's the whole point, isn't it, half-pint? Nothing but Mississippi River sounds and home."

Callie's hair was the golden kind of blond, not silver, her figure fuller, nice womanly curves, very pretty. Though Attila the Hun could be standing in the hall keeping Bonnie quiet and Keefe would think he was pretty, too. "Heard you used to nanny for the Louises over in Riverside. Have we met before? When I came home at Christmas?" He gave her his best smile. "I'm going to be in town for a while. Maybe we can get acquainted, go to dinner. I owe you for saving my ass."

She gently swayed as she stood, rocking the baby side to side. "We didn't meet at Christmas, but I've seen you, of course, on TV. Everyone knows Lex Zandor, mob boss and all-around ladies' man, but why no interviews or appearances on *The View* or Letterman or Leno? Bet your fans would like to know more about you."

Keefe hooked his thumbs in his pockets. "My fans get to see plenty. S and S has my shirt off more than on, and if I do one more bedroom scene, I'll set a record for near nakedness on daytime TV. One of the best things about the Landing is being with family. Fans and the press don't have a damn clue where the hell I am. That's why I drive in from New York. Being here is like falling off the face of the earth."

The doorbell rang, and Keefe answered it. A woman, mid-twenties with green eyes, highlighted hair and tight jeans and a fuchsia spandex halter top. "There you are, you no-good creep." She poked him in the chest with her index finger, driving him two steps back inside as she entered. "I've looked all over this blasted state for you. You owe me, Keefe O'Fallon. You owe me big-time, and I'm here to collect."

"Excuse me? How'd you find me? Who the hell are you?"

"Georgette Cooper, and I followed you from New York till we got to Memphis; then I got lost when you left the expressway. But I asked around, and here I am, and I'm not excusing one blasted thing."

"I don't even know you. How could I—"

"I entered that 'Fantasy Weekend Contest with Keefe O'Fallon' that *Sins and Secrets* had, and I didn't win." She jabbed her finger again, her eyes drawing together. "How could that happen? Look at me." She held her arms wide, which was better than getting poked. "I'm absolutely perfect. These"— she jutted her breasts at him—"cost me a damn fortune. I had a complete makeover, head to toe, just for you, just to win. I got sucked, implanted, stapled, tucked and puckered. I want my weekend, dammit. I want my name in the papers, my picture on TV. I want you!"

Oh, shit! He stepped away from the boobs. "Look, I didn't do the picking, I swear. A computer did and—"

"I intend to cause a lot of problems if you don't pay up, buster. That whole contest was fixed. Rigged! That gal who won wasn't as gorgeous as I am. Am I not gorgeous?"

"Absolutely. Terrific. Incredible. Wonderful."

"Don't you patronize me!" She poked his chest again. "I'm going to file complaints with the network and the FCC and anyone else who will listen. I'm going to ruin your reputation unless you pay up. How are you going to make that happen, huh? I want notoriety!"

"I . . . uh . . ."

"Well, you better think of something fast. I'm staying at that Hastings Bed and Breakfast. I want answers, and I want them fast."

She turned in a snit and whisked out the door. She

tramped down the four steps to the circular driveway that separated the rambling white-frame house from the large expanse of lawn and oaks and the Mississippi River rolling beyond. Keefe followed her out onto the porch and called, "Would you settle for dinner at Slim's while you're here? Great barbecue ribs? Cold beer? Fried chicken? The blues? How about that?"

"How about you go to hell!" she shot back as she opened the car door. "I didn't get all fixed up to eat ribs. This is my chance to shine, and I'm going to do it. It's important to me—more important than you can imagine—and you're going to make it happen or else." She climbed in the red Ford, slammed the door shut and sped off, her tires spitting gravel.

Callie joined Keefe as the car squealed onto the main road, Bonnie now asleep in her arms. The kid could sleep through anything . . . except him. Callie said, "Well, so much for dropping off the earth. Next time you have a contest give away potholders."

"Hell, I don't need her making trouble with the studio. I'm up for contract renewal in a month. S and S could kill off Lex Zandor in a shoot-out with the cops or a gang war, and bam, I'm out of a job just like that. Can't believe a contestant followed me here. The press and disgruntled fans have no conscience."

"About that conscience . . ." She looked at him and smiled sweetly. "Maybe you should rethink your position on the press a little." She walked around Bonnie's stroller parked by the side of the house and sat on the porch railing. A puff of summer breeze floated off the Mississippi as a towboat pushed barges upriver, and the July humidity curled Callie's golden hair into spirals. He didn't remember seeing her around when he was in high school, and he sure would have remembered. She must have moved in after he went off to college. She added, "You got it all wrong about publicity; the right kind can be good for your career."

"Or it can kill it."

A silver Honda Civic pulled into the drive. It stopped, and a middle-aged woman in a navy jumper, white blouse and graying hair pulled back tight enough to eradicate the most stubborn crow's-feet wiggled out. Max ran and barked. Callie offered, "Another disgruntled fan? That must have been some contest. It's too late to hide."

"Fuck!" Keefe put his hands over Bonnie's ears. "Oops. Sorry, Little Bit. Hope you didn't hear that." He watched the woman come their way. "I knew that damn contest was a bad idea. But did the producers listen? Hell, no. Drive up the ratings is all they could think about. They're not the one who had women tearing off his clothes outside the studio, throwing themselves in front of his taxi on Madison Avenue and following him all the way home."

"Women like Lex, the brooding, tortured mob boss with a soft spot for women and kids."

"What they like is using me to get their names and faces in the press. They'd run after Barney the purple dinosaur if it would get them what they wanted."

"I take it you had some pretty bad experiences with women lately? I read about that one gal who handcuffed you to a pole in Times Square while she stripped."

"Mr. Keefe O'Fallon?" the woman asked as she tramped up the steps.

He said, "Look, I'm really sorry for the contest and that you didn't win the fantasy weekend. You're lovely, you really are, and the weekend wasn't that great of a time anyway. Lots of reporters and commotion and the limo got a flat tire and the lobster was stringy and—"

"I'm the baby-sitter." She patted her graying bun. "I got lost coming in from Riverside."

"Excuse me?" Didn't he just say that a few minutes ago? This day was not improving.

The woman continued, "Sally, that lady who runs Slim's with her daddy, called me, said you asked her to find you a sitter real fast. Now, I'm not cheap, and I'm charging for mileage, of course, but I know how to mind offspring well enough and make them behave."

Busted! Callie thought as she took in the pinched-faced woman standing in front of her. Keefe pointed to the woman and cut his gaze to Callie. "If she's the baby-sitter, who the hell are you?"

Someone who's had the hots for Lex Zandor for two years, volunteered to get his interview, and one look at his bare chest and low-riding jeans affirmed her choice was a darn good one! "That's what we need to talk about."

The woman stepped around Keefe, dropped a canvas bag on the porch floor and snagged Bonnie from Callie's arms before she could stop her. Bonnie opened one blue eye, then the other, wrinkled her body into a tight mass and yowled.

"Don't you worry about a thing," the real sitter instructed as she clomped inside. "I'm Eleanor Stick, and I'll mind the baby. I get an hourly rate," she continued as she climbed the steps, calling over Bonnie's yelling, "Double after six o'clock and it's getting near that now. I get lunch and dinner served to me, so you better get to it."

Callie stared at the retreating figure. "Are you really going to leave Bonnie with her?"

"Better to leave her with someone who's a liar? Who the hell are you?"

"I didn't lie. I just didn't tell the whole truth, yet, but I was working up to it. In case you missed something, it's been a little hectic around this place for any kind of meaningful conversation."

Keefe glared, and it wasn't aimed at Eleanor. Even with a scowl the man was more handsome in person than on TV, and that was going some. Long sandy hair that nearly reached his shoulders, that killer half smile, those piercing blue eyes with a thin scar at the left corner, incredible biceps, no wonder he was voted Mr. Love-in-the-afternoon. She'd voted for him twenty times, not that she'd ever admit it to a living soul.

This thing she had for Lex Zandor was so . . . juvenile. Being gaga over a TV star was pathetic. But no matter how she tried to talk herself out of it, she was plain loopy over him anyway. "Before you go ballistic, just hear me out. I'm with *Soap Scoops*, and your fans really do want to see more of you off the show."

"Dammit! That's where I know you from. You're one of those nosy reporters always hanging around the studio and getting in everyone's face."

"Other actors cooperate, you don't and we receive a ton of letters wanting your interview with pictures and—"

"What the hell's *Soap Scoops*?"

"A magazine that gives the lowdown on what soap opera stars do in their real lives, their families, their kids, hobbies, charities and—"

"Made-up affairs, erroneous weddings, fake pregnancies, alien abductions, sex-change operations and anything else you can dream up to sell your rag. Out!"

"That's not what we're about. Rags like *The Dirt* do that. They give all soap magazines a bad name. We're about the person behind the character, the real you, though sometimes it's hard to tell the difference. Like the hacked-off expression you have on your face now is the same one you had on *Sins and Secrets* in that episode where you held a gun on that undercover FBI agent and made her strip to see if she was wearing a wire. That was some bedroom scene. Everyone's favorite. And you'd know it if you answered your fan mail, which I'm sure you never do."

It was also the episode where she really started to connect with Lex Zandor—aka, Keefe O'Fallon—because he had a certain inner sincerity, a caring that seemed to shine through to the character he played.

Who was she kidding! The reason she watched S and S was Keefe O'Fallon's dynamite looks and especially his great ass. "Think of an interview as free publicity, a chance to tell your adoring fans about the real Keefe O'Fallon. Give me a chance to make you even more popular."

"I'll give you a chance to get out of here before I call the sheriff. The last interview I did five years ago nearly killed my career before it started. Implied I was gay, had a lover and I was the secret love child of Hillary Clinton and Arnold Schwarzenegger. Try getting any kind of acting gig after press like that!"

Callie folded her arms. "So you had one little bad experience."

"Bad?" His eyes beaded. "Lady, bad is having a waiter spill a drink in your lap. My experience with the rags is way beyond bad. It sucked!"

"Well, you're successful because the fans like you. You're a personality, you owe them and your life is an open book whether you like it or not. It's the price you pay for fame; that's what fame means. If you have some hard knocks along the way, get over it and deal. You're rich, famous." *Gorgeous!*

"Hard to deal when you can't find a job, your rent's due and the fridge is empty. The soaps were the only ones that would give me a chance. I took a small part no one wanted and made Lex Zandor into the mob boss from hell. I'm not risking it all again because you hunt me down and can rock a baby to sleep."

"Well, she's not asleep now. You need to do something fast because she's getting more upset by the minute." Bonnie's crying carried outside, and the big yellow dog sat on the porch and howled in sympathy.

Keefe glared at the dog. "Max, knock it off. You're not helping."

Max howled all the louder, sounding more pitiful, and Callie said, "Least let me calm the baby before I go. Even your dog knows how miserable she is."

"Nothing to calm," the Stick said as she bustled out. "Best to let babies cry is my motto. They get over it in a few hours, and then they know who the boss is." She tipped her chin. "That would be me." She glared at Max, and he yelped and ran under the wicker settee.

Stick said, "I take it that my dinner has been delayed?" She snagged her canvas bag, parked herself in the white wicker rocker and pulled out her knitting. "I'm waiting and not patiently, I might add."

"Get out of here," Keefe growled to Callie, Stick's knitting needles clicking in the background.

"Fine, suit yourself, Uncle Keefe."

"It's brother."

"I'm waiting," grumbled Stick as Callie threw in, "Some big brother." She clambered down the wooden steps and traipsed across the gravel driveway. To think she'd panted over Lex Zandor, even had some wild sexy dreams about the man, followed him from New York just to interview him. Well, Keefe O'Fallon was a long way from Lex Zandor. Lex might be a mob boss, but he had a heart . . . and a great ass. Keefe was a first-class jerk, and she didn't give a flying fig what kind of ass he had!

She got into her blue Taurus rental and fired the engine. She felt ill and not from the interview rejection and having her Lex Zandor fantasies shot to heck, but because there was a baby involved who didn't deserve to be left crying since some egomaniac chose to protect himself and not a child.

What to do? She didn't have any authority to do anything. Callie started off, stopped, then killed the engine.

She got out and doubled back as Keefe jogged down the drive toward her, handsome chin set, hair mussed as if he'd run his fingers through it too many times, a worried look in his eyes and a slight sheen of sweat across his chest that made her a little woozy. *No woozy!* She steeled herself for a fight, determined to get her way for the sake of the baby, reminding herself not to touch . . . anything! "You can yell and threaten me with a sheriff and jail or whatever, Keefe O'Fallon, but I am not leaving Bonnie with that—"

"I just remembered that the Louis kids stuttered and had eye twitches. Now I understand why. How about I'll pay you to take care of Bonnie till someone gets home who knows what they're doing, because I sure don't. I'll get rid of Stick. What do you say, is it a deal?"

"Well, there you go," she said, a little smile slipping across her lips. "I declared you a complete and total dick, and then you redeem yourself, sort of. I didn't expect that."

She started for the house, and he caught her arm, turning her back. "Just like that you agree? No negotiating on the price? No insisting on an interview in return?"

"A baby's welfare is at stake, and right now that's what matters to both of us." Then she patted his very nice, slightly stubbled, incredibly masculine cheek because being this close to Lex Zandor was simply too much temptation, and she hadn't driven four hours to just look at the man. "Consider this a freebie."

Chapter 2

Callie felt her eyes widen to cover half her face, heat cooked her cheeks to red, she was sure, and her heart stopped dead . . . Least it felt as if it did. Freebie! Where'd that crack come from? Why would she even think such a thing?

Fallout from watching Lex fool around with half the population of Crimson Falls for the last two years on TV and then being this close to him for real. She ran up the steps, past Stick and into the house, following the cries to Bonnie's room. An unhappy baby she could deal with; the sexy stud outside was something else.

Get over it, Callie! The man's an actor, and this trip is for an interview and the chance to see him in the flesh. And he has such great flesh! She cuddled the baby into her arms and hugged her tight. "It's all right, sweetie. I'll take care of you. You're going to be fine. I hope I am." She pictured Keefe. "Dear Lord, it's hot in here." She turned on the ceiling fan, but that didn't help at all.

A car came to life in the driveway, and Callie went to the open window framed with pink gingham curtains and watched the Honda disappear down the road. She held

Bonnie's little hand and did a wave to the retreating Civic. "Say, bye-bye, you old battle-ax."

A scent of river and sun and warm earth wandered inside as she found a pair of baby scissors, cut Bonnie out of her duct tape diaper and changed her. A sense of peace and calm settled over the house . . . except for Callie. She was a reporter, interviewed really handsome men all the time, but now . . . here . . . Keefe! She hadn't planned on this. Footsteps sounded up the stairs, and Keefe came into the room.

"Well, I don't know how you do what you do, Callie Cahill, but whatever it is, Bonnie thinks you're the best." He picked up the roll of tape from the bassinet, studied it for a moment, then put it back. "I might need it again."

She handed him a diaper. "The little sticky things go on the sides and hold it together, built-in duct tape."

"I get it now, but when Bonnie's in a snit I sort of freak out."

Callie sat in the rocker, looking into Bonnie's smiling face and focusing on her and not Keefe. "My sister's younger than me, and I cared for her plenty. I also did a ton of baby-sitting."

"Sure wish I had. Do you always follow people you want to interview to their houses and baby-sit for them?"

"Only the pigheaded ones," and the drop-dead hunky ones she couldn't get out of her brain.

"Hey," came a voice up the steps. "Anybody home? Where's the party?" An older man with graying hair, laughing blue eyes and an electric personality so like Keefe's strode into the room, Max at his side. "Christ in a sidecar, boy, you had me worried spitless there for a minute. I saw Eleanor Stick driving out of here like a bat-out-of-hell and feared you might have asked her to start baby-sitting sweet pea. God help us all! Did you ever see those poor Louis kids? They're grown now, but they're all in therapy, have been for years. Always thought Eleanor Stick was the reason why. What was she doing here anyway?"

Keefe said, "Dad, I didn't know Eleanor was—"

"That bad," Callie chimed in, suddenly getting an idea besides the one that wanted to tackle Keefe to the floor. "Eleanor heard about Keefe needing a baby-sitter, but he'd already hired me. I'm Callie Cahill."

She'd seen a lot of expressions on Lex Zandor's handsome face over the last two years, but complete bewilderment wasn't one of them . . . till now. She continued, "Keefe and I know each other from New York. I do some PR work there, and I stopped in for a visit. He's asked me to help out for a while. He's not too familiar with babies, and you all need help around here."

"Well, damn, son." The man gave Keefe a fatherly pat on the back. "That's mighty considerate. You have no idea what a load you've taken off my shoulders. This is the best idea you've had in a dog's age." He rubbed Max's head and added, "Which we hope is a mighty long time."

He said to Callie, "Thelma, our housekeeper who's really more like a sister, got herself engaged and is opening a bed and breakfast. Ryan, Keefe's twin, and his fiancée are back in San Diego wrapping up their lives there before moving home here. Quaid, the oldest, has a month before he's on leave from the coast guard, and I'm trying to run a tow business and have two barge captains gone, one with a broken leg and the other with the divorce from hell. Keefe's trying to help, but like you said, he doesn't know squat about babies. So how long can we persuade you to stay?"

"Dad, this doesn't have to be a done deal. We can interview other sitters who—"

"Why in blazes do a thing like that? This gal has the magic touch with my baby girl. What more could we ask for? She's your friend, you know her and that's plenty good enough for me."

He scooped up Bonnie and held her up, blowing raspberries on her tummy, making her wiggle and laugh. "Daddy's going to get you a bottle of apple juice." He looked back to Callie. "I know what you're thinking. What's an old guy like me doing with little-bit here?"

He did a two-step around the frilly little-baby-girl room, Bonnie cradled in his arms. "I'm having the time of my life, that's what. Least I will be as soon as we get sweet pea's mama back with us." He held Bonnie to his shoulder with one hand and extended his other. "I'm Rory O'Fallon and pleased as punch that Keefe got you to stay. From what I see you're just what we need."

"Dad, maybe we should try and get Thelma back."

"That isn't going to happen and you know it." Bonnie nuzzled against her daddy's neck and held his shirt in her baby fist as he turned for the door. "I'll let you and Keefe work out the details. Bonnie and I need some liquid refreshment. It's a scorcher today." He kissed her hair. "Don't we, baby girl?" He winked back at Callie. "Welcome aboard, Ms. Cahill. Just make yourself at home and don't let big and ugly here send you away."

Whistling, Rory left the room, and Keefe leaned against the crib, looking totally pissed off. "Well, Mary Poppins, what the hell was that all about? If you think you're going to get away with this—"

"Before you go ape-shit over this, hear me out. I've got a plan."

He did the Lex Zandor eye roll. "Oh, I can't wait. This should be rich."

"Hey, it's a great plan. I'm the Queen of Great Plans. I'll get you references so you know you can trust me with Bonnie, and I'll finesse time off from the magazine and nanny here for three weeks. By then your brother will be home, and you'll be more comfortable with taking care of Bonnie. How's that sound?"

"Like a bribe for the interview from hell."

"And pictures."

He stood straight. "No way. No pictures. I should go downstairs and tell Dad everything."

"Except your dad needs help. I can do that. We all win. I get the interview, you look like a hero and your dad has less stress. Where's the downside of this?"

"I'm looking it straight in the eyes. The press! I hate the press!"

"I'll keep your family out of it. I just want you." Did she have to say that! "There's no sense telling Rory who I really am. If he lets it slip, it will turn your life into a three-ring circus. People go nuts if they think they can get their names in a magazine or paper, you know that. Look how that Georgette person reacted. Everyone around here will be hanging all over you and me."

She stood and fiddled with the bunny mobile in the crib because it was safer than looking at Keefe—too handsome, too close and a little vulnerable at the moment. The vulnerable part really got to her. Could a man be barechested and vulnerable? She peeked. Oh, heck, yes! "What if I throw in something else to sweeten the pot so you'll give me a few exclusive pictures?"

"Like what? You going to pretend to be a plumber or gardener, too?"

"What if I get Ms. Spandex off your back? That's got to be worth a few photo ops."

"There is no way in hell I'm doing another fantasy weekend. Every woman who didn't win will camp out on my doorstep in New York, thinking she'll get a turn. The press will have a field day. I'll have a bazillion blind dates. I hate blind dates. One was more than enough."

"On that we agree. Last week I went out with my neighbor's nephew; he thought he was God's gift to women. I think he was a soap opera star." Callie wound the mobile, and "Twinkle, Twinkle Little Star" tinkled as pink bunnies chased each other in a circle. "I'll think of something besides blind dates, and I want ten pictures."

He picked up a stuffed pink kitten, making him look kind of sweet.

"One picture."

Forget sweet. Back to uncooperative and demanding. "Neutralizing an irate contest loser to save your career is worth way more. Nine."

"Two."

"Five, two without a shirt."

"In your dreams, Cahill!"

And he was so right!

"Damn, woman. Why me? Why this obsession over an interview with Keefe O'Fallon?"

Have you looked in the mirror lately, was what she thought, but said, "Because you're a hot commodity. No one really knows the real you, so you're an enigma, the big mystery man. If I get your interview, that issue will sell like mad. If I can stretch the interview to two issues, that's better still, and it gives me a good chance at getting the editor position that just opened up at *Soap Scoops*."

He put down the rabbit and folded his arms. "You really want to be editor of that rag? That's your life's dream? Aim higher. Hell, anything is higher."

"What I want is the money that goes with the job. You have a sister, and so do I. I convinced mine we could afford law school at Duke in the fall, so now I have to make good on my promise. I need that job."

"Get a real one that doesn't exploit others and tell your sister to get a loan."

She put her hands to her hips and gave him a slit-eyed stare. "For your information what I do is a real job, and *Soap Scoops* doesn't exploit, we provide entertainment for our readers. LuLu's depending on me. I can't disappoint her any more than you would disappoint Bonnie. Isn't that why you finagled time off from the soap and drove straight through to get here? Your little sister?"

He swiped his hand over his face and puffed out a long breath. "Seems the one thing we agree on is family loyalty. But I still don't like what you do."

"And I don't care as long as I get my interview and six pictures and wind up getting that editor's job in the very near future."

"Five pictures and I keep my shirt on. And if it wasn't for the fact that Dad and Bonnie like you and that we need help, I'd tell you to take this great plan of yours and go straight to hell with it."

She smiled. "Then it's a deal, without the going to hell part?"

He grunted. "Like I have a choice. Tell Dad you're on board. I'll get your stuff from your car. You can stay in Quaid's room, though he hasn't been home for over a year. He's known as the O'Fallon badass."

"And you're the polished one?"

Keefe gave a quiet laugh that didn't sound all that polished and a lot more Zandor the rogue than O'Fallon. "I'm the actor, and like you said, no one really knows who the hell I am, and I intend to keep it that way."

She smiled sweetly. "Not if I have anything to say about it, Keefe O'Fallon."

Chapter 3

Keefe went out the front door, and Callie entered the big, cheery yellow and white kitchen, a lot different than her one-room efficiency. With LuLu's tuition and apartment at the University of Georgia, money was tighter than a lid on a honey jar. *Okay, where'd that come from?* How long had she been here? Tennessee-eeze was catching.

Rory looked up from feeding Bonnie. "Well, you're still here, so I figure you and Shakespeare came up with some kind of an agreement that'll work. Can't tell you how much I appreciate this. It was great of Keefe to think to hire you."

"I think he was inspired."

Rory chuckled. "And something else is going on. You two got a look about you, like you know something that the rest of the world doesn't, and you're not about to spill the beans." He winked. "I got it. You're engaged and don't want to tell anyone because it'll hurt his ratings, is that it?"

Callie opened her mouth, but no words came out till finally she managed, "Keefe and I are about as far apart as two people can get and still be friends."

"One of those opposite attracts relationships."

"Attracts is debatable, relationship out of the question."

"I didn't just fall off the cabbage wagon, you know. You're not giving me the whole story. I can tell about these things, and I'll figure you two out sooner or later."

He burped Bonnie with the expertise of someone who'd done it a hundred times before and continued, "Keefe's a fine son but takes himself and his acting too damn serious, if you ask me. Always has, maybe because certain people in this town gave him a ration of crap about running around the stage instead of a baseball field. They just didn't get the acting thing from the kid who was an ace pitcher and could have done a hell of a lot with it. When Keefe went out for the role of Oliver instead of going out for the varsity team a lot of people were pissed as hell. One time he played Noah in the church play and filled the whole dang garage with animals, squawking and snorting all times, day and night. The place stunk like a damn privy, and he built a boat in the side yard and—"

"Dad," Keefe said as he strolled into the kitchen and made for the fridge. "You're telling the Noah story again, aren't you?"

"That's what parents do. They got a right for all the hell their kids put them through over the years. You should tell Callie here about *Romeo and Juliet* and the braces getting locked together. Now that's a great story."

Keefe poured orange juice into a glass. He eyed Callie, then poured juice into another glass and handed it to her, the touching of their fingers making her head spin. Least he had on a shirt now. But three weeks of being this close to Keefe and maintaining a hands-off policy could possibly kill her dead from frustration overload.

"Hey," said another man in his late twenties as he entered the back door with Max at his side. "Sorry to interrupt. Didn't know there was company." He patted the dog's head and nodded at the bandage on the animal's side. "How's he doing? And where's Thelma these days? She's always in this kitchen cooking up something good."

"The vet said Max is okay. As for Thelma she's fixing up Hastings House. Heard she even hired a gal to help her out. Thelma's so in love with Conrad Hastings she doesn't know her knee from her elbow."

Rory hitched his head to Callie. "Digger O'Dell, this is Callie Cahill. She's a friend of Keefe's along with something else they're not telling us, but I intend to find out anyway. She's helping to mind Bonnie."

Digger shoved an old beat-up boat captain's hat to the back of his head. "Did he tell you about the time he played Superman in kindergarten and his cape got caught in the school fan and he started flying backward?"

Rory said, "Digger's one of our barge captains, and he's fixing up an old stern-wheeler. His daddy won the tub in a poker game down in New Orleans years ago. How long you been working on her now, Digger?"

"Been playing in the *Liberty Lee* all my life. Fact is, tomorrow I got a meeting with some investors about turning the *Lee* into an excursion boat. I'm running out of cash faster than a pig going downhill on roller skates. Restoring her's eating me alive." He faced Rory. "I came by to help install that new navigation system for the *Mississippi Miss*. Still can't believe an experienced captain like Ryan ran the *Miss* aground."

Rory smoothed Bonnie's hair. "Considering he and Effie were on that tow alone, I'd say they were watching each other a lot more than the charts. Just the same, the system needs an update, and that's what we're going to do."

He stood and handed the baby to Callie. "Since you're here we can bring Keefe with us to help out. Probably going to take till midnight and we'll see you in the morning. If you have any problems, you can call us down at the docks, number's by the phone."

"And," Callie said to Bonnie, "I'll take you for a spin in your stroller, then feed you dinner when we get back."

"Why not wait till tomorrow when I can go with you," Keefe added a little too quickly. "I need to get more comfortable taking care of a baby. That is one of the reasons you're here, and you probably want to get settled in."

He headed for the side door. "Let's get a move on." He let his dad and Digger go ahead of him, then hung back and said in a low voice to Callie, "Remember. Stay inside. And lock the doors and don't answer to anyone but us. I'll show you how to work the alarm system tomorrow."

Callie watched the door close behind Keefe and turned the dead bolt. Little prickles danced across her shoulders, giving her chills in spite of the hot summer day. What was with all this cloak-and-dagger stuff? TV Land rubbing off on Keefe or was there something more going on in this sleepy little river town? Whatever it was, she'd have to wait to find out.

But for now she had a very cute baby to tend to and clothes to unpack and e-mails to get off to let her editor know what was going on and tell LuLu where she was. This had turned into some interview and a whole lot more. But how much more was the big question.

The next afternoon Keefe followed Callie out to the front porch. How the hell had she conned him into all of this? One minute she'd been cuddling Bonnie in a rocking chair like some sappy greeting card, looking all sweet and innocent. The next minute she'd moved into his house for three weeks, and he was coughing up an interview for the privilege.

Not only was Ms. Cahill pretty, smart, capable as hell

and a rag reporter, but she'd outsmarted him. He wasn't sure which irked him more, the outsmarting or the fact that she was one sensational babe who was strictly off limits.

Damn! Why her? Why did he have to find this one attractive? Even in basic khaki slacks and white T-shirt she made his heart beat double-time. He'd avoided her all morning, trying to figure out why he found her special, but got nowhere. He had women falling all over him, so why was he hot for Callie Cahill, the one person who could eighty-six his career with one swipe of a poisoned pen?

She held Bonnie out to him. "Want to put her in the stroller?"

"M-me?"

"That's why we're doing this walk together, right?"

"I needed to talk to you, and this was the best excuse I could come up with on the spot." He looked at the baby and swallowed. Dammit. He'd played King Lear and the Grinch and everything in between. He could darn-well play confident brother. He took the baby between his hands, holding her tight out in front of him.

"Bring her next to you so she'll feel secure."

"Right. Secure." He curled her into his arms and tried to relax. "Howdy, half-pint."

She looked up at him. "I think she winked at me. That's a good sign, right?"

"Or she has gas."

He rocked her for a minute, and she winked again. It wasn't gas; she liked him, and he was overwhelmed by how happy that made him. He remembered to breathe and kissed her head. "I think we're bonding."

"And this time without duct tape."

He carefully placed Bonnie in the stroller, fastened the straps and lifted the contraption down the steps and onto the driveway.

"See," Callie said as she stood beside him, dapples of sunlight in her hair making it more golden than ever. "Not so much as a whimper from the youngest O'Fallon sibling. Babies know if they're safe and cared for. Part of their survival instinct."

Survival. The word struck home. "Is that the kind of instinct I'm going to need around you so every detail of my life doesn't get blown out of proportion and my career shot to hell and back?" He noticed her soft shirt clung to very nice curves and her brown eyes sparkled like aged brandy in a cut-glass tumbler. "You think because you're sexy as hell you can strut in here and I'll give you what you want."

Did he just say what he thought he said? This baby thing had scrambled his brain.

"You . . . You think I'm sexy?"

"Mostly I think you're an opportunist." And that was the part he had to concentrate on.

"Hey. That's not fair. I tried the straightforward approach and asked for the interview, remember? It didn't work, and you threw me out, so you left me no choice but to get creative. I need this interview. I won't print anything that's not the truth."

He pushed the stroller down the driveway. Oaks that had been here all his life and beyond stretched overhead. A tow pushed a string of barges upriver, leaving a trail of white rollers in its wake. Contentment washed over him, except when he looked at Callie. Between liking her a lot because she was really good-looking and not liking her at all because she was a reporter, the woman was the last word in discontent. "What are my chances of getting editorial rights over this damn interview?"

"'Bout the same as you doing handsprings down this driveway and a swan dive into the Mississippi. Where are we going? Why did I have to wait for you to take a walk?"

"We're going to Slim's and to tell Sally her taste in baby-sitters sucks. If we bellyache enough, maybe we can wheedle a plate of ribs."

"You eating ribs, now that's a great shot." She felt in her pocket. "I even have my camera."

They turned onto the road and headed for town. "No pictures until we get rid of Ms. Spandex, that was the deal. As for the town no pictures of that either. I live here, and no one needs to know that." He stared at her. "Right?"

"You're not making this easy, O'Fallon."

"I don't need Lex Zandor fans running around here. It's fine just the way it is. My great-great-granddad started O'Fallon's Transport. He built the docks below the bluff." Keefe nodded toward the river. "The town sprang up because of the river captains and dockworkers. My brother, Ryan, and his fiancée, Effie, are designing a residential area connected to the town and overlooking the Mississippi. Sally's finagling a grant to renovate the place."

They cut across the street to the hardware store and where the sidewalk began. Callie looked around. "Hope they don't renovate too much: River towns are a dying breed. So, we really are going to eat, except you don't have a let's just eat look about you."

"What the hell's that mean?"

"You got that same look as when Zandor broke into the warehouse to save that woman and her daughter from that bad cop."

He studied her hard. "Do you watch all the episodes of *Sins and Secrets?*"

"It's my job."

"Are you blushing, Cahill?"

"It's like a hundred in the shade, O'Fallon. What you're looking at is basic heatstroke." She took Keefe's arm. "You didn't come to the Landing just to baby-sit, and I can maneuver a stroller by myself, and I sure can't get lost

in a town that has one road and a handful of old build-
ings. Why are you here with me now? Don't you trust me
with Bonnie? And why are you here on the Landing in the
first place. Rory could have found local help."

Keefe stopped under the faded blue awning of the bank,
the town mostly empty in the late afternoon heat. Her
hand still held his arm, making him almost as fevered as
she looked. He slipped his arm from her fingers, hoping
that would help alleviate his condition. It didn't. "Two
weeks ago someone tried to take Bonnie, probably to get
her mama to come out of hiding because she's got something they want. They shot Max; that's why he has the
bandage on his side. The whole town's got their eyes peeled
for strangers and knows what's going on, so if you yell,
everyone will come running. Dad thinks the bad guys won't
go after Bonnie again because we're on to them, but I'm not
so sure. If you stroll Bonnie out in the open during the day,
avoid alleys and out-of-the-way places, you'll be fine."

"What's Bonnie's mother running from?"

He ran his fingers through his hair. "She was an office
manager for River Environs, a company that did work on
the Mississippi with levees and docks. They're under investigation for fraud, for overcharging for work done. She
went to the attorney general a year and a half ago saying
there were two sets of books and she had them both. Then
she disappeared. She probably realized they were on to her
and ran."

"To O'Fallon's Landing."

"And worked for Dad using the name Mimi. She knows
how to run an office, and she knows the river. She and
Dad fell in love, planned to marry; then she just disappeared. Two months ago we guess that Mimi recognized
someone from the company or heard something that made
her think they were close by; that's why she left. Then she
had left Bonnie here on Dad's porch so he could protect

her. I'm telling you all this because I'm going to use you. You're a reporter and notice things. If anyone looks or acts suspicious, you'll pick up on it. As a baby-sitter you can ask questions, be a pest, all the things you do best, and no one will think much of it. You have good instincts, use them."

"I take it your dad doesn't know what you're up to?"

"He's got enough on his mind. He thinks I'm here for moral support and to help with the baby. If he knows I'm out here poking around, he'll want details, and I'd rather not get his hopes up. Dad hired a PI, but it seems Mimi's dropped off the face of the earth. The way I figure it Bonnie's the key. As long as the baby's with Dad, Mimi will stay put. I want to find her so Dad knows she's safe, and I want to put away the men who are after her."

"If the bad guys get Bonnie, they'll use her to draw out Mimi."

"Bingo. If you want that interview, you'll have to work for it. And one word about this better not hit the papers. My family has enough problems."

She parked her hand on her hip and glared. "In spite of what you think, I am trustworthy, and the one and only thing we happen to agree on is taking care of little sisters. Besides, I'm here for a story about you, not Bonnie."

"And what's this burst of cooperation going to cost me? A kidney?"

Suddenly she looked dreamy, her eyes kind of rolling around in her head. He knew that look on a woman's face, had seen it hundreds of times from female fans. Holy crap, she wanted him. That was good because he wanted her, too, all warm and soft in his arms, then in his bed. But it was bad in that getting mixed up with a reporter was like jumping into a volcano . . . death by stupidity.

"To get me to cooperate you can buy me anything cooking in there." She pointed to Slim's.

"C-cooking?"

She licked her lush lips. "Whatever's in that building is way beyond cooking. Cooking is meat loaf in the oven. This aroma means food to die for. I'm starving. Standing here inhaling is torture. I want food, O'Fallon, that food." She elbowed him out of the way, commandeered the pusher position on the stroller and took off in a near run. "Come on, time's a wasting."

What the hell! He was thinking sex, and she was thinking food! He needed to get out more. The tabloids might have him pegged as the human sex machine, but like most of their stuff that wasn't true either. Getting it on with a woman who would probably blab everything to the first reporter to shove a microphone in her face was not his idea of a relationship.

"What do they serve?" she asked as they headed down the broken sidewalk.

"Chicken, ribs, sausage, catfish grilling on Slim's back porch. Slim uses a fifty-gallon drum cut in half, and everything simmers long and low and tender, and for God's sake can you slow down a little."

"Can we take Bonnie inside?"

He stumbled to catch up. "Some kids go to their grandparents' and have cookies and milk, Dad takes Bonnie here, and she babbles to BB King and gnaws on a chicken bone. Turned Slim's into a no-smoking bar overnight and got Slim to put a changing table in the men's restroom." He grinned. "A proud papa and his baby girl."

They pulled up to the porch, and this time Callie hauled the stroller up, not waiting for him. Some women wanted money or power. For Cahill it was obviously food. She said, "Rory's the perfect dad. Wish LuLu had more of that. One older sister isn't much of a substitute for no parents. Think I'll get one of everything on Slim's menu. How much money do you have on you? I left my purse at your place."

"How convenient." He stopped and bit back a laugh as he tucked a strand of hair behind her left ear. Callie Cahill was life on steroids. He'd never seen so much enthusiasm for . . . everything. The way she cared for her sister and Bonnie and her love of Memphis cooking . . . She got to him, and that was bad . . . very, very bad. He remembered another time, another reporter. Sasha. She'd wowed him, wooed him and screwed him in more ways than one.

"Come on, what are you waiting for? We have to eat." Callie nudged him toward the door, the contact like a flash of light out of the blue that jarred him to his toes. No contact with Sasha had ever done that. He'd have to keep his distance, use Callie as a baby-sitter and to help find Mimi, and that was all.

Callie opened the door, and he navigated the stroller inside. The familiar recording of Blind Boy Fuller and *Cat Man Blues* flowed over him like a warm spring rain when fishing the river for striped bass. He had the CD at his apartment in New York, of course, but here it was different. Everything was different, slower, down-home, close to the earth, the water, the people.

"We're between the lunch and dinner crowd," he said as they took a table. He sat across from Callie, not trusting himself to sit next to her. He'd want to touch her, look into her eyes, think of ways the two of them could get to know each other better. Stupid, stupid, stupid idea. No reporters! "The towns folk won't arrive till dinner, then later on into the night. More times than not someone will pick up the sax or get to the piano or bring in a guitar." This was good. Keep the conversation light, keep it simple and non-personal. With Callie he sure as hell didn't need personal.

She hauled Bonnie onto her lap. "Do you play?"

"Took piano lessons for three years, then Dad paid me to quit. Ryan got the music genes. He does a mean sax, and when Sally sings it brings down the house."

Sally ambled over and held out her hand to Callie. "I must say you are certainly an improvement over what I sent to Keefe as a baby-sitter."

Callie shook Sally's hand; then she focused on Keefe, her dark brown eyes in perfect harmony with her dark skin. "I swear I didn't know that woman was Cruella Deville till Dad clued me in, and by that time you had already sent her packing, thank God. You sounded so desperate on the phone with Bonnie crying in the background, Eleanor was the only name I could think of on short notice."

She stroked Bonnie's cheek. "Sorry about that, sugar. But now I got the name of a nanny service in Memphis that's supposed to be the best." Sally fished in her pocket and pulled out a paper. "Tot Tenders. They come very highly recommended, and you can call them anytime day or night." She passed the paper to Keefe. "Put it in your wallet in case of an emergency so we never have to go through this again. Can't believe I sent the Stick to you."

Callie said to Sally, "How'd you find out about this so fast?"

"Fast?" Sally's dazzling smile split her face. "It's been twenty-four hours. I knew five minutes after it all happened. That's the way things are around here. Besides, Eleanor stopped and demanded I pay her fifty bucks for sending her on a wild-goose chase."

Keefe grumbled, "Damn, I gave her a hundred just to get rid of her. She'd make a killing on Wall Street. Sort of like you." He said to Callie, "Not only is Sally Slim's daughter, she's the town egghead. MBA from Harvard, investment guru, Wall Street wonder girl."

"And ulcer victim extraordinaire," Sally added, then pulled Keefe's hair, tilting his head back so she could look him in the face. "We do not mention Wall Street and things New York in this fine restaurant. Gives the place bad karma. I left all that crap behind and came home, thank God and Delta Airlines."

She gave Keefe a quick friendly kiss and let him go. "So you brought home the pretty lady of your very own because the locals aren't good enough for a big TV star?" She winked at Callie.

She smiled. "I'm just here to watch Bonnie for a few weeks, but right now I'm supposed to whine for barbecue ribs or anything else you have grilling out back."

Sally laughed and cut her gaze to the door. "You got it, but first you have to tell me who that is coming in. Anybody in poison green and stilettos has got to be related to a soap opera star; it sure isn't typical dress around this neck of the woods."

Keefe let out a long, deep sigh. "Oh, hell, it's Ms. Spandex."

Sally parked her hand on her waist. "Now, there's a descriptive name. Not exactly Paris Hilton but real close. A fan?"

"A pain in the ass."

Spandex gave a little finger wave and sauntered over to Keefe. "Hi there, big boy." She patted his cheek. "Got any ideas about getting us together?"

"I'm working on it." He glanced at Callie. "I hope."

Spandex gave him a sultry smile. "Well, I'll be waiting." She strolled over to the bar, her hips swaying with every step. She hiked herself onto a stool, showing more leg than most women possessed. She said something to the older man next to her, making him laugh and suddenly look ten years younger.

Sally knocked Keefe's head. "Gotten your little titty in a wringer this time, Lex Zandor?"

"This is my week for trouble. The sun, moon and stars have all lined up and decided to dump on me."

"Don't know if heavenly bodies can do that, but they

sure seem to be stirring things up around here one way or the other, isn't that right?" She gave Keefe a sly look that took in Callie. "You two fit together real well. I can tell that right off." Sally strolled off humming a BB King tune.

Coming home had its good points and some tricky ones. Callie said, "Childhood sweetheart?"

"Not exactly sweetheart. More like partner in trouble. Sally, Ryan, and I grew up together. Learned the facts of life when Sally snuck copies of *Playboy* from her daddy's stash and the three of us read aloud in total wonder."

Sally picking up on the fact that he had a thing for Callie was inevitable. But did she have to do it so fast? She'd needle him till he looked like a dog who'd lost a fight with a porcupine. "Got any brilliant ideas what to do with Georgette?"

"Every guy in the place is watching her, and she sure is enjoying the attention. Holy cow," she stage whispered and grabbed Keefe's hand, the sudden contact blowing his mind like confetti out of a popper. "What if we get her interested in someone else, someone like you but better than you. We divert her attention to some hunky guy, and you're off the hook. What do you think of that?"

"Think?" With her hand on his arm he couldn't put two sentences together.

"Georgette? Getting her interested in someone else? Are you with me here, O'Fallon?"

And he so wished he wasn't. He took his hand back. "Uh, right. Georgette." He did a mental headshake. "Except I don't see an abundance of male soap stars hanging around that she'd be interested in. And another thing, who do we dislike that much to hook them up with her?"

"Can we get Quaid to come home? He sounds like someone who can handle Georgette."

"Quaid can handle anything, but he's in Alaska doing sea rescue on Kodiak Island. Don't think he can come home to rescue his little brother from Ms. Spandex, though he'd have one hell of a time with it."

"Okay, no Quaid. So you'll pay somebody. Get a guy who needs money. That'll work."

"Me pay? Why me? This was your show, remember?"

"I have to put LuLu through law school. Besides, I'm going to make you famous with my great article."

"I don't want to be famous. I just want to act, do theater."

Sally brought over a big plate of all things grilled and delicious, put it in the middle of the table along with a pile of napkins, then took a seat. "Okay, what's going on? You two got your heads together, you're planning something." She picked up a piece of sausage and plunked it in her mouth. "Give," she said around a mouthful.

Callie balanced Bonnie with one hand, grabbed a sausage with the other and ate. "Oh, this is good. This is really good." She licked barbecue sauce from her thumb.

"No changing the subject. I know a dodge when I see one. Spill it."

Callie said, "We're trying to divert Georgette's attention from Keefe and get her involved with someone else. He's paying me to get the job done. Any suggestions?"

Sally pursed her lips. "Yeah, think of something else to do. That woman gives a whole new meaning to the term 'high maintenance.' "

Callie found a rattle in the diaper bag for Bonnie. "So, we need someone really, really desperate."

"Honey, I have never in all my life met a man that desperate."

An older woman with dyed red hair, a blue and pink seersucker suit and hobbling on crutches came up to the table. "Keefe O'Fallon? Oh, my Lord, is it really you? After all these years? Usually you buzz in and out of town so fast and keep to yourself we never even know you're here and gone. And to think you got your start right on our own high school stage. This is so exciting."

"Mrs. Stanley? Tenth and twelfth grade English class. How could I forget?" His stomach rolled, and it took all his effort to plaster a smile on his face and not tell her just how much he'd like to forget her.

"You remembered? I'm tickled to my toes. I heard you were in town visiting the family for a spell, and I was wondering if you might help with the summer play."

Keefe reached into his back pocket and pulled out his wallet. "I can always make a contribution to the community theater and—"

"Well, isn't that so nice of you to give of yourself like that, so I know you'll love directing the play they're putting on. I can't because of my ankle, but you could take over. Part of the Education and the Community program for the summer and mostly it's the senior citizens who showed up. They always do for some reason. The play is scheduled in two weeks, *A Hundred Dresses*. All you have to do is put on the finishing touches. They're all ready to go. You can do that for your old teacher, can't you?"

He looked at Callie, who was soaking this all in like a giant sponge. If he didn't do this, something like "Heartless Soap Star Too Good For Hometown Stage" would for sure be the topic of *Soap Scoops'* next issue. He gave Stanley his best Lex Zandor smile because he knew how to fake that. "I'd be delighted to help out."

Then he gave Callie a smug look that reeked sainthood and said *I'm so damn near perfect you'll never find one thing wrong with me for the next three weeks. And*—he added as he felt every muscle in his body suddenly become more attracted to her by the minute—*that includes getting involved with you.*

*   *   *

Callie watched Keefe leave with the teacher, and Sally said, "I don't know what hold you have over Keefe, but it must be a doozy to make him go off with Stanley and agree to do her a favor. She hates Keefe, and the feeling's mutual. I remember one time in a school production of the *Wizard of Oz* she made him one of the monkeys and told him he'd never make it as an actor and he should just quit trying. He was twelve. Rotten thing to do to a kid."

"If Stanley's such a witch, why in the world did Keefe go with her now? He should have told her to take a flying leap off a tall bridge."

"Mentally, I'm betting he did and a whole lot more." Sally stood and smiled. "But he's a theater junkie. If you shine so much as a flashlight in his direction, he thinks he's on stage. But there's more going on this time, and I'm betting the bar you're involved. You and Keefe kind of dance around each other when you're together, all restless like, prowling and sizing each other up for the . . . pounce. You know what they call that around here?"

"If you take the last chicken leg you're dead meat?"

"Foreplay. Be careful, girl. You got the tiger by the tail and just don't know it yet, but it's my guess you'll find out soon enough."

Sally strolled off, and Callie's heart kicked up a notch. Foreplay? She wasn't even sure how foreplay worked anymore. For the last ten years her focus had been on LuLu. Besides, men weren't all that interested in a woman with a younger sister to raise. Callie said to Bonnie in a quiet voice, "Tiger? Don't think I'd know what to do with a tiger if I had one. Been a long, long time since I had . . . tiger or anything that remotely resembled it."

"If you're counting on that baby answering you anytime soon," Digger said as he stood by her table and snagged a sausage, "you need a drink more than I do, and I need one plenty bad."

He looked like the actors she'd interviewed who'd just been kicked off a soap, their dreams suddenly shattered and not sure how to pick up the pieces and go on. She hated those interviews where they had to put on a good front for the press when all the while their lives were falling apart around them. "What's wrong, Digger? Sit down and I'll buy you a beer, and you can tell me about it. Can I help?"

Sally set a long neck down in front of him and claimed the seat she'd left earlier. "Saw you come in looking like you lost your best friend. Anything I can do?"

"Yeah, give me the winning numbers to the lottery. The investors I had lined up for the *Liberty Lee* took one look at her and laughed. They really did laugh, damn their miserable Yankee hides. I should have known a group of suits from Connecticut would never understand a riverboat on the Mississippi."

He ran his hand over his handsome face now lined with fatigue and worry. "What were they expecting? If the *Lee* was perfect, I wouldn't need their dang money. She's docked down at Rory's landing, so she's seaworthy enough. Guess that the paddle wheel being rotted along with the railings sort of put them off. And there aren't any smokestacks yet and some of the windows are still cracked and she's only half painted and . . . Ah, hell, what was I thinking? No wonder they wouldn't invest in the *Lee*. She's still a mess. No matter how much money I sink into her and how many hours I spend, it doesn't seem to make a dent. I need a crew."

"Which means you're desperate for money?" Callie offered as she rocked Bonnie in her arms.

Sally gave a sassy grin. "Uh-oh. Here we go. Digger, if you have any sense, you better high-tail it right for the door and don't stop till you get home. Callie Cahill might sound like a nice, sweet, innocent name, but the girl's got big plans for you, and it ain't going to be pretty."

Sally was fun and smart and friendly and loyal, not something Callie ran across every day in her line of work. There it was mostly a lot of backstabbing for better interviews or inside scoops. "Don't listen to her, Digger, it really is going to be pretty, very pretty. Sally's an alarmist. I got a real sweet deal for you. Something that's going to make your day a whole lot better. What if Keefe pays you to do him a favor? That could give you some extra money. See that good-looking gal at the bar? The favor involves her and getting to know her real well. See, told you it was a pretty deal."

Digger took a gulp of beer and gave a wolfish grin. "Well, hell, you are so right about that. Whatever it is, it can't be totally bad. She's a fox. This is the best offer I had all day, make that all year."

Laughing, Sally picked up a drumstick, took a bite and said, "That's what you think, country boy. You better hold on to your butt; the favor's going to get a lot more interesting, and you're the guinea pig."

Callie continued, "It involves dating the fox. Her name's Georgette. How's that sound?"

Digger's grin dove into a frown. "Like it's not going to happen. Flashy gals want smooth and suave. That leaves me out. I've been raised on the riverbanks all my life and now run barges up and down the river. That's a long way from Miss Long-and-Lean."

"So Keefe can give you a few pointers. When it comes to women he knows all the angles. Then you'll get the girl and get paid for the trouble."

Digger stroked his chin. "So, why are *we* doing this anyway?"

Sally laughed again as she headed off to wait on people

at the bar. "You be careful what you get yourself into, Digger, but I got to admit it'll give us all plenty to talk about around here for years to come."

Callie said to Digger in a quiet voice that wouldn't carry over the music from the jukebox, "Here's the deal. Georgette thinks she got gypped out of a dream weekend with Keefe. We're going to make her fall for you instead."

He rolled his eyes. Me take the place of Keefe? All the pointers in the world aren't going to make me Keefe."

"You'll be better than Keefe, and you'll have fun and a pretty gal on your arm. It's a win-win situation, Digger. What do you say? A pretty girl, a working crew, how can this not be a good thing?"

Chapter 4

Digger didn't know what in blazes to say as he studied Georgette sitting at the bar. Her short white skirt exposed long tan legs that probably went clear up to her armpits, and her green blouse not only matched her eyes, but showed off incredible cleavage that made his eyes bulge and his mouth water. She'd put her hair up on top of her head in a pile of curls, leaving a few sexy strands hanging loose to frame her perfectly made-up face and drive him totally bonkers.

If there was a hotter babe east of the Mississippi, he couldn't imagine who it might be. But why in the world would a gal like that want anything to do with him?

"Well," coaxed Callie. "What do you think? Going out with Georgette is not a life commitment, you know. She's just passing through town and wants—"

"A TV star," Digger added. "She wants Keefe O'Fallon, not me."

"Maybe, maybe not. She sure seems to be having a good time with the guy she's talking to now, and you have all the basic qualities any woman wants." She gave Digger a head-to-foot once-over. "You're tall, well-built, hardworking, handsome, smart, fun—"

"Is this the flattery approach to convincing me?" he asked on a chuckle.

"It's the truth, I mean it. With a little help from Keefe every woman within a hundred miles will be after you, panting at your doorstep."

Digger turned his beer in little circles on the table, watching the sweat rings form on the worn wood. What to do. Getting all gussied up to impress a woman wasn't exactly his style; then again, he hadn't been with a woman in so long he doubted if he had a style. Hell, he wasn't sure if his style even worked! "If I'm going after Georgette, I'll be taking more time away from working on the *Lee*. With running barges up and down the river two out of every three months I'm gone a lot already."

"Keefe will help you fix up the *Lee,* and I'll pitch in when I can. You help us with Georgette, and we'll help you."

Digger raised his eyebrows, a sly grin on his lips. "Tell me, Callie Cahill, does Keefe know about all your great plans for him?"

"It's for his benefit. And then he'll owe me for saving him from Georgette. He'll be thankful."

"He'll be something, all right." Digger rolled his shoulders, the stress of losing the funding for the *Lee* pulling his muscles tight across his back. "Oh, hell. Why not? It's not like I got anything else going on in my life right now. I got a month's vacation coming, and I can sure use the money and the help. Let's do it."

"That's the spirit." Callie beamed. "You won't be sorry." She kissed Bonnie, then kissed Digger on the cheek. "This will be fun for everyone. You're going to be Georgette's perfect beau. You're going to dazzle her, sweep her off her feet."

He grumbled, "I just hope I don't step on them if we have to dance."

"Of course you'll dance," Callie said as she set Bonnie

in the stroller and fastened her in. "And you'll be great. Keefe can teach you. I remember that episode on *Sins and Secrets* where he waltzed at a charity ball. He was pretty good until the bad guys came in shooting up the place. Lex Zandor's been shot so many times his poor old body must look like a piece of Swiss cheese. I have to feed the wee one here or she's going to get crabby, and she can kick up one fuss when she's not happy. I think the saying goes, 'When Bonnie's not happy, no one's happy.' Come on over to the O'Fallons' tonight. Keefe should be done with play practice, and we'll get a plan worked out."

"Play practice? I can't wait to hear that story. And you'll have to tell Keefe his part of this little plan you just cooked up. I got a feeling that little scene is going to make this all worthwhile."

Callie parked her hand on her hip. "He'll love it. I fixed his little problem."

He watched Callie push the stroller to the door and wondered just what the hell he'd gotten himself into this time. Sometimes he was the master of disaster. Getting expelled from school at sixteen and not going back, running away from home a year later that left him living in his car for a year till he swallowed his pride and came back and now thinking he could fix up the *Lee*.

The only real intelligent decision he'd ever made was going to work for Rory O'Fallon and becoming a damn good barge captain. Gave him purpose, friends, money, respectability. He'd never gotten much of any of those things from a family who made their living gambling and swindling folks out of their savings. But that was behind him now, and a pretty woman was in his future, sort of. And he had the promise of money and hands-on help for the *Liberty Lee*. What seemed like a screwed-up day was turning into a damn good one, thanks to Callie Cahill. He didn't know where Keefe found her, but she was a keeper.

Digger gulped down the last of his beer, then headed for the bar, Sally coming his way after serving up a long neck and a smile to another customer. When she got to Digger, he said, "Hey, thanks for the beer. I needed it, and I needed to talk more than anything. You and Callie were just the ticket."

"Callie seems like an okay gal, and she sure has a way with Bonnie, but she and Keefe have got something between them, and I just don't know what." She cut her gaze to Georgette. "And you're sure in for a ride with that one."

"Hell, I hope so. I could use some spice in my life, just like you have going on in yours. Heard there's a cop working with the Tennessee Attorney General's Office who came up here looking for Rory's fiancée and had his eye on you as well. How's that going?"

"Piss poor, not that I'd go telling it to just anyone. Demar, that lily-livered snake in the grass, never leveled with me on who he was and what he was doing here. He played me for information about Rory and Mimi." Sally stepped back and opened her arms wide. "Do I look like a woman who can't be trusted with a little information?"

Digger folded his arms on the bar and leaned forward. "My guess is you had that boy in such a lather he didn't know what to think and probably still doesn't."

She narrowed her eyes. "Don't you go standing up for that jackass. He's long gone, and that's just peachy-keen by me."

Digger cupped Sally's chin in his hand. "Let me know what happens, pretty girl. You deserve the best." Then he winked and headed for the door. Even with her big fancy education and him not even finishing high school Sally Donaldson never made him feel anything but her equal. He'd keep an eye on her, and if this cop guy came back, maybe they'd have a little talk on how men treated women in this neck of the woods and how friends always stood up for friends.

Digger turned for the docks, catching a glimpse of the sun perched on the Arkansas shore sending rays of gold shimmering across the Mississippi. The earth stilled as if waiting for the cool of evening. He'd squeeze in a few hours of work on the *Lee* while he had the light, then head on over to Keefe's and get his take on dating Georgette. Deep down inside Digger felt it was never ever going to happen. He was too rough around the edges, too backwater to ever be appealing to the likes of city-girl Georgette.

Georgette flirted with Mike . . . least she thought his name was Mike. Maybe it was Charlie or Jim. Since she'd developed her foolproof brand of flirting that got guys asking for her phone number and wanting to dance with her she couldn't remember the names of them all. They sort of blended together into one big testosterone blob. Before her days of rounded boobs, flat stomach and jazzy hair no one paid her any mind no matter what she said or how she said it unless they wanted to file for bankruptcy or Chapter 11.

She drummed her perfectly manicured fingernails on the bar and eyed the local-yokel in the beat-up captain's hat as he headed for the door. That guy had been eyeing her since he came in, but a lot of men did that these days. Whoever thought wallflower Georgette Cooper of the stunning—except for her—Savannah, Georgia, Coopers would ever, ever have that experience?

She turned back to Mike, or whoever he was, hoping something he said was marginally interesting, until she heard behind her, "Georgette!"

Oh, God! It was a familiar voice that sent chills up her

spine and turned her stomach to jelly. Slowly she spun on the bar stool, hoping it was not the person she thought it was. But her hoping hadn't worked. "Rachel?"

Georgette blinked a few times to make sure that her eyes weren't deceiving her, that her sister was indeed in O'Fallon's Landing. That alone was astounding. That Rachel—in pristine white blouse, pressed khakis and matching mules and purse—was in a bar in Tennessee was incredible. "What in the world are you doing here?"

Rachel huffed. "Mother sent me, of course. Why else would I be in this dive? She's busy with the wedding and wrestling with the florist over my orchids. It's so awful. We distinctly ordered peach, and the ones they showed us are much too pink. I'm too emotional to handle this catastrophe with only a month to the wedding, so I was sent to deal with you instead."

"Deal?" *Oh, goodie,* Georgette thought as Rachel tossed her shimmering auburn hair in a way Georgette would never master, no matter how many makeovers she had. Rachel glared at Mike. "Excuse us, we have private family matters to discuss." She pulled Georgette off the stool onto her stilettos. "And you and I need to talk right now."

Teetering, Georgette stumbled across the room as Rachel hauled her toward a table in the corner where only one man, dressed in a blue polo shirt, sat sipping a beer. Rachel took a napkin, dusted the chair, gave a quick disapproving glance that only the rich and ultraperfect can do, then sat and pulled Georgette down with her. "So," she started in. "When are you coming home and putting an end to this insane nonsense of running all over after Keefe O'Fallon like some besotted teenager with half a brain? When Mother called you last night and demanded to know where you were she nearly fainted when she found out."

Georgette massaged her left foot and said, "I think I broke an ankle."

"It'll heal. This place is disgusting. Mother would be horrified. I'm horrified. Why are you wearing spandex? Spandex is so . . . tawdry. And lime green? Your chest looks like mounded Jell–O. And green's a disastrous color on you. You need taupe and cream, maybe a splash of persimmon."

"Like I told Mother last night, I'm not coming home."

Rachel leaned across the table a little farther, her mouth pulled into a perfect tight crimson bow—from lipstick or anger it was hard to tell—her eyes shrunk to the size of frozen peas. "Georgette, you're embarrassing yourself and me and Mother and Father and Rex—for God's sake think of Rex—with this foul behavior of yours."

"So tell me, how is the faultless soon-to-be addition to our family?"

Rachel sat back and tsked. "He's wonderful, of course. His father just made him partner in the law firm, and there's talk of running for state representative that will lead to running for a senate seat in the future. We'll live in Washington."

Rex was a slimy pig. He hit on Georgette when she was in her big girl state, which meant he must have hit on every female in Georgia. When Georgette told Rachel she'd brushed it aside, saying it was Georgette's overactive imagination because of her lack of understanding of men. "God help the state of Georgia," slipped from her mouth.

Rachel's eyes widened. "What was that?"

"God bless the great state of Georgia. I'm sure Rex will be a fine senator."

"And I will be the perfect senator's wife, of course. This is all so exciting." For a moment Rachel actually grinned, then sophistication and proper behavior resurfaced, shutting down the full smile to a thin-lipped smirk. "Your bridesmaid dress needs a final fitting; I think you've lost more weight. There are two more showers at the country club for me that Mother's friends insisted on, though etiquette dictates the timing is completely unacceptable. Then there's a luncheon and a dinner and—"

"All of which you can handle fine without me. I'll be in the way. You have a maid of honor. You're having yellow chiffon and tiaras and ten other bridesmaids. I won't be missed."

Rachel folded her hands together on the tabletop. "You're my sister, for crying out loud. How will that look? What will people think? What will the Montgomerys think?"

"Me being in your wedding was not what you wanted but felt obligated to do. We both know that."

"Perhaps, but then you were so . . . large. But now you're not offensive, so all's well. You look pretty good, in fact, except for your ears; they're still too big. Why didn't you have the doctors fix your ears?"

Georgette resisted the urge to feel her ears. Were they really too big? That was the one part of her she thought was okay. "Rachel, I intend on staying here for a while."

Her sister's face pinched in a tight frown, and she drummed her fingers on the table. "Why do you insist on torturing me like this?"

Georgette eyed the drumming fingers. How could they be so alike in some ways and totally different in others? Same genes, same upbringing, same schools.

Rachel continued, "It's still that Lex Zandor thing, isn't it? You're obsessed, you know that? You've lost the dim-witted competition, and it's time to forget about it."

Georgette's stomach cramped, and her shoulders drooped as she felt herself sink into the chair like she always did when Rachel and Mother were around and harping on her about her looks, her friends, her grades, her ideas that never seemed to mesh with theirs. "I didn't have all this work done on me for nothing. I'm going to get Keefe O'Fallon to pay attention to me, and people will notice. For once I want my day in the sun. I want to see what it feels like."

"Lex Zandor is a character on a soap opera. He's a fantasy that didn't work out. Come home, make Mother happy."

"You getting married to Rex-the-wonder-boy is what's making her happy."

Rachel patted her hair and assumed an air of importance, even more important than usual. "She's beyond happy over this engagement to one of the finest families in Georgia. It's her dream come true, what she's groomed us for. I imagine you'll meet someone at the wedding and get married someday, too, and be content."

"I don't want to be just content."

"That's painfully obvious. You have no sense of what's important in life." Rachel checked her watch. "I have a cab waiting out front to get back to the airport. I so hope Mother has this orchid situation straightened out. I'll tell her to expect you in two days. We have a list of things that need to be done, and with your accounting ability you're good at accomplishing tasks. I still can't believe you quit your job for the likes of this." She swept her hand over the room like a reigning queen.

"Thanks."

"It's just a sisterly observation. And for heaven sake sit up straight. You always did have a unique knack for looking . . . ordinary." She stood. "I'll have an airplane ticket waiting for you at the terminal. Be sure you're on that plane in two days or I'll never forgive you, you hear me, Georgette, never and neither will Mother." Without looking back Rachel pranced out the door.

Feeling as if a tornado had swept through the place, Georgette sat back in her chair and pulled in a deep breath. What just happened? The same thing that had happened for the last twenty-nine years of her life, Rachel and Mother. They ruled everything they touched, and that included her, Dad and Ralph. Course, Ralph got to run away from time to time until the dog warden found him and dragged him home, tail between his legs.

All that waited for Georgette back home was unemployment, Rachel saying "I told you so" and the wedding from hell. Gone were Georgette's dreams of making everyone sit up and take notice and being someone important. She wanted a big chocolate sundae with double whipped cream to drown her misery, but that would so mess up her liquid diet and put on two pounds just by looking at it. What the hell was she going to do?

"Hello," said the tall man from the next table as he put a glass of white wine in front of Georgette. He took a seat across the table. "My name is—"

She held up her hand to stop him. "I'm sure you're very nice, but I'm not in the mood for male companionship right now. Go away. My life is in the toilet."

"Maybe I can help you fish it out." He smiled, his black mustache barely moving. The rest of him didn't budge either, and he made himself comfortable as he parked across from her. He smoothed back his hair. "I'm not here to hit on you but to help and not just by buying you a glass of wine. I overheard your conversation with your sister, and I can see why you really wanted to get that weekend with Keefe O'Fallon. She's obviously the shining star in your family, has been your whole life. and you'd like to try it once, am I right?"

"Oversimplified but close enough. But since I lost that contest what does it matter? Unless I come up with a loophole where no one ever has to pay income taxes again my days of notoriety are history."

He leaned across the paint-chipped table and kept his voice under the din to some bluesy song humming through the saloon. "I work for a magazine, and they sent me here to get a story on Keefe O'Fallon, but he's not cooperating. If you can get close to him, find out what he's really like, you can write the story for me. Your name will be all over as the woman who exposed the man behind the star. I'll pay you, get you interviewed on Entertainment Today and radio shows and the like. The only thing is I get to publish the story in my magazine first."

"What is your magazine?"

"Uh, TV Unplugged." He grinned. "We're new. Anyway, this story will launch our publication. Great exposure for us and for you. You're a pretty fresh face, a new voice, and this is a new story."

"If I do something like that my family will go completely ballistic."

"A little revenge for making your life miserable?" He arched his brow. "Least they'll notice they have two daughters and not just one for a change."

As much as that stung it was the truth. Everything was Rachel, Rachel, Rachel. No matter what she did it was always perfect. "And how would I get close to him? I've even threatened to go to the papers and say that stupid contest was rigged, but I'm getting nowhere fast. I'm not his favorite person at the moment."

"There are other ways to get what you want." The man nodded at the table where the local-yokel had sat earlier. "The guy in the captain's hat who was there couldn't take his eyes off you, and from what I saw he's a good friend of Keefe's. Getting close to Keefe O'Fallon's friends is a great way to get close to the man himself. It's a perfect in. Keefe will trust you by association, especially if you apologize and make nice to him and his family. That'll get you into his house, and you can talk to him, his family, see what's going on and what makes the man tick. You should have won that contest. You're incredibly lovely, you know. I personally think the whole Fantasy Weekend thing was rigged just like you said, so you have a right to the fame you were robbed of."

Georgette fluffed her hair like she'd seen Rachel do, but it felt awkward. "You really think I'm beautiful?"

"Incredible, and this is your chance to get even with Keefe and *Sins and Secrets* and to get on your parents' radar as the daughter who takes control of her life and makes things happen. They might be embarrassed, but they'll know you have moxie and are someone to be reckoned with and not just summoned home when a situation arises."

He took a cell phone from his pocket. "This has a digital recorder device built in; it records up to five hundred hours. Your purse has an open top. Just click on the recorder. The play and record buttons are on the side so you don't get confused with making a call. When you're in the O'Fallon house you can record everything, and no one will suspect."

"I just do it when Keefe's around."

"And his dad. He's a pretty interesting character, and I bet he has lots of information about Keefe and the family that would make for an interesting story. Record everything they say in case you want to use it later. You never know what little tidbits of information can grow into something more. Better safe than regret not getting something right."

"This is kind of underhanded."

"It could land you a whole new career in TV. New stars are born like this. Someone sees you on an interview or reads your stuff, and bam, you got yourself a nice spot on a national network. The best revenge is living well."

Georgette eyed the recorder.

"You'll never get this chance again, Georgette. *TV Today* is just what you need."

"Thought you said the magazine was called *TV Un-plugged*."

"Yeah, right. The column you'd be writing for is, uh, TV Today. We're better than all the other TV magazines out there. If you do a good job, the column could be yours on a permanent basis. Just think of the limelight, dressing up in pretty clothes, going to all the best places, chauffeurs, meeting important people, your pretty face everywhere. And you do have a lovely face."

He sat back and shrugged. "If you don't do it, I'll just find someone else around here and give them the chance. You deserve a break. The gold ring is yours for the taking, Georgette. Grab it."

Using his index finger, he pushed the recorder across the table toward her and looked her in the eyes. His were gray, blank, unreadable. "I'm Bob Smith. You can call me every night and play the recording for me so I know what's going on. I really need the information now so I can put this all together and make it work."

"I'm going to need two weeks to write my article. I'd rather meet up with you then."

His eyes went from soft to steel, not that anyone else would notice, but telling people they owed the IRS money had let her witness that look a lot. His mustache twitched. "Ten days. But call me every night and let me know how it's going. Tell me what you find out. My number's on the phone. I guess that'll do, but ten days is the limit."

He relaxed a little, though it looked more forced than for real. "So, tell me, what do you do when you're not sitting here being a beauty queen?"

"Taxes."

He laughed deep in his throat, and her skin prickled. It wasn't a nice laugh but more of a gotcha kind of laugh. "Well, this is your big chance to do more than other people's taxes, Georgette."

Except something felt off, as if Bob was taking a deduction he wasn't entitled to. Then again, she was probably overreacting, and Bob was a fine person who just wanted a story and was willing to get a little pushy to get it. Her experiences with men were nil before her great fix-up, paint-up and beautification project—unless she counted that time in Larry Bender's dorm room when she lost her virginity and decided sex was not all that it was cracked up to be.

"Okay," she said. This was her chance, her time to do something different. If her family didn't like it, too bad. She didn't like them a lot of times either. It was their turn to see what it felt like. "People report on celebrities all the time, so it's not that devious. Now all I have to do is figure out how to get that guy in the captain's hat to go out with me."

Bob took her hand and smiled. "Georgette, with your looks that won't be a problem."

Then why did she suddenly have this queasy feeling as if her problems were just beginning and she should run like the devil and get the heck out of here? She took her hand away. "Maybe I shouldn't—"

"And live in Rachel's shadow for the rest of your life? This is your chance, right?"

Georgette took the recorder and put it in her purse. She couldn't go back to her old life without trying something new. She couldn't let all her efforts and resolutions about changing count for nothing. "Be back here in ten days and I'll have all that you need."

He stood and grinned. "I'm counting on it, Georgette."

Chapter 5

Keefe followed Mrs. Stanley around a small wooden sign in front of the gym that said *Actors rehearsing. Stay out.* He opened the white doors with *Go Rockets* painted in the school colors of green and gold and let Stanley hobble into the gym. The place smelled of musty wax just as it had fifteen years ago when he was there practicing for one play or another. He followed Stanley, the thump of her crutches on the hardwood echoing off the concrete block walls as they made their way toward the elevated stage at the front. He recognized everyone standing there. He'd known them all his life.

"Well, here he is," Stanley said to the eight actors. "Told you I'd get him to come. Now I got to run. I'll see you all in two weeks or so." She turned to Keefe. "If you have any questions, just do what you think best. I trust you. I'll be visiting my . . . uh, sister for a week or so, something to do while I'm hobbling about. I sure can't be jumping on and off the stage to direct."

She flashed a toothy grin, then scurried toward the side door. He'd never seen someone move so fast on crutches, and hadn't she been favoring her left foot before and not her right?

The door closed with a bang behind her, and Keefe eyed the cast. They were older than he remembered, probably sixty-five or so now. There was Joe from the hardware store, who had given him his first after-school job, Nellie, who had run the newspaper and given his acting great reviews, Nick, the retired sheriff who had let him off with more warnings than he deserved, and Betty, who had taught second grade for probably all her life. Hell, she'd taught him how to read. Blanche used to wait tables at Slim's and always served him extra ribs, and Frank had pumped gas by day and played a mean guitar at Slim's at night; more than likely he still did. Roberta and Ty had been tellers at the bank and had taught him how to balance his checkbook.

"How's the play coming?"

"How you been?" Joe asked, shifting his weight from one foot to the other.

"Okay, and how have you all been?" They all nodded and mumbled they were fine but didn't look him in the eye. "Are you all really putting on a play about dresses? You don't look like the dress type."

Nellie shrugged, fiddled with a silver-gray curl by her left ear and looked up at Nick. "Not really."

Joe straightened Betty's collar. "We got to level with you, Keefe, because we know you so well and all and you seem to have gotten yourself into this trying to do the right thing for the community. There isn't any play, not a single line. Stanley lets us in the gym, then goes off and does whatever. We all talk for a while and . . . and that's the end of it. She just thinks there's a play."

"Then what the hell are you doing here? You can talk at Slim's. What the hell am I doing here?"

Betty huffed. "Okay, here's the deal, kid. This play thing is just a front for something else. Something bigger. Something a heck of a lot better; least we all think so." She looked around and lowered her voice. "We're trusting you to keep this information confidential. You're a big-city guy now but try and remember what it's like living in a small town."

She took Joe's hand. "You see, we're sweet on each other. Nellie and Nick are the same way and so are Frank and Blanche and Roberta and Ty. The play gives us an excuse to be together, really together. We come in here big as you please every afternoon. Put the sign out front that says we're rehearsing and no one should enter . . . That was Ty's idea." She winked and gave Ty a thumbs-up. "Then we leave out the side door and come back in a few hours, and no one knows the difference."

Keefe stroked his chin. "Okay, I don't get it. Why do you leave? What the hell do you do?"

"Sweet Jesus, boy," said Nick. "You live in New York City. You're a hip guy; do we have to go and spell it out for you? We fool around."

Keefe felt his eyes bulge. "You . . . you . . ."

"I love Nellie," Nick continued. "But we can't get married. She'd lose her late husband's pension, and for two to try and live off my savings as sheriff is a joke." The others nodded in agreement. "It's the same with all of us. Financially marriage is out because we're on fixed incomes, and there's not much employment around here for the older folks, so we can't supplement incomes. But we enjoy each other socially and other ways, if you get my drift. If the townsfolk figured it out, tongues would be wagging a mile-a-minute and fingers pointing and snickering and the like, and none of us want that. We're all pillars of the community. We're respectable folk, and we have families here. We have to protect our good names. We sure can't have scandal."

Roberta sighed, "My daughter would shrivel up and die if she found out I was sleeping with Ty, and his son wouldn't fair any better. The kids just don't get it. Guess they think they got delivered by the stork."

Keefe arched his eyebrows. "Until Bonnie showed up that's pretty much how I had it pegged."

"Good grief," Betty said, then added, "I don't think Stanley ever caught on to what we were up to and didn't care as long as she got paid. Then she went and won a trip to Vegas from some radio show in Memphis—least that's what we surmise—and now you're here taking over."

Keefe said, "What the hell were you going to do when it came time to put on a play and there wasn't one?"

Ty said, "Figured we'd cross that bridge when we came to it. We'd all get sick or something."

Frank added, "We're desperate here, son. Bible study used to be how we got together before. We'd troop in the front door of Betty's house all proper like with our Bibles in hand and our potluck dinner. Then the other six would sneak out the back and be gone for a few hours. They'd come back; we'd eat and leave through the front door looking respectable as all get-out. Pretty slick, huh?"

"Bible study?" Keefe leaned against the stage for support, half expecting a bolt of lightning to strike them all dead on the spot.

Betty said, "Except meeting three times a week for four years started to look kind of suspicious. There is just so much Bible to study, you know, and none of us could quote scripture for squat. When Ty told Reverend Adler we were reading Matthew, Mac, Luke, and Jack we knew we were treading on thin ice."

"Three times a week? You're all . . . What? Sixty-five? Older? Really, three times a week! Holy shit."

Nellie blushed. "We're not dead, Keefe, just on the better side of fifty, and being retired doesn't mean we retire from everything."

And they had one hell of a more active sex life than he

did! Dammit, he was the young one, the TV star; he should be the one fooling around. Then he thought of Callie, and fooling around was just what he wanted to do. "I don't believe this."

"What's not to believe?"

That they had incredible sex lives and his sucked goose droppings. Damn. "You're right," he said and held up his hands in surrender. "I believe every word, and I'm jealous."

They all gave him a laugh that said they knew he was kidding . . . except he wasn't. That was the pathetic part. "So now you expect me to cover for you?"

"Piece of cake. All you need to do is show up here with us around five so we can enter together and then at eight so we can leave together. And you can come up with a reason there won't be a play. You got two weeks to figure out something."

"Why me? All this so you can have your clandestine affairs?"

"Yep," Nick said. "That pretty much covers it, and since you're the creative one around here and can act for real you can fabricate a lie and make it believable."

Keefe let out a long sigh. "Look, I can't do this. I could never pull it off. There's got to be another way for you to . . . you know."

Ty shook his head. "We've racked our brains, and this is the best we could come up with till Stanley took off. Can't you help us out for old-time's sake?"

"What the hell am I supposed to do here for three hours? Make noises like there's activity? And how do you know someone won't come nosing around?"

Ty pushed a tape into a player sitting on the edge of the stage. He cranked up the volume, and *Dial M for Murder* came to life. "One play pretty much sounds like any other from a distance and through heavy doors. I got it to loop so there's continuous voices. And what you do is your business as long as you keep your mouth shut about our business. No one's going to come in. Adults mind the sign, and the kids don't care diddly about a senior citizens' play rehearsal."

Keefe watched the couples sneak out the side door one at a time. If the CIA needed undercover senior personnel, the Energetic Eight of O'Fallon's Landing were prime candidates. Hell, they were prime in more ways than one, had him outprimed all to hell and back.

It was his choosing, no doubt about that. But even with that damn contest and more women than ever hanging around him, he wasn't interested. They all seemed . . . artificial. Ms. Spandex done a hundred times over and there was nothing appealing about that. Callie might be the press, but she was not a fake. She leveled with him about what she wanted. He hated fake . . . except on the stage where it belonged.

Which was why he couldn't lie for the seniors. He'd help them think of something else . . . but what?

He checked his watch. He'd sneak back to his house and see what was happening there, then come back at eight. He waited a few minutes, then opened the side door to, "Callie? What are you doing here? Didn't you see the sign out front?"

"I never pay attention to signs; it's an occupational privilege." She looked around as she came inside. "I dropped off Bonnie, and Rory said he wanted to feed her. Where are your actors, and why is there a recording on instead of a rehearsal? I wanted to see you in action, take some pictures. Isn't that *Dial M for Murder*? I love that play. The key is the key."

She laughed, the happy sound making him laugh, too. How'd she do that, turn a simple meeting into something more. "So," she pressed. "What's going on? From the looks of things nothing much. How do you feel about sawing and hammering?"

She'd changed from her khakis and T-shirt into one of those long peasant skirts and a red sleeveless cotton blouse with a scooped neck. Her skin was creamy, no suntan for Callie Cahill. She really was a workaholic, but right now she looked as refreshing as a gin and tonic on the back porch.

"I know a saw from a hammer, but other than that I'm a lost cause." And getting more lost in Callie by the minute. "Why do you ask?"

"Well, there's a glitch," she said as she paced in front of the stage. "Not exactly a glitch so much as an added event. Yeah, that sounds better."

"I think this town is full of added events."

"Digger's the one who's going to woo Georgette, and we're going to help him with some suggestions because he feels he's not socially up to the task. In payment for his efforts you're going to give him a nice big check, and we're going to help him fix up the *Lee*."

She had on white sandals, her toenails painted red to match her top. Why couldn't she have changed into a . . . garment bag. "When did this *we* stuff come into play? Georgette was your responsibility in exchange for pictures. How'd I get roped in?" Though just looking at Callie he figured she could probably rope him into anything right now.

"You're Georgette's target. She's making your life miserable. You get to help solve the problem. I did my part by convincing Digger. It's not a bad idea, and it could work with some help. Wanna help?"

"Since I can't think of any other way to deter Ms. Spandex, your way is worth a shot."

She stopped pacing, smiled and held her arms wide. "Well there you go. We actually agree on something. So, you never did tell me where everyone went. Taking a break?"

"That's one way of looking at it. Since we're into a little flim-flam as Dad calls it, here's another secret to add to the list. The play is really a front for the actors to mess around on the side. They're older, living on a fixed income, but that's the only thing fixed about them. They use this time to . . . And then they return and leave and—they're screwing like rabbits." The words hung between them, and their gazes connected.

"Screwing?" she whispered, then swallowed, her eyes dark as the Mississippi in a storm. Golden curls framed her face, the blouse showing a hint of cleavage. God, he wanted to touch her . . . just one touch to see if she was as soft and sweet as she looked. His heart thudded; she could probably hear it. After talking about sex for the last half hour and thinking about Callie and having her here now, what did he expect?

He felt her hair, the silky strands slipping between his fingers. Holy crap, one touch was not near enough. He wanted all of her, and he took her into his arms and kissed her.

His brain sizzled; his body went granite-hard. If she pulled away and slapped him silly, he'd understand, but she didn't . . . Oh, thank God she didn't!

She kissed him back! Her mouth parted, her lips warm, moist, accepting as her arms twined around his neck. His tongue laid claim to hers, and his hands splayed across her back, fusing their bodies. Her whimpers accompanied his primal moan, the sensual sounds drowned out by the recording. *Thanks, Ty, for the tape.*

Her breasts swelling against his chest made him even

more crazy for her, and he backed her against the stage as her fingers wound into his hair and her body wiggled closer to him.

"What are we doing?" she asked in a shaky breath.

His tongue stroking hers suggested exactly what was on his mind. She pulled her head back, her face flushed and eyes bright with the same passion possessing him.

"I don't have a clue, but I really like it," he replied.

Her eyes never left his as her palms trailed down his neck, his chest, then stopped at the snap to his jeans. His skin burned for wanting her and then she claimed his mouth in a wet kiss as she unzipped his jeans. She stroked his erection through his briefs, and the gym tilted on its foundation.

The play droned on, but he had no idea what was said, and when she pushed down his briefs and cradled him between her palms he nearly lost it.

"What if someone comes in," she gasped. "I did."

"They'll get one hell of a performance. Damn, woman, you are something else." Reluctantly he let her go and retrieved a condom. Four shaky hands slid it on, and he looked her in the eyes. "You sure about this."

"Good grief, Keefe!" She scooped her skirt onto one arm, exposing bare legs, a patch of blue silk and soft curls beneath. She hooked her thumb into the waistband of her panties and peeled them down her legs, and she stepped out. She took the lace and stuck it into the neck of his shirt; then she slid her tongue halfway down his throat. Guess that meant yes she was sure.

Heat poured through him, and desire feasted on his insides. He bunched her skirt into his hands, then slid his hands beneath the filmy material and cupped her derriere. She took a quick breath, her eyes wide. "Oh, God."

"Yeah, me, too." The smooth mounds fit perfectly in his

palms, and her legs parted, straddling his. She tucked the material of her skirt into her waistband and braced her arms on the stage. "This is a little complicated."

"Life's complicated." He kissed her again and lifted her as her legs circled his waist. His body shuddered for wanting her, his muscles rippled and slowly he pushed into her, giving her time to adjust to him, till she suddenly arched her hips, taking him in one thrust.

He choked in surprise, his whole body in a fever reacting to the connection that was more mind-boggling than he thought possible. He fought for control, lost it, then climaxed as if this were the first time he'd ever had sex in his entire fucking life. Callie's head swayed back, the scent of her filling his head and her cries of delight mixing with the recording.

He'd done the quickie thing before, but this elevated it to a whole new experience. "Holy moly, Callie," he finally whispered, his lips against hers, the heat from her body a match for his. He rested his forehead against her. "What the hell was that all about?"

"Sex." She panted, then swallowed. "Really, really good sex. I think I'm going to die."

"Dad would be pissed if I killed the baby-sitter." He eased himself out of her and let her down, his muscles like pudding now. Her skirt cascaded over her legs, covering her, but if he said she looked as if nothing happened, he'd be lying. She looked erotic as hell. She took her panties from his shirt and handed them to him. "You can put the condom in these; I have more . . . panties, I mean. Lord, I don't know what I mean."

She blushed. He found it endearing that she behaved that way considering what had just transpired between them in his high school gym. "Recreational sex isn't my thing, but that's got to be some of the best recreation I've ever had. I don't know how or why—"

"It's all my fault." She swiped her hair back from her face. "I . . . I always wanted to make it with Lex Zandor."

He felt as if he'd been kicked in the gut. Every inch of him got ice cold. "Lex?"

She rolled her shoulders. "For over two years I've—"

"Y-you were having sex with a TV character?"

She held up her hand. "What can I say? It's the truth, and today when I came in here there you were and here I was and we were talking sex and then there we were. But it's over now, fantasy is fulfilled. Thanks. It was . . . memorable."

She smiled. "Guess I better be on my way. Rory may need help. I'll see you back at the house. Digger's stopping over later so we can get Operation Georgette under way." Callie took a breath, made for the side door and was gone.

"What the fucking hell?" he said into the empty gym as he stood there like an idiot and adjusted his clothes. "All that great sex was with Zandor?" The door slowly opened. Callie was back. He knew she'd reconsider and realize it was him, not Zandor, she was with and . . .

Except it wasn't Callie. It was a kid about fourteen or so in his baseball uniform. He looked uneasy. Keefe was sure he, himself, looked a whole lot worse than uneasy . . . more like a damn fool. The boy stopped just inside the gym, the door swinging closed behind him. "Are you Keefe O'Fallon? I . . . I want to be in your play," he blurted out all at once.

Keefe hid the panties behind his back. What happened to no one coming into the gym? No one having any interest? This was Grand Central Station. "Look, kid, I—"

"I'm Barry. Mrs. Stanley says I can't act at all and I'm terrible and I should give up the theater, but I can't. I think about it all the time, even act stuff in front of a mirror. I'm such a loser, but I can't help it because I really like being in plays and she won't put me in anything and I just want a chance, just a small part and—"

"Ah, hell."

Barry held up his hand. "Please, just give me a walk-on. I swear I'll work my ass off to make it right." Barry finally took a breath, looking depressed but a flicker of hope shining in his eyes. "Please?"

"The *ah, hell* wasn't for you; it was for me. It's just been a very complicated day." And was about to get more complicated. Stanley strikes again. Damn her miserable hide. "Look, Barry, about that play, there . . . there . . ." *There isn't any play* stuck in Keefe's throat. How could he tell this kid there was no play going on?

Barry was Keefe fifteen years ago right down to the pitcher's glove. Keefe knew how Barry felt, that sick feeling in the gut where something you want so bad you can taste it is out of reach and you don't know how to make it happen. Stanley had demoralized Keefe, and the old goat was not doing the same thing to this kid.

Keefe said, "Come back tomorrow around six, bring a girl about your age who likes to act as much as you do." Keefe gave him a manly kind of grin. "I'm sure you know someone." He went to Barry and put his hand on the kid's shoulder and looked him in the eyes. "And don't listen to Stanley, ever. She's a lazy nutcase who wouldn't know good acting if it bit her in the butt. All she's really interested in is getting paid for doing as little as possible and the school board not finding out about it."

Barry grinned, his eyes dancing. "I . . . I . . . Thanks, Mr. O'Fallon." He grabbed Keefe around the shoulders, hugging him tight and surprising the heck out of both of them. Barry stepped back. "Sorry about that; it's just that—"

"You got a chance. I know what you mean. Call me Keefe; my dad's the mister in our family. See you tomorrow."

"Yeah, tomorrow, wow." Barry floated to the door and

turned back. "Thanks. And you won't tell anyone about the hug, will you?"

"Heck no." Barry blushed and went out the door just as the seniors entered. Was he ever going to get rid of this damn condom that he still held behind his back? "What happened to three hours and everyone coming back here at eight?"

Joe looked at the others, then Keefe. "None of us could keep our mind on . . . Well, you know what I mean. We couldn't concentrate. Are you going to help us, or not? What did you decide? We have a lot riding on this decision of yours."

Keefe said, "Here's the deal. Too many people over at Slim's heard Stanley commandeer me into doing a play. They'll expect a production, or it's going to look more suspicious than the Bible study for all of you."

"Well, dang," Frank grumbled. "A real play? If that don't beat all. Now we got to do a show about a bunch of stupid dresses." He ran his hand around the back of his neck. "Guess it's the price we pay for a little nookie around here."

Little? Keefe wondered what they considered a lot! "It doesn't have to be about dresses. In fact, there are no adult male parts in that play, and it's a kid's play anyway. I'm betting Stanley hoped you'd all get fed up with it and leave, and she could get paid for doing nothing. What about the play *Arsenic and Old Lace*?"

"Don't think I like that 'old' reference," Roberta said in a pout.

Keefe said, "You know the story. Two sisters, an eccentric brother, a con artist and his evil pal. We can use the radio script; it's shorter. We need ten actors, two younger, and I got that covered. We'll meet every night for three hours and—"

"No way," Joe said, holding up his hands in protest. "Too long. We got other stuff on our minds besides this dang play that you got us roped into." He draped his arm around Betty and brought her close, and Keefe remembered how he liked having Callie close. Couldn't he think of something else besides Callie! Hell, she was thinking about Lex!

"Fine. Two hours but we meet every day, and you all have to memorize your lines on your own time and do it quick. No fooling around while you're here. We work hard, and we start tomorrow, six sharp."

This was a good idea. He'd help the seniors and Barry, and it would keep him away from Callie. She might have imagined she was having sex with Lex Zandor, but it was Keefe O'Fallon who couldn't keep his hands off her, even though he knew he had to with every brain cell he possessed. Getting too close to a reporter was a really, really dumb thing to do.

The problem was every cell in his body wanted her again. Not just because the sex was really great, but to clear up once and for all exactly with whom she'd had sex.

Max lay sprawled across the front porch as Callie rocked Bonnie in the swing. Digger had persuaded Rory to join him for a beer at Slim's, leaving her alone to appreciate the sky painted with pinks and blues. A perfect moment, a perfect house, a perfect baby. Tranquility hugged the earth as if paying homage to the glorious moment.

Except it sure as heck wasn't going to last. Keefe would come home, and then what? If he didn't buy her fantasy story of thinking of him as Lex Zandor when they had made love, the situation between them could get real darn embarrassing.

Not for him, of course. Keefe was a player, and Callie Cahill was just another female conquest, another notch on that overly notched belt she'd heard about. The good part was the Lex Zandor lie had come across as a one-time fling that was now over with. And that part was true. Lex or Keefe, or whatever his name, was out of her system . . .

Least that's what she thought till she saw him walking down the driveway with his hands in his pockets, hair mussed and five o'clock stubble darkening his jaw. He looked rough, a little risky, more Zandor than O'Fallon, without a doubt the most gorgeous hunk of mankind God saw fit to put on the earth, and he was not out of her system one bit.

Chapter 6

Callie went cold, then hot, then very hot, just looking at Keefe as he came toward her. What could she say to a man she had just had sex with, but then insisted it wasn't him at all but someone else? How had she gotten into this mess? Duh! She'd screwed around when she shouldn't have.

Maybe she could steer the conversation in the direction of getting Digger and Georgette together and keep the talk far, far away from the gym. Maybe Keefe was as ready as she to forget what happened there. She considered the set of his determined chin and the purpose in his step. Maybe pigs could fly!

Max wagged his tail like a windshield wiper in high gear as Keefe came up the steps. *Think, Callie, think. Say something smooth and sophisticated. Something trite.* "Ah, what's going on with the senior citizens and their sex lives?"

Sex lives was not trite!

He leaned against the post and stared down at her. "I didn't ask them. I've got enough problems with my own sex life and a bad case of mistaken identity. You know this isn't over."

She swallowed. Her insides dissolved into goo.

"When I make love to a woman she knows it's me and not some TV character." Keefe's eyes turned black. "Next time you won't get confused who you're screwing around with. You'll damn well remember it's me."

"Next time?" Was that croak really her pathetic voice? She felt herself blush to the bottoms of her feet.

"Oh, yeah," Keefe said, his voice low and smoky, swirling around her. Her skin prickled and felt clammy, and it had nothing to do with the hot summer night and everything to do with Keefe right here in front of her now. If there was one thing that made a handsome man even more so, it was him wanting a woman and doing whatever it took to get her. And this time she was the woman.

Okay, this had gone far enough. She had to level with him about not thinking he was Lex. It couldn't be any worse than him thinking he needed to convince her. If he did . . . If they did . . . Again . . . "Look, Keefe, about the gym and what I said about you being Lex. I—"

"This isn't about Lex; it's about you and me."

How the heck could she get over this guy when he said things like that? How could she not strap Bonnie in the stroller and ravage Keefe right here on the porch swing. After doing it in the gym the swing would be a snap and a lot more comfortable. She had to stop thinking about Keefe and sex!

She heard voices and cut her gaze to the driveway and Rory and Digger ambling toward the house. Thank the Lord! Nothing like an audience to kill a bad case of raging hormones. "We have company."

"Like I said, this isn't over."

As the two men came up on the porch, Rory said, "Looks like my sweet pea's doing just great." He scooped Bonnie into his arms. "And she's all mine." He swayed back and forth, grinning like the happiest man on earth, and Keefe asked in an even voice, "Did you happen to hear anything about Mimi when you were at Slim's?"

How could he be so calm? She was a wreck. Then again he wasn't the one who lied and got caught. Digger parked in the swing beside her. "If someone is in town keeping an eye out, they're going to hang low and do more listening than talking. They know we're looking for a connection to Mimi's past, and they won't want to make us suspicious. But now that we have contractors coming in for the new residential area strangers are a dime a dozen, so we have no idea who to suspect."

If she looked at Keefe, she'd probably break out in nervous hives, so she tipped her head, focusing on Digger and Rory, and concentrated on keeping the conversation going. "Was Georgette at Slim's?"

Rory said, "You bet. Digger pointed her out to me right off. What a dishy gal. Flirting with some young deckhand I just hired on. She sure can dance. Looked like she was having the time of her life at Slim's tonight, but she kept looking over at Digger here, giving him the eye."

Digger rolled his broad shoulders. "That woman's way out of my league. One look at her and I knew that."

Callie nudged Digger. "You're a barge captain."

"I'm a river rat."

"A very nice, really handsome river rat with great green eyes and a terrific body, who's getting the come-on from the new girl in town."

Digger blushed, and Rory chuckled as Callie added, "You should ask Georgette to go dancing. Take her into Memphis. The town is music central; you can have a great time."

"Except I dance like an elephant with a hernia, and Georgette was looking real good tonight, like she goes to all those fancy places in the big cities. The only dance I know is a country two-step, and then I got to have a few beers in me to do that much."

Keefe said, "Hell, if you can two-step, you got it made. Add a few of your own moves, and you're there. If I can play the part of a mob boss, you can dance."

"What about the slow dancing? That's me leaving the bar three sheets to the wind and walking home real easy like."

Callie said, "There's a radio in the kitchen. I'll get it, and we'll have you dancing like Fred Astaire in no time."

Rory turned for the door. "Okay, that's my cue to skedaddle on out of here. Bonnie and I need our beauty rest. Try not to step on too many toes. 'Course, if my Mimi was here, she and I could show you a thing or two about dancing."

Keefe put his hand on Rory's shoulder. "We'll find her, Dad. I swear it. You know what you used to tell me when things were going right to hell. That goes double from me now."

Rory nodded as if trying to convince himself as much as agree with Keefe. "We have to find Mimi. My baby needs her mama." Rory went inside, Callie following. He said to her, "You best get some beer along with that radio. I'm betting it's going to be a beer kind of night."

She touched Rory's arm, and when he turned she kissed him on the cheek. "If Keefe said he's going to find Mimi, he will. When that man sets his mind to something it happens . . . no matter what it is." She gulped, thinking how she fit into that picture.

Rory smiled, but his weathered face was more worried than happy. "Mimi's out there, and we are going to get her back. I really believe that. And I want you to know I'm real glad you're here. You're good with Bonnie and my son. You understand him, and not everyone does. Got made fun of when he was kid. He and Ryan used to get beat up regular like by a gang of punks at school. Called Keefe pansy and faggot and a lot of other nasty stuff. Then one day badass Quaid came along and saw what was what and set things to right. The three of them have been joined at the hip ever since."

"I thought Quaid was Keefe and Ryan's brother?"

"Quaid came from a crappy home, raised by his grandpa who let him run wild, then walloped him good when he got into trouble. He was a hair away from going to some juvenile detention place, so I took him in. Grandpa was more than happy to get rid of him . . . for a price of course." He winked at Callie. "Never told anyone that before. Best keep it to yourself. All my boys are strong as bears. Ryan made it as a big-time architect in San Diego, Quaid's off with the coast guard, still rescuing folks and still part badass from what I hear. Keefe never gave up on his dreams and made it on his own." Rory nodded. "I like that you keep him on his toes, don't get all moony-eyed over him being on TV and you don't let him get away with anything."

"I think that works both ways."

Rory gave a soft laugh as he headed for the upstairs, Bonnie cradled lovingly in his arms. "I bet it does."

She wasn't sure what that meant, but no matter what happened with her and Keefe she was going to help find Mimi. That mattered more than anything. If there was one thing Callie Cahill understood, it was family first no matter what it took.

She headed for the kitchen, put the radio on a tray along with cold chicken, long necks and pretzels, then returned to the porch. She put the things on a wicker side table and plugged in the radio.

Keefe came over and said, "I'll get the oldies station on.

Those songs are easier to dance to." He flipped through the stations till he found Elton John singing about feeling the love tonight. "That'll do."

Keefe stood and took Digger in a traditional dance position. Digger's eyes rounded. "Uh, what are we doing?" Digger squirmed and gave a quick look around. "Hey, man, if anyone sees us like this . . ."

"Don't worry, you're not my type. Max is sworn to secrecy, and this was Callie's idea, so she's safe. Stand straight, shoulders back and hold your partner tight like you mean it, not like some sissy."

Keefe did those things with Digger and added, "You lead with your hands." He glanced at Callie. "A man always leads with his hands. The pressure tells which way your partner is to go and how fast or slow to move. It sets the rhythm." He directed his gaze to Callie again. "Right?"

Pressure? Fast? Slow? Rhythm? The man was not talking dancing here.

Keefe said to Digger, "Step in a box pattern; it's the basic move in a slow dance. Basic moves are good, but variations and innovations are interesting, too." He cut his gaze to Callie again. "Don't you agree?"

And doing the deed in the school gym was about as innovative as it got.

"How do you know all this?" Digger asked as his feet tried to follow Keefe's. "Guess that's a dumb question since you're a ladies' man living in New York."

"The ladies' man part is the press talking. I learned to dance at an Arthur Murray's studio. When *Sins and Secrets* announced auditions for Lex they wanted someone who could dance. I'd been without a job for so long, I would have learned to fly if that's what they needed. I was broke, so I made a deal with the dance instructor. I'd be a partner for the older women in the class and get the lessons free.

Those gals could outdance me anytime, and when I got the job of Lex they gave me a party and started my fan club. Really helped my career. They were great."

Digger stepped on Keefe's foot for the third time, then pulled away. "I'm not one of the old ladies. I can't do this, Keefe. I can't get everything to move together. My feet go one way, my shoulders the other way." He looked at Callie. "It might help if you two show me how it's done."

Callie nearly swallowed her teeth but instead gave Digger her biggest smile. No way was she slipping into Keefe's arms. It would be like walking into a minefield not knowing what to expect. Oh, nothing would happen with Digger here, but he would leave and then what? After all the suggestive comments and the promise of next time she could only imagine. "Keefe already knows how to dance, and so do I. Let's concentrate on you."

Digger said, "Here's what we'll do; while Keefe dances I'll stand behind him and copy the steps."

Keefe eyed Callie as Elvis sang about a cold Kentucky rain. She didn't know which gave her more chills. He said, "It's just a dance, Callie."

His eyes were dark as he took her firmly into his arms. Their bodies close but not touching, his warm breath on her face. A man in control who really did know how to dance. Too bad she wasn't a woman in control. Bodies moved as one . . . like when they were in the gym. His thigh brushed hers; her hip touched his. Her body tingled, every nerve ending alive and wanting him more than ever.

"Okay," she said to Digger when the song ended, and she stepped away from Keefe, her body temperature close to that of the sun. "Your turn." She slipped her hand into Digger's and slapped his other hand around her waist. "Let's count, sometimes that helps."

Faith Hill sang about a kiss, and dancing with Digger

was like driving a semi that kept running over her toes. Least he wasn't running over her heart, and if she got too close to Keefe, that just might happen.

Keefe stood behind Digger, his hands on Digger's shoulders directing his movements. "That's better," she said. "You're starting to get the hang of it."

Keefe added, "Loosen up. Have fun. Dancing is all about having fun."

She had to get this misunderstanding straightened out with Keefe tonight. She'd tromped on his ego and hurt his feelings. She understood that. If he'd told her he'd imagined she was J-Lo in that gym, Callie wouldn't have liked it much either. She didn't mean to hurt him so much as put space between them. Well, that sure didn't happen. All it did was make him determined, and a determined Keefe O'Fallon with sex on his mind had only one place to go.

She and Keefe took turns dancing with Digger till the beers were gone and the oldies station turned into some midnight talk show where people called in about the problems they had with their love lives. Did relationships have to be so darn stressful, that they even had radio shows about it. Maybe she should call in. Couldn't be any worse advice than the mess she'd gotten herself into.

Digger snagged a handful of pretzels and sat on the porch railing. "You guys have done worn me out. If I can't dance now, it's never going to happen."

Keefe said, "Keep it simple and throw in some turns and dips as you feel more comfortable with Georgette."

Callie sat in the swing and tucked her legs under her as she nibbled a pretzel. She said to Digger, "So, are you going to ask her out or is all this for nothing?"

Digger swiped his forehead. "If I want the *Lee* worked on, I don't have much choice." He glanced from Callie to Keefe. "That was a hint, you guys. Are you two coming to help me paint?"

Keefe grinned. "It's a deal. You lay on the charm and that'll get Georgette off my back. I'll write you a check so you can get what you need."

Digger said, "There is a little problem. What if I crash and burn. What if Georgette won't go with me? Then what happens?"

"Then I pay you for trying, and we still help." He looked at Callie, who nodded in agreement. Keefe added, "I got some new clothes I bought before I left New York. You can have them. Too bad Conrad Hastings sold off his Ferrari or you could borrow it and really wow her."

"I got an old Harley I've been working on. What about that?"

Keefe grinned. "Perfect. The woman wears poison green spandex that probably glows in the dark. She's got to have some fun in her somewhere. Bet she'll jump at a Hog. I'll go get those clothes."

Keefe left, and Digger sat down next to Callie. "So, spill it. What's with you and Keefe? I feel like I've been dancing on eggs all night and it has nothing to do with my two left feet."

She sat up. "Uh, nothing's with us. What do you mean?"

"You guys got something going on, but you're fighting it all the way. It's like Rory said, we don't know the whole story."

"There is no story." Least not one she was going to tell.

Keefe returned and handed Digger some slacks and shirts. "These are Armani, guaranteed to impress the socks off any gal, especially someone like Georgette."

Digger raked back his hair. "This shirt is . . . orange. I'm supposed to wear an orange shirt?"

"It's rust and all the rage in New York."

"Probably get me shot at in Tennessee. I'll ask Georgette tomorrow morning before I lose my nerve and let you know what happens that afternoon when you come to work." He winked. "I'm not letting you forget." Digger gave a little salute, then clambered down the stairs and headed toward the docks.

"Well," Keefe said to Callie. "That just leaves the two of us. Want to . . . dance?"

She stood and paced the porch. "Look, I lied, okay? You have nothing to prove. I knew it was you all along when we were in the gym and not Zandor. If I hurt your feelings, I'm sorry, but I thought it was the best thing to do. We can't get involved, Keefe. You don't trust me. I don't want to be a . . . piece of ass to fill the time while you're here. The gym was a one-time thing, sex on over-drive. Now we steer clear of each other and live happily ever after."

She stopped pacing and peered back at Keefe. He sat on the porch railing, arms crossed over his broad chest. "I know."

An uneasy feeling crept up her spine, and she walked over to him. "You know what? About the hormones?"

"That you lied when you said you thought of me as Lex. If it was true, you wouldn't have been so jumpy tonight."

"You knew that? And you didn't say anything. You let me sweat and go on and on about being a piece of ass?"

"When would I have told you? Digger was here the whole time."

"Oh, that is such a lame excuse. You could have dragged me into the kitchen and said, 'Callie, old girl, the jig's up, I know what's going on. We—as in Keefe and Callie and no Lex—had sex in the gym.' But did you do that? No! Why didn't you level with me? You could have stopped me in the middle of my little speech if nothing else."

"Like you leveled with me?"

Ouch. "I did . . . eventually." She sighed. "And you

eventually did, too, so I guess we're even. Least this confrontation makes being together less appealing than ever. The sex might be good but—"

"The sex is great," he said in a quiet voice that made her insides quiver.

She fought the heat creeping into her cheeks. "Right, great. But that's all, and it's over and we both know it." She snagged up the tray and headed for the kitchen.

"Are you still going to help me with finding Mimi?"

She stopped at the doorway. "Of course. But that and Bonnie are the only connections between us for the next three weeks, so we can stay out of each other's way."

"What about the two of us helping Digger with the stern-wheeler and helping him win over Georgette? And we live in the same house; you're staying in my brother's room. And there's the interview and the photos and eating at Slim's. The Landing isn't all that big, Callie. We'll be tripping over each other at every turn."

"Well, then we can mentally keep our distance, and that's exactly what I intend to do. You have a lot on your mind with the play and the seniors and trying to get a lead on Mimi. I have Bonnie to care for and watching for anything or anyone suspicious. I think we both have enough to keep us busy."

Keefe watched the door close behind Callie, and he ran his hand over his face. Well, hell. That didn't go the way he wanted at all. He'd planned on leveling with Callie and telling her that he knew she didn't think he was Lex. Then they'd laugh over it and get to know each other a whole lot better while they were here at the Landing and maybe sleep together tonight. His dick swelled at the thought. Damn, he wanted her again.

But then what? After three weeks they'd go their separate ways, him at the soap and her beating the bushes for interviews? That didn't feel right either, and she'd never just be a piece of ass. He knew how her eyes danced when she made love, how a whimper crept up her throat when he kissed her neck, how her legs held him just right and how good she felt in his arms. And she cared about his family. That counted for a hell of a lot in his book.

So now what? His plan hadn't worked, no sex with Callie tonight. But what was he going to do about this attraction for Callie Cahill?

Nothing, that's what. Let it go. Hell of a lot easier said than done. He gazed across the driveway to the front lawn and the oaks big and strong like sentries protecting the O'Fallon family. A line of rhododendrons blocked the road; the mighty Mississippi rolled beyond just as it had since the dawn of time. Peace and permanence surrounded him, but tonight it didn't include him.

There was another hour or so before Slim's closed, and conversation and a beer sounded good, get his mind off himself, who was piss-poor company at the moment, and off Callie. Why did his thoughts always circle back to her?

He started down the steps with Max at his side, gravel from the driveway crunching under his shoes, night things scurrying in the bushes, an owl hooting and fireflies playing catch in the trees.

He knew this town and the people like he knew his own name. Most of the people were great. Most of the memories the same, least the ones involving his family were. He crossed the street to Slim's, and Max lay down on the saloon porch to wait as Keefe opened the door. "I'll bring back sausage."

Max wagged his tail, and Keefe went inside. The aroma of great food, good beer and mellow blues surrounded him like a blanket on a cold night. He needed that, something familiar to latch on to.

Sally signaled from the nearly deserted bar, and he ambled over and took a seat. She said, "Howdy, Keefe O'Fallon. What are you doing here at this hour when you got a pretty little thing at home waiting for you?"

She put a beer in front of him and smiled big. "Woman troubles?"

"Isn't it always?"

Unless you are a woman, then it's man troubles." She nodded to a big guy in his early thirties at the end of the bar nursing a beer. "That's Demar, my latest and greatest breakup."

"Doesn't look like Demar's ready to take no for an answer. What happened?"

"He's working with the Attorney General's Office and used me to get information on your family. He was with your dad when they saved Bonnie from the kidnappers." She gave Demar a steely look. "Least he did something right," Sally said as Keefe grinned, held his beer in salute and took a sip. "Surly bastard."

"And you've still got your knickers in a twist?"

Demar ambled on down. He held out his hand to Keefe. "I'm the boyfriend in the doghouse and figured I'd come on down and defend my good name."

Sally gave him an evil look. "The doghouse part is true enough, but the boyfriend part is a figment of your imagination."

"But I'm working on changing that."

Sally tipped her chin. "You can work all you want, big boy. It's not going to happen." Then she gave Keefe a sly smile. "I forgot to tell you the best gossip tonight, and it involves you."

"Ah, hell. Somebody saw me and Callie—"

"Try you and Digger, sweet thing." She winked and pinched his cheek. "I must say the rest of us around here had no idea. Last time I saw Digger he was salivating over that sexy piece from the city in here, and now I hear you and him? Very interesting." Sally laughed.

"Digger?"

She laughed harder. "Rumor has it you and the captain were dancing on your porch real close like to Elton John music."

Keefe choked, and Sally added, "Where would someone get a story like that?"

Keefe took another drink of beer. "It's true."

Sally's jaw dropped, and her eyes bugged.

"Not true that way, true like I was teaching Digger how to dance, part of his plan to hook up with Georgette. He needed a few pointers."

Sally leaned against the bar, and Demar handed her his beer. She took a long drink. "Holy mother of pearl, you had me real worried there for a minute. Thought that New York scene had gotten to you."

"You understand what this means," Demar said.

Sally took another drink of his beer. "Don't remember anyone asking the likes of you."

Demar grinned, swiped a drop from her lips and said to Keefe, "She's really crazy about me." He took Sally's hand and kissed the back. Then he looked at Keefe and added, "Someone's watching you, close. And it's no accident or drive-by encounter. Your house is the last one on the road before it drops down to the docks, and it's blocked from the road by those bushes. You got yourself a spy. Not a bright one since they're spreading rumors."

Keefe felt his blood run cold. "Think they're after Bonnie?"

"I'd say they're out to hurt you. I'd be careful. I hear you got a baby-sitter, and if I were you, I'd keep her and Bonnie with me as much as possible."

"Dad had a security system put on the house, so that should help. 'Course, it would be nice if we used the blasted thing. It's hard to adjust to setting alarms when the Landing's been so peaceful for so long."

Sally said, "Since Demar's hanging around here occupying space at my bar he can help you out if you need him."

Demar gave her a little smile. "Told you she's crazy about me."

Sally smoothed back her curls. "I got to make sacrifices for that little baby, and putting up with you is part of my contribution."

Keefe finished off his beer. He said to Demar, "I'll let you know if I find out anything. I better get back to the house." He stood. "Thanks for hanging out here. You've been a big help."

Demar hitched his chin at Sally and winked. "It's a tough job, but somebody's got to watch out for this one."

Sally sucker punched his arm, but she couldn't hold back the smile pulling at her lips. "He's nothing but a smartass cop."

Keefe headed for the door till Sally called, "Hey, wait up. There's something else."

He turned, and she tossed him a baggie and said, "Sausage for Max. He'll be gnawing on your foot if you forget his treat, and I know he's waiting right outside that door. You need to come home more often; you're starting to forget what living here's all about. Aren't you the one who talked me into getting out of Wall Street and getting myself home?"

Keefe held up the bag. "Thanks for this."

He went outside and fed Max the sausage and took in the dilapidated shops closed for the night as if resting before the next day's business. He remembered the shops painted and kept up with flower boxes and shiny clean windows. With luck and hard work the town would be that way again. Keefe turned for his house, feeling more like a tourist than a resident. And he didn't like that at all.

The front porch was lit. He crept up the steps so as not to wake anyone, opened the door and let himself and Max inside. Tomorrow he'd show Callie how to use the security system Rory had installed. He headed upstairs, reached the top landing and barely missed getting knocked in the head by a baseball bat. "Callie! What are you doing?"

"Keefe?"

Rory's bedroom door flew open. He scrambled into the hall, great-granddad's Confederate sword drawn. He looked from Callie to Keefe. "What the hell's going on," he thundered as Bonnie started to fuss. "Who the hell needed an alarm system with all this homeland security in place?"

"I was just coming upstairs to go to bed."

Callie looked from him to the bat. "Thought you were already in bed."

"Christ in a sidecar," Rory grumbled as he headed for Bonnie's room, the crying threatening to strip the paper off the walls. "You went and woke my sweet pea. If you two don't settle what's eating you, you'll drive us all nuts, and we're not going to get a stick of sleep. Just when you think your kids are off on their own they come back to torment the daylights out of you all over again."

Keefe studied Callie in her pink pj's, baseball bat in hand, nipples nudging through the soft cotton. Fatigue vanished; horniness rode him hard. Callie Cahill was going to be the death of him, and she didn't need a bat to make it happen. She just needed to show up looking like this.

She turned back for her room. "I'll grab a robe and see if I can help Rory."

Keefe headed toward the crying. "I'll see what I can do to help."

She snagged his arm, and he spun around, the contact nearly making him lose his balance, and the deep set of her eyes suggested she felt the same. She said, "Don't. I can do this . . . alone."

"You think alone is better?"

"Definitely." Her voice was hoarse, just a whisper.

"I agree." He could see her nipples bead under her top now, making his dick hard. Since she'd got here he'd spent a lot of waking hours in this condition. He had to get out of here. Painfully he headed for his room. Next time he'd just give the damn interview and pictures and whatever else and take his chances.

Chapter 7

Digger drove the Harley into the circular driveway of Hastings House, killed the engine and checked his watch. Holy shit, it was noon. That meant it had taken him three hours to scrounge up the courage to get here, get off the bike, ring the bell and ask for Georgette. Actually, it had taken longer because the only thing he'd accomplished so far was dragging his sorry ass to their spot. The rest was still in the planning stage.

What would a gal like Georgette ever see in him? She was here for Keefe. Except for the O in their last names, Digger O'Dell and Keefe O'Fallon were as far apart as two men could be. The ladies' man and the reject man. Dang! He turned the ignition, put the Hog in gear, and Thelma McAllister, one-time nanny for the O'Fallons, great cook and now the future Mrs. Conrad Hastings, darted from the front door and stood in front of him, blocking his path.

"Digger O'Dell, you've driven up this blasted driveway of mine three times, making racket enough to raise the dead on that machine of yours. You going to come in and ask Georgette out on a date and go dancing or just buzz around in circles all day driving me nuts? Least this time you shut off the engine for a minute, guess that means you're getting closer to doing something."

As he turned off the motorcycle, Digger groused, "Why don't you just mind your own beeswax."

She craned her neck toward him, her eyes determined. "And whose drive do you think this is? Mickey Mouse's?" She stepped back and pointed a stiff finger at the front door with a shiny brass knocker. "Get going. All this procrastinating's wasting gas and polluting the peace and quiet of my house. Get on with it, boy."

He didn't budge. "How do you know about my plans anyway? It's no business of yours."

She laughed and parked her hands on her hips. "It's the Landing. That makes it my business. You've been living here all your life, so you know that." She nodded toward the front door. "Well?"

"Bossy woman."

"Somebody's got to take charge or you'll be old and gray and still be parked here cluttering up my drive." She stood aside. "I don't have all day. Got a pineapple upside-down cake and scones in the oven. Right now it's me and Georgette Cooper, but I've got another reservation coming in at three. There's work to do, and you better get to it."

"Lordy, woman, you've been telling me what to do like a second mother all my life." Digger hiked his leg over the Harley. He had to ask Georgette out for the sake of the *Liberty Lee* or she'd stay in the sad state she was in now. He straightened his spine and followed Thelma up the brick steps and through the heavy oak door with beveled glass sidelights.

Inside she asked, "Ever been here before?"

"The Hastings and the O'Dells don't exactly travel in the same social circles."

"Same with me but things changed. Conrad's better now."

Digger grinned. "So I hear." He looked around at the polished wood staircase, the gold-leafed portraits, the antique furniture in the front room. "You really keep this place nice, Thelma, but why is there a broken vase on the entrance table here."

"I shot the hell out of it. Was aiming for Conrad at the time and missed. Not like me to do that . . . miss, I mean. It's a reminder to uppity guests to mind their manners."

"And for Conrad to mind his manners as well?"

"There is that. Great conversation piece."

"Pieces." Digger bit back a laugh, suddenly feeling a little less stressed. Least Georgette wouldn't be gunning for him and hitting vases instead. He nodded at the stairs. "Can you get Georgette for me, or do I just go up and knock on her door myself?"

"She's out back on the patio, talking to her sister on her cell phone. I think my back patio is the only place on the Landing with reception. And this time it's not a good thing. The arguing I hear going on makes me glad I was an only child." She slapped Digger on the back. "If you're going to ask Georgette dancing in Memphis, go to BB King's. Get there early, they pack them in like sardines."

He held out his hands. "Thelma, I live here. I know the drill."

"Well, then act like it, boy." She strode off into the living room, and Digger followed the hall straight back to the screen door and the outside beyond. He could hear Georgette talking, and she sounded none too happy. Digger opened the door and stepped onto the brick patio bedecked with baskets of flowers, comfortable wicker furniture, a hammock and an old Memphis-style grill almost as fine as his own. Georgette continued to talk, not paying him any mind. What to do to get her attention? Clear his throat? Say "excuse me, ma'am?" Step on her toe?

"Are you waiting for me?" Georgette finally asked, looking perturbed.

Digger faced her, swallowed, then stabbed himself in his chest with his index finger. "You . . . You talking to me?" This was not going well. He sounded like a country bumpkin, and that was a generous assessment. Mostly he just sounded plain stupid. He was doomed.

Then he thought of the *Lee* and rounded up his courage. "Uh, yeah . . . I know you're talking to me 'cause there's no one else out here. I mean . . ." He closed his eyes to calm down before his heart jumped out of his chest. "I mean, yes, I'm here to talk to you, if you don't mind."

High school boys had more finesse than this.

"Well, what do you want?" She shook her head and held up her hand, warning him not to speak, then said into the phone, "Rachel, someone's here. I have to go. I'm sure Rex is indeed as wonderful as you say." She continued on a sigh, "And I'll be home in time for the wedding just for you." She disconnected and looked at Digger.

Okay, this had to be the worst experience of his life. There had to be another way to save the *Lee*. "I should never have come. Never mind. Sorry I bothered—"

"You're that friend of Keefe O'Fallon's. I saw you in the saloon." Her face softened; the hard glint in her eyes vanished. She smiled at him, though it looked more forced than real, but right now he'd take what he could get. She patted the place beside her on the wicker settee. "Why don't you sit down here and make yourself comfy and talk to me?"

He stared, speechless.

"That is why you're here, right? To see me? Or to admire the flowers?"

He glanced at his shirt and pants. It was the clothes.

Keefe said they would make a difference. He sat and tried not to fidget. She had on white slacks with some red flowers and a red shimmery top to match. The only women he ever saw who looked like this were on the cover of magazines. Heaven help him . . . literally.

"You had something to say?" she purred.

"How would you like to go dancing . . . with me . . . in Memphis . . . tonight?"

"Why, sure."

He nearly slipped off his seat.

"What time?" she asked in a perfect Southern lilt. "Is Keefe coming with us? I mean, he has that baby-sitter glued to him half the time, and I thought they might be joining us for some fun."

"Probably not."

Her face got serious again, and she drummed her fingers against her arm as if considering something. "Well, maybe we could meet up with him for drinks or dinner?"

Digger felt his stomach tighten. "If you're hung up on Keefe, maybe we should forget this." He stood, and she yanked him back down with a force he never suspected.

"Don't be silly," she blurted along with more of her fake smile. "I want to go dancing, with you. Keefe is a curiosity. He is a TV star, after all. You don't run into them every day. I followed him here just to meet him. At first I thought I wanted a date with him, but now I know that's not going to happen." The last part sounded more like a growl than a purr. She continued, "I just want to get to know him better, maybe have lunch, talk. You know, so when I go home I get to say I met Keefe O'Fallon, Lex Zandor of *Sins and Secrets*."

Digger checked his watch. "Well, he should be working on my boat right now." Her eyes widened in surprise, and Digger chuckled as much from pent-up nerves as the thought of a real TV star hammering and sawing and ruining a hundred-dollar manicure. Hard to think of Keefe with a manicure. "We can go see him now if you want."

Georgette sprang from the settee as if she had coils mounted on her butt . . . her very nice butt. "Great idea. We can all be friends. Let's go, but I have to get my purse. Never go anywhere without that. I'll meet you out front."

She took off for the house, and he followed, trying to make some sense of what just went on.

Thelma joined him in the hallway and said, "Well, that had to be the worst example of asking someone on a date I ever heard."

Digger glared. "Women scare the hell out of me. I'm supposed to be protective, but you all seem to know what's going on more than I do. And do you listen to every single thing that goes on around here?"

Thelma gave him a cocky grin, and he added, "That was a dumb question, wasn't it?"

"The dumbest. Seems like she's a bit hung up on Keefe, but if you have a real good time tonight, I bet she changes her tune."

"I still can't get over the fact that she wants to have anything at all to do with me. Doesn't that seem a little strange?"

"Well, maybe a little. I'll have to think about it. But with Conrad and me winding up together I suppose nothing's stranger than that." Thelma patted him on the back. "Don't look a gift horse in the mouth, Digger O'Dell, just go along for the ride."

The door closed upstairs, then another. Digger said, "Thought it was only you and Georgette here."

"And a cleaning lady." Thelma hurried off as Georgette skipped down the stairs. She smiled at him, driving the air right out of his lungs. He gripped the newel post for support. "You look lovely."

"Same clothes I had on before."

"Well, you looked lovely then, too."

"Right. Whatever. Come on, let's go." She hurried out the front door and stopped dead. "A motorcycle?"

"Actually it's a—"

"Nineteen eighty Harley Davidson FLH Shovelhead with police seat. What a beauty."

"My dad won it in a poker game down in Nashville. He ran it into a tree, and I bought it from him. And how do you even know what it is?"

"I'm an accountant, and one of my clients owns a Harley dealership. He takes me for rides because I get him refunds, and he always sends me a Harley calendar. I got hooked. More fun than looking at numbers all day." She looped her purse on her arm, then hitched her leg over the seat. She patted the vacant area in front of her and said on a laugh, "Let's go."

Until now the only thing he and Georgette had in common was Keefe, and an admiration for Georgette's fine looks. But at this moment she was truly happy being with him. Harleys were incredible machines for more reasons than one. Not just awesome transportation, but they impressed the hell out of Georgette Cooper. He climbed on, and she said, "We need helmets."

"I have some back at my place. I usually wear one, but I didn't want helmet hair."

"You should always wear one. Helmet hair beats the heck out of being roadkill."

Smart, funny and beautiful. What a combination! He laughed, feeling as happy as Georgette looked. He turned the ignition, and the Harley came to life, the unmistakable low rumble replacing the quiet. He slid on sunglasses, put the Hog into gear, and Georgette's arms circled his waist, sending chills right through him. With a great bike and a hot babe on the back, life was damn sweet right now.

He took off down the drive, catching a glimpse of

Thelma smiling from the front window. He offered a little salute and turned right onto the main road, giving the bike more power over the country road. Oaks formed a canopy of green overhead; sunlight slipped through here and there as the ribbon of asphalt curved and dipped, offering glimpses of the Mississippi and tows pushing barges. As much as he loved the excitement of being in the wheelhouse of a tow, being here with Georgette was even better.

He took the turn to O'Fallon's docks and glided into the parking area next to his pickup that had definitely seen better days. He killed the Hog and turned to Georgette, her hair a froth of curls, her cheeks rosy and not from the excellent makeup job, but the kind of exhilaration that radiated clear through to her eyes. She was genuinely happy, not forced or phony. She made him giddy inside, which was better than outside. That could be downright embarrassing. "We can walk from here."

"My hair must be a mess."

"You look incredible," he said, meaning every word.

"And you're sweet." She kissed him on the cheek and dismounted. He nearly did handsprings over the front fender. She said, "That was a great ride. You have a great bike." She patted the black seat and pulled out her cell phone. "Just checking if I have reception here."

She pushed the buttons on the side and held it to her ear. "Nope, not a thing." She hooked her arm through Digger's. "But let's talk about your boat. It's here? And Keefe really is working on it today?"

"Rory's letting me tie up and use his equipment to make repairs."

"Repairs?"

"Oh, yeah. A lot of repairs. That's where Keefe comes in. He's helping."

"Then he'll be here for a while?"

"Every afternoon."

Her smile morphed into a full grin. "Well, isn't that nice of him to help you out like that. If you and I are going to spend time together, I'll have to make it a point to get to know him just to see what a really great guy he is."

She wanted to spend time with him? Could life get any better? The love gods had waved some magic wand to make up for all the times they'd pissed on him. He led the way down the path, and they rounded the bend, the Mississippi coming into view. Muddy water lapped the shore, swaying the cattails and scattering dragonflies here and there. Blazing sunlight turned the river's surface into a giant mirror, making it hard to see and upping the temperature into the high nineties. Summer on the river.

He gazed down to the *Lee* floating peaceful like the tired old lady she was, but in his mind he always saw her all fresh and new. If someone could have a love affair with a boat, he did with the *Liberty Lee*.

A few deckhands worked the trip boat *Delta Dee*, getting her ready for a haul upriver. They gave Georgette a male once-over and Digger the *you dog* look.

Georgette dug into her purse, and two phones tumbled out onto the concrete dock. One of the hands picked them up and handed them back, a big dopey smile on his face. "Here you go, little lady. You sure must talk a lot. One of these is usually enough."

Georgette snagged them away. "I . . . I was just trying to get my sunglasses." She dropped the phones back in her purse and pulled out her glasses and slipped them on. "Thanks," she said to the deckhand. Then she pointed and said to Digger, "Is that your boat? Let's go see it." Before he could answer she grabbed a handful of his shirt and yanked him in that direction.

And here he thought Georgette would be all put-off by the *Lee*. Fact was she loved it, just like the Harley. What had he done to suddenly make things go so perfectly?

Perfect was not his usual lifestyle. Keefe came out onto the open lower deck, and Digger called, "Hey."

He looked up and gave a halfhearted wave as Digger held out his hand to Georgette, but she ignored it and hopped on board as if she'd done it all her life. What a gal. He said to Keefe, "You know Georgette."

Keefe's expression was one of *What the hell is she doing here* more than howdy as Georgette offered him her hand. She said, "I'm afraid we got off to a poor start." They shook; then she hooked her arm through Digger's and cuddled close, taking his heart into the danger zone.

Georgette continued, "Now I'm here as a friend and to tell you I'm sorry I caused a commotion at your place the other day." She held her purse in her free hand and waved the other hand at the boat. "This is . . . great. Yep, just terrific. How have you been, Keefe? What are you doing here? Got any plans while you're visiting on the Landing?"

"Well, right now I'm helping Digger. Digger's a fine dancer; you should get him to take you into Memphis and show you around."

Georgette smiled sweetly. "Well, isn't that a coincidence that you would say such a thing. Digger and I are going dancing tonight. Why don't you and that gal you have baby-sitting for you come with us? Sort of a double date. I'd love to hear all about your family and where you live and how you got to be a big TV star."

"I'm sort of busy with this boat and—"

Georgette chimed in. "Then I'll help, too. The boat needs it, and I'll have an excuse to be with you . . . and Digger."

Georgette work on the boat? Digger couldn't have been more surprised if she stole the Harley and roared off into the sunset. "I appreciate it. What kind of work would you want to do?" he asked her.

"I can get everyone water or change the channel on the

radio station when you get tired of it and maybe run for sandwiches or something like that."

"Guess that will work," Digger said, thinking that having Georgette around was more ornamental than substance, and taking another look at her, he decided the ornamental part was just fine and dandy by him. Keefe handed Digger a sheet of paper. "While you were gone the guy from the shipyard in Memphis dropped off this estimate of the materials you need for repairs."

Digger took the sheet. "Wow, this is more than I expected. Delivery is a fortune."

Georgette studied her fingernails, turning her head one way, then the other. "So go into Memphis and get whatever it is you need yourself. I saw a pickup when we parked the Harley, use that to fetch your order. If you need something bigger, I bet you can have one of the tugs here stop in at the marina in Memphis and pick it up for you. I'm sure they have a dock and can off-load there."

Keefe and Digger looked at each other. Keefe said, "That's a really good idea. If it's on the way to a job, Dad wouldn't mind."

Georgette continued, "And the store helps load for free; that's half of the work done for nothing. Like them paying you instead of the other way around."

She let out a sigh and shagged the paper from his hands. "Oh, for heaven sake, let me see that." As she read her eyes drew together, and she made huffing sounds, the kind the tellers did when he didn't add his bank deposit right. She snapped the paper with her index finger. "And they're screwing you ten ways to Tuesday on a lot of other items. First of all there's no mention of a discount for paying cash up front. Always pay cash up front and get a discount unless you have your money tied up in something that's making you a ten-percent return."

"They cut me a deal?"

"Of course. They have use of your money right away instead of waiting on a credit card payout. And why are they charging you more for special orders? Look at this, right there." She pointed to the paper. "They should be quoting less, give you a deduction because there's no stock inventoried for them. When they special order they use your money to purchase and have none of their own money tied up or labor in shelving it. What a bogus charge."

Keefe raked back his hair. "How the heck do you know all this?"

She sighed, "I am an accountant; numbers is my game like being an actor is yours. I try to get away from it, but it always comes back and gets me because someone's messing over someone else and it just hacks me off. I'll call these people and get you a better price."

Digger said, "I don't know how to thank you."

She smiled. "My pleasure. It's lunchtime; I'll walk up to that Slim's place and get us something to eat and make that call. My cell doesn't work down here. When I come back we'll talk and have a picnic. Sure would like to get to know this town better." She looked at Digger. "And about you and all about your friends."

She kissed his cheek and patted his hand, then skipped onto the dock and strolled toward the road they'd come down earlier. Digger watched the gentle swing of her hips, the way she glided instead of walked, the way her whole body moved in harmony, turning him on, making his dick hard and his throat dry.

Keefe said, "Down, boy. She'll be back, and you can ogle more then."

Digger blushed; he could feel the heat rush to his face. "I . . . I—"

"Got it bad," Keefe filled in on a chuckle as he slapped him on the back.

"I was going to say I think she's really smart and . . ."

"Right. You're attracted to her brains. I'm sure that's what's got you hot as a Fourth of July rocket."

"What the hell am I doing? This was supposed to be a business arrangement, a favor to you and now . . ."

"Now you're behaving like any man would when he sees a woman he's really attracted to. Georgette seems friendly. Complete turnaround from when she stormed my house with threats and accusations. I think she really likes you or she wouldn't have changed like that."

Digger watched Georgette take the road up the hill. Never in a million years had he thought a babe like Georgette would be attracted to him. But she truly seemed to be. He was one hell of a lucky guy.

Georgette mumbled curses as she concentrated on stepping around the loose gravel that led down to the docks. She gripped the bag of food from Slim's in one hand and her purse in the other and stopped under the big tree where the road turned for the river. She put down the bag and clicked the side button on the cell phone Bob had given her and laid it on top of her other stuff in her purse. She put the button up so the darn thing wouldn't click off by accident.

Ten days didn't give her much time to get the information for the article, but it was doable. She swatted at some insect that found her makeup tasty. Then pulled her damp blouse from her heated skin. Lugging lunch and getting eaten alive by flying things was not the thrilling weekend she had envisioned with Keefe O'Fallon, but publishing the story about the elusive soap star would make her famous. There'd be plenty of notoriety just like Bob promised. TV interviews, maybe a new job, and her family would certainly sit up and take notice.

She picked up the bag and her purse and headed for the dock. Lord love-a-duck! It had to be a hundred in the shade. Perspiration slithered down her back and between her C-cup boobs. What an improvement from her barely B's where there wasn't enough cleavage to have a between.

She headed to the *Lee,* knowing every guy around had his gaze glued to her. Showtime! She rotated her hips a little more, arched her shoulders back to give them a nice view of enhanced endowments and gave a mental thanks to the modeling course she took that taught her how to move, stand, talk, dress and make herself up.

Waving to Digger, he smiled back, a gleam in his eyes. She'd seen it before when men appreciated what they saw, and they usually appreciated a lot these days. Digger had on work clothes now. They were stained with sweat and dirt, a smear of something across his cheek. Nice enough guy but a basic loser, like she used to be. Then she'd changed, and life was oh, so much better.

"Time to eat," she said as she climbed on board and held up the bag. Keefe came around the corner, shirt off, sandy hair mussed, eyes blue as that new skirt she just bought from DKNY, and she nearly walked right off the boat for staring at him. Now, there was a man!

He grabbed his shirt from the railing and slipped it on, ruining her great view. Digger said, "We can eat up on the top deck." He took the bag from her and pointed to the stairs. "That way. I can take your purse if you want to hold on to the railings with both hands."

"No, thanks," she added a little too quickly. Good grief, she was a terrible spy. Too easily flustered. But she didn't need Digger to see those two phones again. That was weird, and he might start asking questions. She took a breath, smiled sweetly and added in explanation, "My purse isn't heavy, and when I'm out and don't have it with me I feel downright naked."

If the "n" word didn't get his mind off her purse, the man was hopeless. She climbed the stairs and headed down the narrow deck, railing on one side, windows to living quarters on the other side. Bed, couch, table, obviously where Digger lived. Kitchen in the back.

She couldn't imagine staying in such a place. Rex-the-wonderful would condemn it. Probably turn it into something political so he could make a speech, and Rachel would serve up little cucumber sandwiches at the meeting.

Georgette sat at the paint-chipped wrought-iron table under an overhang that offered protection from the sun. Digger turned on a fan that sent up a breeze. Then he sat next to her, with Keefe on the other side. She pulled out sandwiches and sodas and placed her purse on the table. With it being a little flowery thing it looked more like a centerpiece. The phone at the top should pick up everything said. Time to get to work and make her dreams a reality.

"So," she said around a mouthful of veggie sandwich. "Do you guys always get together when Keefe comes into town? What do you do for fun?"

Keefe talked about needing to get out of New York and touch base with friends and family here and how having a little sister was the best thing ever. She asked, "Where's Bonnie's mother?"

Keefe took a bite of dill pickle. "We don't know. Someone's after her because she has information on a company that was defrauding the state out of millions of dollars. If she testifies, some very rich people go to jail."

Digger nodded. "She left Bonnie with Rory for safekeeping. That's why Keefe came home, to help his dad."

Georgette did a mental shrug. She didn't need to know all this family stuff. She needed Keefe-the-manly-man for her article. She said to him, "I heard you like to dance. You sure you can't come with me and Digger tonight?" If she could get some pictures of Keefe dancing at BB King's on Beale Street that would be great for her article.

He said, "You and Digger are just getting to know each other. I don't want to intrude."

She took Digger's hand and smiled at him. "I want to do all the things Digger does. What's important to him is important to me."

The bigger the play she made for Digger and the more attracted she seemed to be to him, the more relaxed Keefe would be that she wasn't going to make waves over the contest. Then he'd loosen up and tell her about himself.

Keefe said, "If I go into Memphis, someone might recognize me. I hate when that happens. It ruins the fun for everyone and some guy gets obnoxious and women start wanting attention and . . . Well, you get the picture."

Great! Now she'd have to spend a boring evening with Digger alone, and there'd be no furthering Operation Keefe O'Fallon. Her only hope was to fake a headache so they could get home early. Then the headache could miraculously get better on the way back, and they could visit Keefe . . . if she could think of an excuse why they should. This spy stuff was very tedious.

"Well," Digger said as he finished off the last bite of sandwich. "We better get back to work." They gathered up the remains and stuffed them in the bag. Then Georgette stood. "And I'll leave you men alone and take some time to get ready for tonight."

Digger said, "I'll run you back to Hastings House."

She shook her head. "No need. I can walk. It's not that far." And maybe she'd stop at Slim's and ask about Keefe there. Get some other views, local-color stuff. She headed for the dock, hoping with all her might tonight wouldn't be as long and boring as she thought.

But by nine o'clock she knew all the hoping in the world hadn't saved her from the most mind-numbing date on planet Earth. Digger and dull were synonymous terms, she decided as she nursed her drink at some little club they found off Beale Street. He'd dressed okay and said all the right things about her new little sparkly dress, and he wasn't that bad of a dancer, but there was nothing to talk about. And that they'd driven here in that truck, an old beat-up rusted hunk of junk, didn't help. Sort of set the tone for the evening.

She leaned across the little table. "I hate to say this, Digger, but I really have a terrible headache. Do you mind if we go?"

"Sure." He looked as relieved as she felt. But how could that happen? She was perfect; guys loved to be with her, though if she wanted to be truthful, they looked more than talked. She picked up her purse and snaked her way through the dancing crowd till they reached the sidewalk. Digger said, "Let's walk for a bit. You might feel better with some fresh air. We'll head for the river. There's a great view, and we can get out of this crowd."

The only thing that would make her feel better was instant escape, except she had to string Digger along in order to get her story. "A walk is a good idea."

"You know, I think we're trying too hard."

She looked at him.

"To make a go of this evening." he added as they jaywalked across Beale Street which was closed to vehicles and teaming with pedestrians. "I think we like each other, but it's not working."

The last part was the understatement of the day, the first part out of the question.

They walked on, the partiers giving way to strollers and the neon signs fading as moonlight on the Mississippi took over. "Tell me about yourself. How you got here."

"I drove?" Too surly. This was not how to keep a guy she had to keep.

He grinned and took her hand in the way a man takes a woman's hand when he's truly interested in her. He had good hands, hardworking male hands with a strong dependable grip and nothing like those soft and squishy office types at Mason, Mackey and Monroe Accounting Offices.

He said, "I mean, what brought you to the Landing chasing after Keefe? You could have any guy you want. I know he's a star and all, but you're more than a soap groupie and interested in some contest you didn't win."

"Nope, actually, that about sums it up."

Talking was better than being bored into a stupor. "And I couldn't always have anyone I wanted. Most of the time I had no one. I used to be fifty pounds heavier on the bottom and three sizes smaller on top. I think that made me a pear. I got tired of being a pear."

He held her away from him and gave her an appreciative look. "You are gorgeous, and I admire that. Not just the obvious physical side, but that you knew what you wanted and went after it."

She'd heard a lot of baloney from guys trying to flatter and impress her but never this line and never one that rang with honest sincerity. "You don't think I'm shallow for taking my appearance to the extreme?" She'd never said that to anyone before but always thought it. Then again, saying it to Digger didn't count because he didn't count. After she got the story she'd never see him again.

"You made your dream come true. What could be wrong with that?"

"And I suppose it's no more far-fetched than wanting to restore an old Mississippi paddle wheeler." She started to laugh.

"You think I'm crazy for doing it, don't you?"

She couldn't take the risk of telling him she thought he'd lost his flipping mind. "You have to follow your—"

"Holy hell." Digger stopped and looked at the telephone pole beside her.

"I was just going to say dream, nothing all that earth-shattering."

He gave her a quick kiss. "Not that."

Not what? Her head started to spin. Her toes tingled. Where had Digger learned to kiss? He was a loser, except the man sure didn't kiss like a loser, even one that fast. On the kissing front he was a pro!

He yanked down the paper with *Reward* printed across the top and a picture. "This is Mimi, Rory's Mimi, but the contact information is not the O'Fallons'. They wouldn't do this because it would make things even more dangerous for her if everyone was out looking for her, and it would drive her farther away." Digger looked at Georgette. "Someone else is after Mimi, and now we have an e-mail contact."

Scrambling to get her brain working after kiss-by-Digger, Georgette added, "Whoever did this is very clever. Phone numbers are too easy to trace. We need to tell Keefe."

What a lucky break. Not only would this bring an end to the date from hell—except for the kiss, that was pure heaven—but she'd get another chance to talk to Keefe. And there was the Mimi factor. A story about Keefe helping to find Bonnie's mother would be a great read.

Georgette grabbed Digger's hand and started for the truck. God, she hated that truck. "We have to go right now."

"What about our date?" He stumbled after her. "The information on Mimi can hold till tomorrow."

"No way. This is really important."

Chapter 8

Keefe lay on his back watching his ceiling fan go round in slow, lazy circles. The nearly full moon cast leafy shadows against the walls as summer insects droned a nightly concert. He loved listening to the sounds of home and the river, and usually they put him right to sleep, except usually Callie Cahill wasn't five damn steps away, all warm and soft and in sexy little pink pj's.

He could still envision her standing in the hallway the other night, bat in hand, ready to bash in his head. Well, it wasn't his head specifically so much as an intruder she'd thought was lurking about the house. Maybe if she'd connected with his head, he'd quit thinking about her. He could still see her face when they'd had sex in the gym, feel her smooth legs around him, feel himself slide so easily inside her.

Ah, hell! He checked the clock. Two A.M. He was never going to get any sleep . . . and with someone knocking on the front door no one in the whole freaking house would either. "God almighty, now what," he muttered as he shrugged into his jeans and grabbed a shirt from the back of a chair and hustled down the stairs. Least it was friend and not foe or Max would be barking his head off.

He opened the door to, "Digger? Georgette? Max. Social call?"

"What's wrong," came Callie's voice in a whisper behind him.

Digger held up a paper in front of him. "We found this in Memphis and thought you needed to know right away, least Georgette thought it was that important."

"What is it?" Callie asked as they both stepped onto the porch and closed the door.

Keefe studied the paper under the porch light. "Someone's offering a reward for Mimi. Oh, boy, and it isn't anyone from our family. Someone thinks she's in the area because of Bonnie, I bet. I wonder what"—he looked at the paper for the name—"M. Perry knows about Mimi, and he must know something because he wants to find her."

Callie said, "Could be that M. Perry is a PI but he's working for someone who wants to know."

Keefe ran his hand over his whiskered chin. "We need to meet this guy."

Digger and Georgette sat in the swing, Georgette cradling her purse in her lap. Callie sat beside Keefe on the wicker settee. Least this time she had on a robe, but she still smelled of warm sunshine and a cozy bed.

Max lounged at his usual perch across the top porch step. Keefe set the flyer on the side table, and Callie asked him, "So, what are you going to do?"

Take you into my bed and have a repeat performance of the gym scene. But he couldn't say that, so he went for, "Go fishing. E-mail whoever this is. We get a reply, and I meet with him and ask some questions and see if he knows more than we do."

Callie smirked. "Like that's going to work, oh, swami of the soap operas. Everyone knows you. M. Perry will take one look at you and realize in a second you want info, not to give it."

Digger said, "So I'll do the meet."

Callie huffed. "That's no better. Everyone around here knows you work for O'Fallon Transport." She beamed. "Guess that leaves little old me. I'll do the meeting, no one knows me at all."

Digger said, "What about Demar?"

Keefe said, "He's a cop and he'd have to tell someone because of the investigation and the whole state of Tennessee would show up and—"

Callie waved her hand. "Hey, yoo-hoo. I'm volunteering here. Anyone hear what I just said? I'll do the meeting. I can handle this." She said to Keefe, "I told you I'd help with finding Mimi, and I meant it."

"Too dangerous. I'm not letting you anywhere near this Perry person. We have no idea who he is."

Keefe's gaze met Callie's, and he suddenly felt as if he'd been zapped by lightning . . . and it wasn't the good kind of lightning that made him all aware of Callie and want to bed her; it was one of those ouch kinds.

Callie growled, "You're not going to let me? Does that mean you're taking away my car and my allowance?"

"It means what I said; it's dangerous."

"I'm thirty, I can deal."

Max bolted up and cocked his ears. Keefe said, "Someone's coming." He pointed down the drive. "There."

Footsteps crunched on the gravel, and he could make out Sally's silhouette; then he recognized Demar's. Sally waved, and Keefe stage whispered, "No discussing this with Demar around; we don't need the cops in on this."

Demar and Sally came up onto the porch, and Sally looked at them. "What is this, a séance in the moonlight or something? Why are you all here at two-thirty in the morning?"

Callie smiled sweetly. "Keefe let me stay up past midnight. I'm all twitterpated."

Keefe put on his casual Lex expression, and Digger sat back looking relaxed. Hell, he should be the one on TV he was a damn good actor. Digger said, "Same reason you're taking a walk. Too nice of a night to waste indoors."

"What's this?" Demar asked as he snagged the flyer from the end table as he and Sally sat in the double wicker rocker. "Where'd you get it?"

Keefe mentally banged his head against a brick wall. How could he forget to hide the paper? It was the lack of sleep getting to him . . . or maybe Callie. But since one caused the other how could he tell the difference?

He said to Demar, "I can't even think of a good lie at the moment. I'll have to go with the truth. We're going to meet up with whoever's at the end of this e-mail and see what they know about Mimi, and I'd appreciate it if you'd forget I just said that."

Demar studied the yellow paper. "These must have gone up recently. The Memphis cops will probably think this is from your family." He nodded at Keefe. "Least they will at first, then ask you about it, and then they'll set up a sting for this Perry person." He studied Keefe. "Just like you are now, except it will take a lot longer. So, what do you have planned?"

Keefe asked, "That means you're going to help?"

"It means I'm going into Memphis with two friends for a beer, and who knows what will happen."

Sally kissed his cheek. "You are a good man, Demar."

Callie said, "Except you'll ruin any chance we have of meeting with M. Perry and seeing what he knows. You guys are all too well known. I should do the meeting. No one knows me. I'll take Georgette with me. We'll be fine."

Georgette gasped, "Me? We? What? Who?"

Sally huffed. "What am I, the B team? I'm coming, too, and before you go all crazy I've got an idea so no one recognizes me."

Callie grinned. "I've got it. We'll all three dress like hookers, gals who know the rougher side of Memphis and all the street people. It makes sense that they would know who's new to the area and trying to keep a low profile. Perry must have some reason to think she's in Memphis. Maybe because it's near Bonnie and she can keep an eye on her baby."

"And," Sally added, "if we're hookers, we'll look like we need that reward money. It's a perfect cover. I am so impressed with myself."

Demar cleared his throat. "Uh, if you three think that we, as in Digger, Keefe and myself, are letting you—"

"See, there's that word again." Callie huffed.

Demar ignored her and went on, "—meet with this Perry person, you are out of your ever-loving minds."

Sally swiped her hand across Demar's cheek and gave him a slit-eyed stare. "I took my kiss back, and now you can kiss my something else instead. You're not telling me what to do, Demar Thacker, just because you're a cop. This plan we just came up with is perfect."

Demar snorted. "Walking down Beale Street looking like hookers is out of the question. What if you get picked up? You're not doing it, period, end of discussion."

Georgette sat back and said, "Well, thank God for that." And Sally said, "We're not going to do an FBI take-down, Demar, just make the contact, and you badasses can be right there with us, just at another table."

Keefe said, "Not happening. Digger, Demar and I will wear baseball hats and dress down and meet at some bar with Perry. No one will know us."

Sally sat back in the wicker rocker. "That is the worst, most unimaginative plan I have ever heard in my life. It's fraught with problems. Don't you think Perry will suspect that the O'Fallons will want to get a hold of him and already have his guard up? And, someone on the Memphis

PD is bound to blow Demar's cover. Everyone knows Lex Zandor—I don't care what kind of hat you wear—and every woman will come squealing your way, and the M. Perry lead will be gone for good."

Demar rolled his shoulders. "We'll take our chances. It's the best we have on the table right now."

Callie said, "No, it's not, that's the whole point."

Keefe said, "It's the safest and most intelligent idea, how's that?"

"Inaccurate," Sally groused, and Keefe added, "Callie, you have a computer, and Ryan had this place wired for high-speed Internet when he was here. We'll contact Perry right now and get going on this before the police get involved . . . except for the one who's already involved."

Callie sighed and stood. "I'm doing this under protest, you understand. It's a terrible waste of a good lead because men think they know everything."

She turned for the door, giving him a glimpse of very shapely legs and those damn pink shortie pajamas—except he didn't need to be distracted. He needed to focus on this meeting and getting Mimi back and staying away from reporters in cute jammies.

Sally pursed her lips. "I'm bummed."

Demar patted her leg affectionately. "It's for the best, girl."

Sally plucked his hand up as if it were a dead skunk and dropped it back on his own leg. "I doubt that, and you can just keep your paws to yourself."

Callie came back outside and reclaimed her seat. She flipped open her laptop, hit the keys to bring her computer to life and pulled up her e-mail account. "Okay, any suggestions on what to say to this M. Perry person besides no person in their right mind will fall for this stupid hoax but I'm sending it anyway?"

Demar stood and paced. "Keep it simple."

Callie said, "Since you're hell-bent on this how about saying"—she typed—"We've seen the lady in the photo and know where she's hiding out."

Sally added, "Meet tomorrow at nine at Kerby's on Peabody."

Callie typed it in and said, "We should include that we know about her baby. That way Perry's assured you've made contact with Mimi and know something about her and it's not a wild-goose chase."

Callie put in the information, then gazed at the others. "Anything else? Not that it matters because this idea is so doomed."

Keefe huffed. "Will you just send it?"

"There," she said after she hit the send key. "Done."

Demar checked his watch. "It's after three. We won't get a reply till tomorrow, and we've gotten into enough trouble for one night."

Callie sighed, moonlight playing in her hair making Keefe want to do the same. She said, "I'll let everyone know as soon as I hear from Perry."

Demar and Sally walked down the drive. Georgette and Digger left in his pickup while Keefe leaned against the porch post. "I think this is going to work."

"I think you're delusional or Perry's dumber than a box of rocks." She yawned and closed down her computer. "This is going to be the shortest night in history. We'll both be dead tired tomorrow." She stood. "What do you think are our chances of even getting a reply on that e-mail?"

"I think you're so damn beautiful in the moonlight you make my teeth ache." He ran his hand over his face. "God, I shouldn't have said that, but you drive me nuts even when we don't agree. I don't know how to get over you. Callie, no matter what I try it doesn't work." And he snagged her around the waist, not ready to let her go. "God, I want you."

He slipped the computer from her hands, put it on the settee, then took her in his arms, feeling as if this was exactly where she belonged. He looked down at her and kissed her, his mouth hot on hers, his tongue mating with hers, his body pressed tight to hers. He hadn't meant for this to happen but wasn't surprised it had.

He slid his hands into the robe, her warm, soft skin against his palms the most incredible sensation on earth. A little moan slid up her throat, and she wrapped her arms around his neck, bringing herself closer still. He tasted every crevice of her mouth as he wedged his leg between hers, his thigh feeling the mounting heat of her sex as she spread her legs in response. He backed her against the side of the house, shielding her and what they were doing from the street and anyone making an early call at the docks. He ran his hands down her sides, into the waistband on her pj's and cupping her wonderful hips.

Perfect. Not bag-of-bones skinny like so many TV types. Her pelvis arched against him, his erection throbbing as he slipped the waistband down, his hand nestling into the silk curls. His heart slammed against his ribs, and he gulped in air as her hot lips planted wet kisses along his neck and chin, her fingers struggling with his belt buckle . . . until Bonnie's cry split the air.

Callie's fingers stilled, and she rested her head on his shoulder. "What the hell are we doing? We've recited the litany of why we shouldn't get together, and now here we are doing it again anyway."

She stepped away, her breathing fast. He took a step back, trying to put distance between them, but it was only physical. Emotionally they were attached. He was falling for her, dammit. Falling hard and fast and . . . opening himself up to another career disaster. He said, "Least I'm not the only one doing the wanting."

That hadn't come out exactly as he'd intended. He'd meant it as a tease, but it didn't sound that way. "I mean—"

"That's what this was about? To prove a point? To show that I want you, the real you, and not Lex." She adjusted her pj's and gave him an eat-dirt-and-die look.

Hell, no! He didn't play games—he hated them—except maybe this time he should. This misunderstanding was best left that way. She was ticked off just like he'd been when they did the deed in the gym and she said she thought of him as Lex. Ticked he could deal with; Callie more than willing to step into his arms could be career disaster. He needed time to get over her, and this would do it. It was the best for both of them. They were getting more involved at every turn, and there was nowhere for a relationship to go. Their careers didn't exactly mesh.

He slapped on his Lex Zandor face and slid into acting mode. Her attempt to break them up hadn't worked but his sure would. "Just wanted to see if you wanted me as much as I want you. That was one way of doing it."

"You're pond scum. Below pond scum, and I thought you were better than that. Mutual attraction is one thing we could try and get over together, but to do this to feed your ego is something else. I have a baby to tend to." Callie jutted her chin and stormed off into the house.

Well, mission accomplished. No going back. She thought him an ass and wouldn't have anything more to do with him, least on a romantic level. He'd killed any chance of that dead as a skunk on the four-lane. He should feel good because it kept his career safe, except he felt like . . . pond scum. What really got to him was that crack about being disappointed in him and in herself because she'd overestimated him. For some reason he didn't want her to think badly of him. In fact, he realized he wanted just the opposite. Well, that was just too damn bad now because it wasn't going to happen.

Callie lay back against the headboard, staring at the computer propped against her knees, the moon and the glow from the monitor the only lights in the room. After her little groping session with Keefe on the front porch that ended in total humiliation, how could she sleep?

She checked her e-mail again, looking for a message from M. Perry, but still no reply. She clicked back to solitaire to start another game.

She was furious with Keefe, the bastard. Getting her to respond to him just to puff up his male ego was something she'd never dreamed he'd do. She knew the soap set, least she thought she did. There were the actors who were self-absorbed and thought they were the second Tom Cruise on their way to the top, the playmates who were in it for the glam, the press hounds who loved seeing their names and pictures everywhere. But Keefe never fit into any of those categories. He seemed real. Till tonight. Guess that put him in the Tom Cruise category. She lost at solitaire again, checked her in box again, and there it was . . . a reply from M. Perry.

She sat up and took a deep breath, then opened the e-mail. M. Perry said the meeting was a go. "Holy cow," she whispered into the darkness. "We really did it."

This was a big step closer to finding Mimi. If Perry didn't know something about Mimi, the people he worked for had to have a hunch where she was. Why else would they be advertising for her in Memphis? She should tell Keefe. No matter what their differences he needed to know about the note, even if it was the middle of the night, actually almost morning. He should make plans, and she needed to know what to write back to Perry.

Callie slid from the bed, pulled on her robe and tiptoed into the hall. She looked both ways to make sure Rory wasn't around to get suspicious. Then she opened the door to Keefe's room and went in.

Moonlight fell across Keefe's bare back. Did it have to be bare? She tried to resurrect her thoughts of him as a bastard, but it didn't help to see his skin. Lots of it. Didn't the man ever hear of a T-shirt? The sheet just covered his butt. Eyes closed, breathing slow and steady. There was not one thing slow and steady about her right now. She should have never come. What was she thinking? She turned and started for the door, and he said, "Enjoying the view?"

See, bastard! She spun around. "You are the most arrogant, conceited, self-important, smug, high-and-mighty, stuck-up, vain, arrogant—"

"You already said arrogant."

"Well, I'm saying it again because it's double true." He rolled over onto his back, taking the sheet with him. Thank the Lord for that! She didn't need any more maleness to distract her; this was enough. "I came to tell you we heard from M. Perry. The meeting's on. I thought you might like to know and what do you want me to reply?"

"So what the hell are you doing up at this hour?"

"What do you think, waiting for the darn e-mail, like I said. This is important. I need to reply."

"Tell him to look for three guys in Atlanta Braves baseball hats. Now, what else do you need?" He winked.

"I need to beat you about the neck and shoulders." She yanked the door open and resisted the urge to slam it as she left and crept back to her room. Her stomach churned, and she ground her teeth. How could she be attracted to such a jerk? She wasn't; it was over. Two years of ogling and daydreaming about the man had officially ended tonight. Common sense had prevailed over primal lust. In fact, common sense should always prevail, especially in important matters.

And by late the next afternoon as she and Bonnie entered Slim's, Callie was more convinced of that than ever. Sally waved her over to a table where she and Georgette sat, and Callie pushed the stroller in that direction. Dinner customers occupied about half the tables, including Eleanor Stick sitting in the back. Well, what brought that on?

Callie lifted Bonnie onto her lap, and Sally leaned across the table. "Did you see who's graced our presence for dinner tonight? Eleanor's working at the hardware store. Can't seem to find baby-sitting jobs anywhere now that Keefe made a point of telling everyone on the Landing she's way less than a great baby-sitter."

Bonnie started to fuss, and Callie rocked her, but it didn't help. She stood and paced and ran smack into Eleanor Stick. The old bat smirked. "Taking care of young'ns isn't as easy as you think, is it, city-girl?" She harrumphed, then strolled off toward the door, nose in the air, shoulders back.

Bonnie yelled louder, and Callie said, "Now look what she did. That woman brings out the worst in this baby."

Georgette sighed. "Oh, good grief." She stood and lifted Bonnie into her arms. "Crying babies make me nuts. Let me have a go at this. I worked my way through college at a day care." She put Bonnie to her shoulder, her cries gradually decreasing by several decibels.

Georgette slowly grinned, a real grin as if she truly enjoyed the moment. "She likes my earrings. One of my cousins was the same way, into the bling even at this age."

Bonnie cooed as she played with the silver and gold dangles at Georgette's ears, and Sally said, "Georgette, you're a baby genius."

"Just doing what needs to be done."

Callie felt her heart soften toward Georgette. This was a genuine side of her Callie hadn't seen before, and she liked it. "Bonnie wins everyone over, and maybe after tonight we'll be a step closer to getting her mama back."

Sally huffed. "Well, I doubt it. Three men in baseball caps? What the heck kind of disguise is that? That's what happens to men; they never play dress-up when they're growing up. They don't get the fantasy concept. Perry's going to recognize Keefe, someone's bound to know Digger and Demar reeks of cop. The man might as well have *I am the law* written across his forehead. The meeting's never going to come off."

Callie said, "But what if Keefe and his merry men don't do the meeting. What if someone else does . . . like us." Her gaze fused with Sally's, and she sat up straight.

Georgette sat down. "The guys already said it's them and only them, and we weren't invited to the party."

Callie bit at her bottom lip. "Well, that was before I sinned."

Georgette whispered, "Sinned as in little white lie or as in going straight to hell?"

"The hell one. I told M. Perry to look for three women in red boas at nine o'clock at Kerby's. I had to keep the time the same because I mentioned it in the first note, and I didn't want to do anything to scare him off."

Sally put her fingers over her mouth to stifle a laugh, then said, "Honey, if three red boas don't scare him off, nothing will."

Callie said, "I had to do something. The guys' idea sucked, and I suddenly decided I wasn't in the mood to be dictated to by a . . . dick."

This time Sally couldn't contain the laugh. "Oh, boy, that must have been some fight you and Keefe had. So what's your plan, other than to make Keefe madder than a cat in a thunderstorm?"

"I've been thinking about this, and the hooker disguise is the best idea and most believable."

Sally scoffed, "Believable? Have you looked in the mirror lately?"

"We'll have to dress the part, but who else knows the streets better than a streetwalker, huh? It's perfectly logical. And the boas fit on Beale Street; the place is sort of nuts at night. No one will pay much mind."

Sally said, "Bet the cops pay some mind."

"We're not doing anything, just looking like we could if we wanted to. Think of us as faux hookers. That's not breaking any laws."

Georgette patted Bonnie. "And I suppose you need my clothes, am I right?"

"And your presence," Callie said. "Three is safer than two, and we don't know M. Perry." She studied Georgette. "So, are you in?"

She sighed. "The men aren't going to be happy. You sure you want to tick them off like this? Maybe there's another way."

Callie said, "Like what? If we don't intercede, we'll never find out what M. Perry knows. All we have to do is reroute the guys, and we're in business. I think if we tell them the time has changed, that M. Perry is meeting them at ten, not nine, that should work. Then we meet with Perry at the original time. The guys will be a little perturbed, but they'll get over it."

"By the next millennium."

Georgette shook her head. "I got my doubts, but if you need me . . . I . . . I guess I can do this. Callie tells Keefe about the time change. I'll get to Digger. Sally clues in Demar. We meet at Hastings House in an hour, and we'll get all hussied up and go."

Callie stood and took Bonnie from Georgette, placing her in the stroller, then glanced at her watch. "I better get going. Keefe's over at the gym doing play practice." She smiled, gave a little finger wave and practiced strutting her stuff out the saloon while pushing the stroller. No easy feat.

The hardware store had already closed, and Betty Lindel locked up Burgers-n-Bait and told Callie to be extra careful of strangers as the streets would be deserted soon except for Slim's. Callie agreed and crossed to the high school, parked the stroller outside and took Bonnie in.

The cool interior felt good. She stopped at the back, watching Keefe on stage pointing to actors and giving directions, his deep voice a muffled echo off the concrete walls. The actors hung on his every word. They respected him, trusted him; she could tell that right away. Keefe O'Fallon may be a first-class jerk to her, but he knew the theater.

"Hi," came a whispered voice beside her. "Is that Keefe's sister?" A teenager flashed his boyish grin and nodded at Bonnie. "Did you come to watch the play practice? You're Keefe's girlfriend, aren't you? That's what everyone says."

"Everyone's wrong." They should have been on the front porch last night or in Keefe's room. That was enough to kill anyone's notions of romance between her and Keefe. "I'm just the baby-sitter."

They watched the stage for a few beats, and the boy whispered, "Keefe's the best director we've ever had in this town. We're so freaking lucky to have him, and we all know it. This is going to be a real kick-butt play. Mr. Leonard worked at the hardware store and built the stairs for the set. The rest of us are working on the frame and a balcony. Keefe gave me the part of Mortimer, do you believe it? Mortimer. That's the lead part. Stanley told me I couldn't act and wouldn't even give me a walk-on part, but now . . . I . . . I want to be an actor just like Keefe when I grow up. I don't know how to thank him."

Callie patted the boy's shoulder. "I think you just did." It was darn difficult to think evil thoughts about Keefe O'Fallon with a cheering section like this boy in Keefe's corner. She eyed his baseball jersey. "What position do you play?"

He blushed. "I don't. My dad thinks I'm going to base-ball practice, but I'm coming here instead." His eyes rounded. "You won't tell my dad, will you?"

"I don't even know your dad, but maybe you should tell him. He's going to find out, you know."

The boy stood on one foot, then the other. "I'll think of something. I'll tell him I got kicked off the team. That might work."

"Or it might not. Just tell him the truth."

The boy sucked in air through clenched teeth. "You don't know my dad."

A pretty girl with long, straight brown hair and about his age came up beside him. "Do you know your lines, Barry? The next scene is yours again. You did great in the first scene."

He smiled hugely, love of the theater mixing with first love of a girlfriend. "Hi, Helen," he said on a dreamy sigh. "I even know your lines as Elaine, and I know everyone else's in case they forget."

Callie said, "I've heard Keefe used to do the very same thing."

The boy's eyes sparkled, but they didn't stop looking at Helen. "Cool."

Keefe turned to the back of the gym. "Barry, you and Helen and . . ."

His voice trailed off when he caught sight of Callie. For a split second she and Keefe stared at each other. She really wanted to hate his guts for kissing her and labeling it an experiment, except she couldn't. Least not all his guts, the ones that gave Barry the lead in the play were okay. And directing the play for the seniors was nice. And he loved Bonnie and Rory and his brothers and . . . Darn. He did fine with everyone but her. Why was that? "Can I talk to you for a minute? It won't take long."

Keefe nodded and said to the cast as he walked toward her, "Take a five-minute break but no longer. And don't go anywhere or we'll never get this play together." He said to Callie. "Is anything wrong? Bonnie okay?"

Callie nodded at the baby asleep on her shoulder. "Just had her with Georgette and Sally over at Slim's. I'm taking her home to Rory right now. He's starting her on strained peaches tonight, a big step in baby land. I got another message from M. Perry." Lordy, how was she going to pull this off? She wasn't the actor. "The time's changed for the meeting. He wants ten instead of nine."

Keefe nodded. Okay, that was good. He wasn't shaking his head; that would be bad. She continued, "I wrote back and said it was okay."

"That works, but what's going on?"

She froze. Uh-oh! Somehow he knew she was lying through her teeth. "Look, I—"

"You and Sally being friends with Georgette sort of boggles the mind."

She heaved a mental sigh of relief. He was concerned about a friendship not the meeting. "Georgette is okay. She seems to treat Digger all right, and she has Bonnie's best interest at heart. I have to admit I never saw that one coming. Seems she's a member of the little sister club like the rest of us." Uh-oh, she was rambling. Rambling was a dead giveaway to lying. Time to wrap this up and get out of here. "So, good luck at Kerby's. I better go."

Callie turned, and Keefe snagged her arm, the heat from his large hand making her so physically aware of him that no one else seemed to exist. How could one touch do that!

"So what are you doing tonight?"

"What do you mean?"

"You haven't tried to change my mind about the meeting in Memphis. You're just letting it go? And, you seem jumpy."

"Jumpy? It's strained peaches night, what more can I say?"

Chapter 9

Callie followed Georgette down Beale Street and called, "Will you wait up for one second? Not everyone's as proficient in stilettos as you are."

She tried to tug down the candy-apple red mini skirt that fit more like a low belt, wobbled, tripped, grabbed for Sally at her side, making her stumble and hold on to whatever was near . . . a guy in a ripped T-shirt with *Sex 24/7* on it. He grinned. "Want something, baby?"

Sally growled, "Yeah, my head examined for agreeing to this." She let go of the man's arm. "You can leave now."

24/7 frowned. "Hey, you're the one who grabbed me, lady."

"Yeah, well, big mistake on my part." He gave her the middle-finger salute and strode off.

Sally gasped and pointed to his retreating back. "Did you see that? How insulting. I should deck him."

Georgette rolled her eyes. "You look like a gal on the prowl, and you grabbed the man's arm. I think between the three of us we have on every truly slutty thing I own. What do you expect from him, the stock reports?"

Sally said, "I'd know what to do with the stock report."

Callie slipped her left foot from the four-inch heel and massaged her tootsies. "These are torture."

"They're French, cost two hundred dollars." Georgette sighed and pinched the bridge of her nose. "You two are the worst sluts on the planet. Think wicked, think sexy and try not to trip anymore or you'll ruin my shoes."

Sally said, "Okay, this store is Strange Cargo. We can hobble in here and get the boas. They have everything, and I do mean everything. Then we cut down to Peabody to Kerby's and get this over with."

"As long as we sit when we get there." Callie slipped her sore piggies back into their torture chamber, and Georgette said, "When we approach Kerby's remember to stand straight, shoulders back, boobs out, hips gyrating. Got to look like hussies if we want Perry to think we are, and I bet anything he's watching for us."

Sally said, "Honey, every male in Memphis is watching us." She assumed the pose that Georgette described and frowned. "Think I have on more mascara tonight than in the whole rest of my life. My lashes weigh a ton and— yikes." She jumped, her eyes suddenly huge as a guy in a cowboy hat and no shirt strolled past and winked at her. Sally sputtered, "That man just pinched my ass. I'll have a bruise. After all this we better learn something that will help find Mimi."

Callie turned into Strange Cargo. "Next time we dress as street thugs. They get to wear jeans and gym shoes, and no one hits on them."

They ambled past a display of toasters with a picture of Elvis on the front, a hat shaped like a guitar that proclaimed BB King the King and a back-scratcher. They paused and looked around doing the I-am-a-tourist impersonation, and Callie snagged the back-scratcher. After a night in itchy spandex she'd need one of these . . . least that's what she thought till she realized the scratcher was shaped like a very long . . . penis?

Holy cow. She'd gotten into enough trouble with one of these things. She sure didn't need another. She tossed it back onto the stack, but she found a bandanna that said *Wonder Dog*. She'd get that for Max. He deserved it for saving Bonnie. Sally pointed to a pink boa draped around a plastic flamingo's neck. "We're getting close."

They crossed the aisle and found boas in every color imaginable. "Pay dirt," Sally said as she snagged up a red one, flipped it around her neck and assumed a sexy pose. "The real me. Wall Street, eat your heart out."

Callie picked up another one and tossed it to Georgette, who twisted it on. "IRS, eat your heart out."

Callie adorned herself in the third boa, and Sally said, "Keefe, eat your heart out."

Callie said, "Keefe couldn't care less, but M. Perry will have no trouble recognizing us now." She caught sight of two big guys in biker shirts standing by the Elvis toasters giving her, Sally, and Georgette the male once-over. Creepiness danced up her spine. The guys had warned them about this. She'd planned on getting the boas and then hurrying on to Kerby's. Obviously they hadn't hurried fast enough. "Uh, we better get out of here right now. Don't look now but I think we're getting an audience."

Georgette and Sally glanced at the guys, and Sally said, "They're kind of scruffy-looking." She batted her eyes. "And I think I'm allergic to these feathers."

Callie groused, "Didn't I say not to look, and for God's sake don't keep fluttering your eyes."

"They itch, I can't help it."

Callie, followed by Georgette and Sally, elbowed their way through the customers, paid for the boas and bandanna, then joined the crowd on the sidewalk milling about in the muggy night air.

Sally pulled her gold spandex top away from her body. "The humidity must be a hundred and ten out here. Bet we got rain on the way for sure."

Callie gasped. "Oh crap. The two guys from Strange Cargo are following, except now there's four. It's like one of those horror movies where the aliens multiply and you can't stop them." She stuck the bandanna in her purse and took Sally's and Georgette's hands. "We got to get to Kerby's. A bouncer would be good here. Some protection."

"I hate when this happens," Georgette said as they did a fast trot on tiptoes.

Sally said, "We can go down Third Street to Peabody. Hurry up." She cut her gaze to Georgette. "You've experienced this phenomenon before?"

Georgette huffed. "Fallout from stilettos and short skirts." Callie added, "This is as fast as I go. I didn't think a marathon was on the program for tonight."

Sally glanced back, her eyes still twitching. "Something's on the program for tonight, and I think we're the main attraction. They're gaining on us."

Callie dodged around a corner, followed by Georgette and Sally, the men moving fast. Sally pointed to a bar that spilled out onto the sidewalk with tables, chairs and music. "Kerby's!"

Callie huffed. "Never been so flipping happy to see a bar in my life."

Georgette said, "How do we deal with these guys?"

Sally said, "You're asking us? You're the pro on attracting men."

"I'm a newbie sexpot who has no idea what she's doing unless it's on a balance sheet."

"Now she tells us." Callie darted into the entrance of Kerby's, followed by Sally and Georgette . . . until a man, a very big man, stood in front of them. "We don't want your kind in here."

Sally drew herself up tall. Panting, she said, "Excuse me! What do you mean our kind? I have an MBA from Harvard, worked on the floor of the New York Stock Exchange."

Georgette poked his chest. "I'm an accountant. A CPA. I'll do your taxes for free if you let us in. There are unsavory guys following us."

The bouncer scoffed, "Isn't that what you want?"

"No," they all three blurted at once. Callie hissed, "We're not who you think we are. For God's sake let us in, I'm a . . . baby-sitter."

"Well, three cheers for you," the man groused. "And I'm Martha Stewart on parole. Get the hell out of here all of you right now."

Callie puffed, "But—"

"No buts."

"We're supposed to meet someone here. It's really important."

"I just bet it is. Meet them somewhere else."

The four men came up behind them, and the one with a ponytail and gold earring snaked a possessive hand around Callie's waist. "Hi, there, baby. Trying to play hard to get? I'm damn good at playing catch."

Crapolla!

He continued, "Saw you gals giving us the eye back in that store." He smelled of beer and sweat and all things vile and a little dangerous.

Sally said, "That was the evil eye to turn you into a horse's butt. It worked, now go away."

Callie tried to free herself from his grip. Sally squirmed to get away from a guy who looked like a fireplug on steroids, and Georgette tried to do the same with a grungy guy in a leather vest.

A Neanderthal throwback said, "Wait till you get to know me, you'll really like me." He glanced at the others with a menacing glint in his eyes. "You'll like all of us. What do you girls charge?"

Oh, shit! Oh, shit! Callie pushed at ponytail guy. The bouncer said, "Take your business somewhere else or I'm calling the cops," and Keefe was suddenly at Callie's side saying, "You heard the ladies, beat it."

Ponytail guy scoffed, "How about I just beat the hell out of you instead." He threw a punch, Keefe ducked as he grabbed Callie, and Sally got hit in the back of the head, sending her hard against the bouncer.

"Hey." He pushed her aside, and out of nowhere Demar caught Sally with one hand and blocked a punch from vest guy with the other, then did some marshal arts kind of kicking thing at the bouncer coming toward him.

In her peripheral vision Callie caught sight of a man with a black mustache and limp leaving in a hurry. Then Neanderthal socked Keefe, sending him flying across a table. Digger returned the favor to Neanderthal as he grabbed Georgette and tucked her safely behind him. Callie took her boa and flipped it around vest guy, pulling him off balance as he tried to swing at Demar, and Sally elbowed the bouncer as he grabbed for Digger.

Sirens sounded, and Callie felt her hair stand on end. So much for meeting Perry, and Keefe did not need this bad publicity. He swung at ponytail, connected hard, sending him across the room, and grabbed Callie with his other hand. He made eye contact with Demar and Digger for a split second, then pulled Callie through the congested bar, back into the kitchen area, now deserted since no one wanted to miss the fight out front.

Keefe snagged aprons from a rack and slipped through the back door into the alley. He draped one apron over her head, the other over his, did a quick tie, then took her into his arms and kissed her as if she were the only woman on earth. Without a doubt this was the best thing that had happened to her in the last three hours.

"Hey," came a gruff voice and footsteps next to them. "You two see anyone out here?"

Callie fought to focus, and Keefe gave the cop a man-to-man kind of look. "Hell, man. I wasn't exactly paying attention, know what I mean, but someone was running somewhere. Heard steps. Didn't see who. We've got a fifteen-minute break and . . ." He eyed Callie, and a devilish smirk lit his face. "Well, you get the picture."

The cop shrugged. "Yeah, right. Get a room." He ducked back inside the bar, but Keefe didn't let go. His eyes sparked fire and not the good kind that said *I want you, baby.* More like, *give me one good reason why I shouldn't toss your sorry butt into the river.* His lips drew into a firm line. "When we get home I'm going to wring your neck. What did you think you were . . ." His voice trailed off as a downpour of rain fell over them like someone turning on the faucet full blast. Callie put her hands over her head, and Keefe stepped back.

She said, "Oh, great, now what?"

Keefe took her hand. "My car's around the corner. Keep the apron on or another band of horny men will be following us. Whatever possessed you to do something so insane and—"

"We can't leave Digger, Georgette, Sally, and Demar."

Keefe swiped his face. "They all split when we heard the sirens. None of us need cop problems, especially Demar who is one. He'll take care of Sally. Digger knows this town like his name; he'll look after Georgette. Let's get the hell out of here."

"Look, I had no idea these guys would—"

"Can we argue later?"

Her clothes were soaked through and glued to her skin,

though considering how tight they were in the first place, there wasn't much change. "What about M. Perry?"

Keefe put his hands on her shoulders and gazed through the gush of water between them, his breath warm across her lips, even though she was chilled to the core. "I think the cover's blown, babe, don't you?"

"But this was such a really good plan."

"Yeah, fucking terrific."

She glared, suddenly not caring he had sexy breath or if the rain washed her down the nearest drain. She had something to say! "Hey, this was not just some hair-brained idea. It was a good idea and a hell of a lot better than baseball caps on TV stars that was sure to wind up as a photo op for tourists more than an undercover meeting."

"Least my idea wouldn't have overgrown apes running after me down the street." His eye was swelling shut, his lip cut, knuckles raw, and she felt wretched about all those things, no matter how much she and Keefe disagreed. And that he'd come and helped her out of a crappy situation was something she couldn't dismiss. In fact, she owed him big-time.

A slow twinkle sparked in his one good eye, and he folded his arms. "But I gotta say, you do make one hell of a hooker. I'll give you that."

"I've had it, that's it, I'm so out of here." She turned and tramped down the alleyway, splashing water till one of her steps scared a mangy cat trying to squeeze under a Dumpster to escape the rain. She looked down at the torn ear, scraggy tail, obviously the least successful cat in the neighborhood. "Boy, do I know exactly how you feel."

She took off her apron, came toward him, and when he didn't run away she wrapped him up and took him into her arms.

"Now what are you doing?" Keefe asked as he came up beside her.

"Taking this cat home. I can at least rescue something tonight."

"It's a feral cat, Callie."

He meowed pitifully and looked at Keefe, his matted fur plastered to his face, whiskers limp and broken, eyes droopy. Callie said, "Yeah, mean as a snake, this one. I'm terrified all to hell and back. Let's go."

"A souvenir from Memphis. Max is going to love it." Keefe pulled off his apron and put it around Callie's shoulders, and she tucked the cat inside. Keefe nodded up the street. "Swim that way. My car's two blocks over."

They crossed at the corner, not bothering to run. What was the point? She spotted Keefe's Jeep at the next curb. He hit the unlock button on his key chain, and they climbed inside, the sudden absence of water everywhere kind of shocking. Keefe pulled back the apron and studied the mass of fur. "He's either dead or asleep."

"Purring, I can feel his bones going up and down. I bet he has fleas."

"Not after this downpour."

She took an edge of apron and wiped her face, the mascara leaving a long black smear. She looked like a roadie for Kiss. "Let's circle around the block and see if we can find the others."

"They're fine. Digger drove his truck. Demar will get a ride with Sally. By some miracle you didn't get any information we could use before all hell broke loose, did you?"

"Only thing I found out was that they have some really strange back-scratchers in this town. And I bought a bandanna for Max." She fished in her purse and pulled out the red material.

"Wonder Dog. You're going to give him a big head."

"Maybe he won't eat my cat."

She leaned back, droplets slithering down her body into

crevices she didn't know she had. She licked rain from her upper lip and thought of the man with the mustache. For some reason he stuck out in her mind, maybe because he got away from the action as fast as possible while everyone else ran toward it. But was that anything significant? Maybe he was simply someone who didn't want to get involved in a barroom brawl. Besides, what difference did it make now. He was long gone . . . except . . . except she felt as if she'd seen him before, which was impossible because she'd never been to Memphis in her life.

She shivered. From the guy or the rain? She shivered again and realized she wasn't sure which. "We're ruining the interior of your car."

"It's fabric, it'll dry. I just wonder if we will." Keefe turned the ignition, bringing the Jeep to life, then flipped on the heat. "I don't get this wet in the shower."

He eased out into the steady flow of traffic, a stream of cars intent on abandoning Beale Street and the surrounding territory. Lightning zigzagged across the inky sky as more rain fell, and windshield wipers did double-time. He played follow-the-leader, rear lights forming a red ribbon toward the expressway. The cat purred harder, warming the spot on her left side. "I wonder what color this cat is?"

Keefe glanced her way. "Looks like a little dirt ball from here."

"He's just a little dusty is all. We'll call him that, Dusty."

"Better than dirt ball. This rain isn't letting up. You cannot imagine the river when this kind of storm blows in. It's like doing battle with the devil himself. Sure hope Dad or Digger checked on the tows at the dock." He stared into the traffic. "I'm sure not making much progress here to be of any help."

Finally they exited the expressway onto the two-lane. Water streamed across the asphalt; visibility shrank as total darkness closed in around them. She felt as if they were the only two people and one cat on the planet. Keefe slowed the Jeep around a bend. She needed to apologize for dragging him into this mess, and now was as good a time as any. Besides, he had to keep both hands on the steering wheel, so he couldn't make good on his wringing-her-neck idea.

She petted the cat, and Keefe downshifted the car, slowing more. Rain hammered the roof, the sound like rocks dropped from a high place. "I'm sorry about this, you know. I was really trying to help, so were Sally and Georgette. But it was my idea, and I dragged them into it. You weren't listening to us, and the hooker idea seemed like it would work, and yours was really rotten. We would have pulled the Perry meeting off if those creeps hadn't descended on us. But they did, so thanks for showing up early. How did you know to do that?"

"We realized you were up to something when you and Sally weren't haranguing us anymore. Neither of you give up that easily. Actually, neither of you give up ever. We put one and one and one together and went to Memphis."

"Can you see out of your eye at all? It looks pretty swollen."

"It's been worse." They started down a hill.

"Barroom fights a way of life for Keefe O'Fallon?"

He gave her a Lex Zandor half grin. She knew that sexy-as-hell expression even in the dark.

"I have two brothers, and we've gotten into our share of battles for one reason or another, but usually not with each other and not in bars. When I was in junior high I used to get the crap beat out of me on a regular basis by Butch Longford and his buddies for being the sissy who liked plays instead of baseball. Then big bad Quaid came along and I didn't get beat up anymore." Keefe shifted gears and accelerated as they started back up the other side of the hill.

"I got the feeling there's something more going on with Quaid than you're saying."

"You'll have to ask him about that and—"

Something darted across the road, Dusty hissed and dove for the floor and Keefe veered hard left. "Damn!" Callie grabbed the cat as the Jeep spun, skidded to the edge, then slid over the side into the ditch, airbags deploying.

"Fuck a duck," Keefe said as the bags shriveled. He looked at her. "Are you okay? Cat okay? I think this is the night that'll never end."

"We're fine. What the heck was that in front of us? I couldn't make it out. Sure spooked Dusty; he puffed out like a scrub brush. Are you all right?"

"No new bruises here." He gazed into the dark, his profile sure and strong and dependable. If she had to get stuck in a ditch on a rotten night in the middle of God knew where, she was glad she was here with Keefe. Not only was he good to look at in any situation, but he didn't go on a testosterone high and pound the dashboard and cuss a blue streak like a lot of guys.

She hated that; it only made things worse. Keefe was calm in a crisis, a man who got the job done no matter what and who really didn't care all that much for her. Trouble was she was more attracted to him than ever and couldn't deny it, no matter how hard she tried. Darn! Did he have to be all the things she admired most? "Want to pound on the dashboard and cuss?"

He gave her a have-you-lost-your-mind look, then pointed to the road. "Bet it was Grant who ran us off the road. I forgot about him being out here."

"A man? In this rain? It didn't exactly look like a man, more like a blur of something."

Keefe sighed. "A blue blur to be exact and it's General Grant. He haunts the woods around here. Used to quarter his troops at Hastings House just up the drive on the other side of the road. He never really left. Word has it he's out looking for his troops."

"We're talking Ulysses S., as in the guy who fought the Civil War?"

"Yeah, the one buried in the tomb. You saw him with your own eyes . . . sort of. Dusty knew. That's why he freaked out. Animals got this instinct about things. Grant doesn't like Southerners much, and you're from Georgia and just got here and on his land. He's pissed."

"And where the heck do you think you're from, Ontario?"

"I work in New York, so I'm innocent, and cats don't count. There's talk of putting up a warning sign, but ghost crossing seemed a little over the top."

Callie massaged her forehead. "I'm so tired I'm willing to believe anything, and what you said actually makes sense. What do you suggest we do now, Yankee boy?"

"The Jeep has four-wheel drive; we'll see how well it does in a monsoon." He put the car in reverse and hit the accelerator. The tires spun, and the car went nowhere in the Mississippi mud. He put the Jeep in drive, and the tires spun again, the vehicle staying snugly imbedded. He looked at Callie. "What I suggest we do now, Southern gal, is walk."

Keefe hated to drag Callie back out into the storm, but they sure as hell couldn't stay in the car all night. Not only would it be damn uncomfortable, but it wasn't safe with the threat of flash floods, and truth be told, he didn't want to be in such tight quarters with her.

In spite of her deception over meeting with Perry and his attempts to get her permanently ticked off at him, he still wanted her more than ever. He admired her for trying to help with Perry, even though her idea had been damn dangerous.

He hitched his thumb to the right side of the road. "Over there is that driveway I mentioned. It leads to Hastings House. We'll spend the night there. I don't see any lights, so the electricity is blown, but I'm sure Thelma is in and probably Conrad, too. It used to be his house till he gave it to Thelma to make up for being a total ass, and he wanted to convince her he loved her. They're going to be married next month. I'm sure they have some extra beds somewhere."

"The way things are going tonight, I'm betting those beds are in a dungeon, and I don't even care." She stared ahead, no expression on her face. "When I get done with this assignment I'm going to Vegas and taking a long walk in the very dry desert." She cut her gaze back to Keefe, sat straight and squared her shoulders. "Okay, enough whining, I can do this. We have a cat to protect." She put her hand on the doorknob. "On the count of three we go. One, two—"

"Wait! I'll take the cat. I'm not the one running in heels. Maybe I should carry you."

"Oh, good grief, O'Fallon. I can do this. Three!" She shoved open the door, scurried out and slammed it shut. Keefe did the same and took off after her. She was running flat out in bare feet, holding her side where she'd tucked Dusty. More lightning cut across the sky, silhouetting her, and he realized he'd never forget Callie Cahill charging up the hill as the wind howled and rain swirled from all directions. The woman was a lot of things, but for her timid and whiny didn't exist.

"Over here," he yelled through the storm as he headed for the front porch, finding the door more from memory than sight. He spotted the knocker in the next blast of lightning and rapped the handle down hard. He hammered it again and again till the door to the huge brick house flew open, and Thelma McAllister stood in the arched entranceway, lit candelabra in her hand.

"Keefe? Keefe! What . . . What are you doing here?"

She narrowed her eyes. "I've got a bone to pick with you. You've been home what, almost a week, and you're just getting around to visiting me and—"

"Can we pick bones later, if you don't mind. It's a little wet out here."

"You . . . want to come in? Now?" She shook her head as if coming to her senses. What was that all about? She continued, "Oh, heavenly days, of course you do. What am I thinking? Where in the world are my manners? What are you doing out in this cranky weather? Why is your face swollen? Is that a busted lip, and what's wrong with your eye?"

She stepped back, and he hauled Callie inside, then followed, Thelma closing the door behind them. Another burst of lightning reflected off the brass chandelier in the hall, fine antiques in the living room and Callie dripping wet and barefoot next to him. Keefe swiped water from his face; he'd been doing that a lot tonight. "We were coming home from Memphis and ran off the road. The eye's from a skirmish at Kerby's."

"Skirmish my old tomato. You've been fighting, and I don't even want to know why. Bet you got run off the road because of Grant." Candlelight set a glow to the staircase and polished floors.

"Callie's from Atlanta, and you already have Georgette from Savannah staying with you."

Thelma tsked. "Lordy, that man and his Southerners. As soon as new ones come to town he goes on a tirade and starts looking for his troops, especially if it rains."

She held out her hand to Callie. "Welcome. Sorry I haven't been around to introduce myself sooner. This place keeps me busier than a paperhanger in a windstorm, but I've heard you're a first-rate fan of our Bonnie." She glanced back to Keefe. "Uh, how long do you think you'll be here?"

"There's no way I can get the car out. Can we spend the night?"

She glanced around and bit her bottom lip. "I have an extra two bedrooms."

"And a box of litter?" Keefe pulled back the apron around Callie. "Meet Dusty from operation Dumpster rescue."

Thelma's face softened as she stroked the cat. "I'll put you all on the third floor. There's a big bath up there, and you can clean him up and yourselves. I have sand on the back porch from repotting ferns for the breakfast room, and I'll make up a litter box and get this ragamuffin some food and a blanket. That should hold him till—" A door squeaked upstairs.

Keefe said, "You have guests besides Georgette staying here?"

"Guests? Yes, yes I do." She grabbed a candle in a brass holder sitting on the hall table, lit it from her array of tapers and handed it to Keefe. "You'll be in the Beauregard and Jefferson Davis rooms, right next to each other, bath across the hall for the litter. My other guests are on the second floor, and I don't want you to wake them."

"Yeah, cats can be so damn noisy." What was up with Thelma?

She said on a fake yawn, "Now, we better get to bed. You both look beat and cold and tired."

She herded them along to the steps, and as they climbed Callie said, "This house is lovely."

"It's big but sometimes not big enough; you'd be surprised." They turned for the next flight, and Keefe said, "Your guests must have a baby, thought I heard it cry for a second there."

"Wind. Just the wind. Here we are now," she said, drawing up to a door and opening it. They entered, and she lit two candles on the mahogany dresser. "We have our share of power outages, so we're prepared." She faced Callie. "You're in here. It's a little bigger than the other room. We'll put Keefe in there since he didn't see fit to visit till now." She winked at Callie. That was good because it meant she liked Callie and bad because it meant he'd have to dig himself out of the doghouse with Thelma.

Thelma continued, "If you need more candles, they're in the dresser drawers. Make sure you snuff them before you go to sleep. Robes are in the closet. Some older towels are under the sink in the bathroom for Dusty." She pointed to a door in the wall. "The rooms are connecting. Up here used to be the maids' quarters."

Callie gave an appreciative sigh. "I'll mind the cat so he doesn't scratch your things. I think this room is a little piece of heaven."

Thelma smiled. "It's just Hastings House."

Keefe asked, "Where's Conrad?"

"Drumming up business in New Orleans." She beamed. "The dry dock's got a few more boats scheduled for repair, and he just hired a second welder." She left the door open as she went into the hall and opened the door to the next room. She said to Keefe, "You can stay in here."

He held the candle high to cast light around the area, except there wasn't all that much area. "Don't think I've ever seen such a small bed or room."

She harrumphed. "Guess next time you'll pay me a call when you come to town. Besides"—she lowered her voice—"I figure with that pretty girl next door you won't be spending all that much time in here anyway."

This was not good. He was on the ragged edge of caving and going back to Callie, to beg her forgiveness and confess all . . . though she'd probably tell him to take his apology and shove it. "Maybe I can sleep on your couch."

"I don't think so," Thelma said in a rush, then turned on her heel and strolled out.

He listened as her footsteps retreated down the hall. Why was she so agitated, and it wasn't just his failure to pay a visit. Then again, this storm was enough to set anyone on edge. He started for Callie's room, stopping in the doorway, not quite trusting himself to go inside and be alone with her. The warm candlelight gave the room a soft vintage feeling, offering safety and comfort from the mayhem outside. That Callie was there made it all the more appealing. He didn't need an appealing reporter. He needed self-control. "You got the better end of this deal. My room's the broom closet."

She chuckled. "So I heard." She held Dusty up to the dim light. "Well, him's a her, and she's so dirty I can't let her down. She really needs a bath."

Dusty's eyes shot wide open, her back arched and she squirmed right out of Callie's hands and hit the floor on a run. Keefe lunged to catch the black streak as she tore out the door. "I think she's had enough water for one day."

He studied Callie. No shoes, wet clothes, shivering. He wanted to make her stop shivering and knew just how to do that. No way! "You get a bath. I'll go cat hunting."

Her brows drew together. "Okay, why are you being so nice to me now when you should be mad as a hornet, and why so rotten last night without any cause? You're not acting too logical here."

When it came to Callie there was no logic, just lust. Well, that wasn't exactly true; there was more to her than sex appeal. "You have goose bumps the size of small chicken eggs, and you're going to get sick if you don't get out of those wet clothes, and then poor Bonnie will have me as her caretaker again. I'm not ready. I'll get Dusty, and after you get cleaned up you can raid Thelma's fridge for us."

"Seems a little crass, we're her guests here for the night."

"I got a feeling I'll get a bill." Keefe headed down the hall, then the steps. "Here, kitty, kitty," he whispered. Nothing. He went down the second steps to the first floor, rounded the corner and came face-to-face with . . . "D-dad? What the heck are you doing here?"

Chapter 10

Rain fell in waves across the windshield as Georgette snuggled into Digger's jacket. Denim! She was actually wearing denim. When she'd made her transformation to the new Georgette she'd tossed every piece of the stuff she owned and replaced it with silk and satin . . . till now. And to make matters worse she was riding in a disgusting hee-haw truck next to a guy named Digger O'Dell, who wore denim and a stupid captain's hat that looked as if he'd scrubbed floors with it.

God Bless America, how had this happened? The only consolation to being with Digger was it helped her get the scoop on Keefe. That's why she went to Memphis with Sally and Callie. She had to keep Keefe's friends close to get to him so she could do the article, the article that would change her life. She focused on her family. For a change she'd be the one noticed, the other daughter.

Digger slowed the truck to a crawl and made the turn onto the two-lane. Lightning split the sky, and she caught the outline of the Landing. "I don't remember Sally passing the town on our way to Memphis. Why are we here?"

"This is the back route. A little longer but I need to check the docks to make sure everything is secure. Then we'll head for Hastings House. The Mississippi on a rampage is nothing to mess with, and O'Fallon Transport can't afford to lose a tow."

"Isn't that the O'Fallons' problem?"

He smiled. He had a nice smile for a hick. "They pay me to make it my problem. And I'd do it no matter what; they're my friends."

She sat up straight and pointed to herself. "Well, that's nice but what about me and getting me home?"

He patted her knee. "In a minute. I'll take care of you, Georgette. I would never let anything happen to you."

"Well, you did save my bacon tonight, and I do appreciate it." She sat back and sulked. Not only was she wearing clothes she hated but now she was taking a backseat to boats.

Digger drove past the town and the O'Fallons' house, slowed more and took the road that dipped down to the river, going past the parking lot to get closer to the dock itself. Headlights picked out the Mississippi right in front of them all wild, angry and the color of two-day-old coffee. Dock lights undoubtedly working on emergency generator power illuminated the area.

He pulled the truck to a stop, shifted into park, put on the emergency brake and kept the engine and wipers running. "You stay here, pretty girl. I'm going to check the office and make sure everything's okay and we're not getting any distress calls from a tow in trouble. I'll be right back."

He stepped out into the downpour and tugged his hat down on his head. Good grief, he hadn't even asked for his jacket back. Crazy man. He faded into the rain, and she watched the river build into angry white-capped waves that pounded the shore as the winds howled and beat the truck. Five minutes passed, then ten. No Digger. Well, heck. Had he fallen in? She wanted to go home, climb in bed, forget today ever happened.

She looked at the keys in the ignition and considered driving herself and leaving Digger O'Dell to his tows and blue-collar way of life. But if anything happened to him when she was with him, Keefe would not be happy and probably never talk to her again, and she could kiss her article good-bye.

She felt the truck sway in the gusts. She'd have to go out into this godawful mess and find Digger O'Dell! She had to make sure he was okay. Son-of-a-sea biscuit! Didn't her dad always say that? How did she get to be Digger's keeper? She killed the engine and the headlights, wrapped the jacket around herself and stepped out into the storm from hell, tripping on her purse and spilling the contents onto the ground. Bob's phone hit the pavement and suddenly played back the conversation she'd recorded earlier.

Damn the phone for making her purse top heavy and for being too easy to play. All this for a freaking article! There must be an easier way to get her parents' attention.

She shoved the purse back into the car and headed across the dock. Rain stung her legs, her ruined shoes now even more ruined. She slid on the gravel nearly losing her balance and kicked off the stilettos into the river. Gravel on her toes was far from comfortable, but sliding into the Mississippi tonight would be a lot worse. A light burned in Digger's stern-wheeler at the end of the dock, and she headed there, her bare feet slapping the concrete as angry waves crashed against the dockside, sending spray skyward and soaking her even more . . . Was that possible? Catching a swell, she jumped from the dock onto the deck of the boat, holding the railing so as not to slip.

"Digger," she yelled and swished water from her face and swept back her hair. She shook her hands to rid them of water, but there was no answer from Digger. Then again, how could he hear her over the wind?

She went toward the side stairs just as Digger swung

around from the back. She asked, "What's wrong? You look worried. Are you okay? Least you didn't fall overboard."

He gave her a half smile along with a towel he'd draped around his neck. His bedraggled hat stuck out of his front pocket. "Back bilge pump isn't working, and the *Lee*'s taking on water. I'm good at steering boats but the engines . . . not my bag."

She wiped her face. "Well, you have lights, so your generator's working. What about the stern pumps and the ones port and starboard?"

"They're all working fine."

"Okay, that helps, keeps the *Lee* out of immediate danger. Let me see that pump."

He stood there staring at her as if she'd told him she was from Mars. "W-why?"

She wiped her legs. "Because I want to add it to my charm bracelet." She handed him the towel and rolled her eyes. "My dad owns the fleet of tugboats in Savannah that push those ocean freighters around like Tinkertoys. I've been around boats of one kind or another all my life."

The half smile morphed into a full one. "Well, I'll be damned."

She poked him in the chest. "And if this boat sinks with us on it, you just might get your wish, depending on what you've been up to, Digger O'Dell." She took his hand. "Come on, show me the pump, time's a wasting." How many years had it been since she said that?

He led her toward the stern, opened the door into an engine room and the familiar smell of diesel fuel and oil. A million memories of tagging along with her father came rushing back. Digger nodded to the back motor. "It's not turning over. I just bought the blasted thing when I put the *Lee* in the water."

"Hit it."

His eyes widened. "Hit it?" He smacked the casing with the flat of his hand.

"Oh, good grief, Digger, that's not a hit; that's a love tap." She opened a toolbox on the floor, took out a hammer and whacked the motor with the flat side, the metal on metal sound echoing in the little room. The motor coughed, sputtered, coughed again and hummed to life. She grinned and parked her hands on her hips, still gripping the hammer. She gave him her best cocky grin. "Am I good or what? Sometimes new motors freeze for no good reason. My dad calls a hammer his own personal persuader."

Digger laughed, the rich sound mixing with the steady drone of all the motors and the relentless rain beating down. He slid his arms under the denim jacket, around her waist and swept her up off the ground, making them face-to-face.

"Oh, Digger," she yelped and laughed, too. She dropped the hammer and held on to his shoulders for support. She'd had no idea he was this strong.

His eyes twinkled, his nose nearly touching hers, his lips a breath away . . . and he had such nice lips. "You, Ms. Georgette Cooper from Savannah, Georgia, are the most amazing woman I've ever met in my life, and you just saved my boat."

"Well, you saved me earlier tonight with those creepy guys, so I guess we're even."

He looked totally happy. "Well then, I guess we are." And he kissed her.

Except kissing Digger O'Dell was so not part of her plan because the man was the king of kissing and that kind of kissing completely fogged her brain. In fact, this was without a doubt the best darn kiss she'd ever gotten. She relaxed into Digger's arms as hers slid easily around his neck. His lips took hers in a slow seductive dance, leading then following then leading again as her heart raced, and she felt warm all over in spite of being thoroughly drenched.

His teeth grazed her bottom lip, and she gasped, letting his tongue touch, then twine, with hers. The intimacy surprised the heck out of her, but then it felt so right, as if she'd been waiting for this particular kiss for a really long time. How could that be? This was Digger O'Dell.

Slowly he let her down, her breasts sliding over his muscled chest, her nipples beading into sensitive nubs. Her abdomen skimmed his tight abs, and as her bare feet touched the cool, wet wood floor, the juncture of her legs hugged his very hard arousal.

She wanted him! Right here, right now, on the deck of this old tub in the pouring rain. It took every ounce of willpower she had not to strip down, then do the very same thing to Digger O'Dell.

He held her close and sucked her tongue into his warm, moist mouth. Her legs parted, bringing his erection closer, deeper. Never in all her twenty-eight years had she kissed a man like this.

Digger gazed down at her, his eyes dark and mysterious. "God, what you do to me, Georgette," he said in a slow Tennessee drawl that turned her insides to mush. Except none of this should be happening. What the heck was she doing? Digger wasn't her type. She wanted . . . Keefe. Well, not the exact man himself, but someone like him. That's why she'd done her own personal rehab. Digger O'Dell was nothing but a pawn in a game to get what she wanted. She stepped back. Panting, she said, "This is not a good idea."

"Oh, honey, I think we both know it's a heck of a good idea." He touched her hair, then tucked the strand behind her left ear, his fingers lingering there, tracing her ear, turning her on more, confusing the hell out of her. Then he said, "But we have to get out of these clothes first." The comment nearly shocked her pants off. Was that the point!

Her eyes widened, and he chuckled, "Because we're wet, river girl, and cold, and making out with you is heaven on earth, but I don't want you to get sick. My place is upstairs. It's not the Plaza, but I have a shower and dry things to put on."

"Okay," she said before the urge to jump back into his arms completely got the better of her. "Dry sounds wonderful."

Sex sounded better.

He took her hand, his grip firm and tender all at the same time. "And I have food."

Food? She was starved. *Think about being hungry, but not for Digger!* "Leftover pizza?" she said, trying to ignore his fingers entwined with hers as they headed out of the engine room. They were under the cover of the upper deck, but the rain fell all around them.

"Stew and biscuits. We'll take the inside steps so we don't have to go back into the storm."

She stopped and stared at him. "You cook?"

He tugged her on and climbed the stairs. "The way I figure, I eat, so I cook."

Again she stopped, making him stop, too, and look back at her, him halfway up the flight, her below him. His wet clothes molded his body, and he had such a nice body to mold. Digger was big, strong like a man who'd worked hard all his life, but his easy manner didn't draw attention to his physique. Well, she was sure paying attention now as she gazed up at him, his clothes more like a second skin than a loose covering. She said, "Shanty boat stew and sourdough biscuits, I bet."

He laughed, looking even more handsome. And it was that kind of laugh that said they shared something neither of them ever thought they'd share at all. "To me it's the perfect food, nothing quite like shanty boat stew cooking on the stove all day making me hungry as a working mule. Your daddy used to fix it for you?"

"And my mama. Lord, I haven't called her that since I was five and we moved off the riverbank and into the brownstone on Jones Street. Mother joined the Savannah Historical Society, Dad the Oglethorpe Club. I went to private school."

"Pissing in the high cotton."

"Not always. When I was little and Daddy was just starting out . . . Well, you get the picture. Caught my first fish when I was three right off our front porch." She shrugged. "Now I can't cook or fish." And something about that made her feel sad. As if she'd lost something important and didn't know how to get it back.

He stepped down and kissed the tip of her nose. "Ah, but you didn't forget how to fix the motor of a bilge pump, so who cares." And he didn't care, she realized, about her being rich or poor or the social clubs or anything else.

He gently tugged her after him till they reached the top deck, and he smiled as he slipped his arm around her to keep her close. No matter how much he wasn't her type his smile was so easy, so perfect, so incredibly contagious. He simply put her in a good mood. . . .

Why couldn't he be more like Keefe, the glitz, the glamour, the fame and notoriety? That's what she wanted, someone to be proud of, make her parents sit up and take notice.

Who could be proud of Digger O'Dell? He was not the man she wanted at all.

Digger slipped his hat back on his head and guided Georgette to the set of rooms he called home. God, he was crazy about her, he realized as he opened the door. Crazier than he thought he'd be and that was a lot. She was a real looker, and she tickled the hell out of him. She also responded to his kisses like no other woman ever had, reduced him to coal ash with one look and had saved his boat. This was a woman he wanted all to himself, not get paid to fall for. Tomorrow he'd tell Keefe and Callie the deal was off. He wanted Georgette free and clear, no strings, and he'd find another way to save the *Lee*.

He turned on the light, and Georgette glanced around just as a crack of lightning illuminated the sky. "Wow," she said as she gazed out the line of windows. "You have some terrific view up here."

He was thankful for the lightning because it drew Georgette's attention away from the worn blue couch with a throw over the back, faded plaid chair, simple oak end tables and cheap lamps. She was used to the good life, and his living quarters were a far cry from that. He opened the windows partway to circulate the stale air trapped inside. "You should see the view from the pilothouse. When the rain's not in the way you'll have to come take a look-see."

"You're so . . . neat and tidy. No messy bachelor pad?"

"This place is too small to clutter up, wouldn't be able to move around if I left stuff sit out. Shower's across the hall. There are six other bedrooms, but they all need work. Kitchen and a living area are in the back. Beyond that the open deck where we ate lunch with Keefe. The *Lee* was originally built to haul cargo, so that's why she's open on the first deck. Then she got turned into a dance boat, and there's a raised platform for the band. I'd like to do that again, go to different towns on the river and take people out for dancing in the moonlight. May through October. When it turns too cold I'll run tows for Rory." He laughed. He was nervous having Georgette here and babbling like a schoolkid. "Sorry about going on like that."

"Why, Digger O'Dell, you're a romantic."

He felt his cheeks warm and knew he was blushing, not so much from the romantic comment as from the fact that

Georgette had said it. He never thought much about romance, but now with Georgette in his life romance seemed like a real great idea. "The *Lee* is just business."

But her eyes turned the color of rich jade, and the expression on her face said she wasn't buying that simple explanation. She took a step toward him, then stopped. Damn, he didn't want her to stop. He wanted her to glide into his arms so he could kiss her again. But maybe that was moving too fast. She may dress all hot and sexy, but he sensed vulnerability, something that suggested Georgette Cooper wasn't what she seemed at all or at least she was new to it. He needed to go slow, let her feel comfortable with him. He doubted if he'd ever feel comfortable with her; she made him edgy.

She said, "Think I'll get that shower now," snapping him back to the moment.

"I'll fetch you some clothes." He walked into his bedroom and took jeans and a denim shirt from the drawer, then came back out and handed them to her. "Damn poor substitute for the pretty clothes you always wear, but these are dry."

She took them. "They're fine." But the set of her mouth said they weren't. She looked back to him, bit her bottom lip, then touched his cheek. She came closer, one step, then two. He knew that look. Georgette wanted him as much as he wanted her, but there was definitely a conflict of some kind running around in her brain. Lightning struck close by, making her jump, her eyes widening in surprise.

"Maybe you should flip a coin," he suggested. "What do you want to do, Georgette? What do you want *me* to do? I want you more than you can imagine, but if you're not ready to—"

"Oh, Digger," she said on a resigned sigh. "You talk too much, you know that." She snagged his cap from his

pocket and put it on, then stepped into his arms and threw
hers around him, knocking them backward and onto the
couch as more lightning crossed the sky. Or, maybe that
wasn't lightning at all but a blast of excitement from having Georgette's body lying across his, and it being all her
idea. How'd he get so damn lucky?

Her lips ravaged his, her fingers curling into his wet
hair. She seemed desperate, as if needing to have him right
away. But he wouldn't let that happen. Having sex with
Georgette was too special to rush through. He pulled his
lips from hers. "I want to make this good for you, honey.
We need to slow down a little."

"No," she said, her lips against his, kissing him between
words. "I don't want to slow down. I want you and me together now and—"

He framed her face with his palms. "But we don't have
to set some record for fastest sex east of the Mississippi. I
want to take you slow, touch and kiss you everywhere, feel
your skin grow warm under my hands, hear you whimper
and give you more pleasure than you thought possible."

She looked surprised. "You can do that?"

He couldn't have kept the smile from his face if he'd
wanted to. "It's going to be a hell of a lot of fun finding
out, I promise." He looked into her eyes that were trou-
bled yet growing heavy with desire. "But something's wrong.
You're not comfortable with this, with me?"

"Digger, I tackled you onto the couch. I want to make
love to you. I really, really do."

"On that we agree. How we get there is another question. Let's try it my way, slow and easy, and then if it's not
working for you, we'll do it your way."

She swallowed. "Digger, I got to tell you. I think I'm up
to doing it my way right now." She squirmed against him,
and his dick went bone-hard.

"Why rush to dessert when there's a whole buffet to experience. You're going to love the buffet, Georgette, I swear you will."

"The last time I had sex he said it was a mercy fuck because he felt sorry for me because he knew I wasn't getting any, and since he was drunk he could do me as a good deed. I didn't always look like this, Digger. I think prolonged sex is ruined for me, but I have urges." She licked her lips, her eyes closing by half as she growled, "Lots and lots of urges."

In one motion he snagged the blanket from the back of the couch, dropped it on the floor and then rolled them both off the couch and onto the comforter, breaking the fall with his hand. "That guy was an ass, Georgette. He made himself feel good by making you feel bad. That's not what we're about here, honey. Wham, bam, slam is not my style."

"But it's my style."

He barked a short laugh. "Let me show you how good sex can be." He kissed her tenderly, wanting to reassure her he was sincere and that she could trust him. "I think you like me, and I know I like you, and that's why I'm going to make this memorable. You won't forget tonight, I promise." He kissed her again. "Trust me, please?"

"I . . . I do." Her eyes turned dark and cloudy, and he slid off her, bracing himself on his elbow, not touching her, just talking. "Nice blouse."

"It's a tube top because it's just a tube of material and no straps."

"Or bra."

"What are you going to do to me?"

"Right now I'm taking inventory. Make you realize how lovely you are and replace all those events of the last time you had sex. Nice skirt."

"Kind of short."

He winked. "Short is good. I'm going to make love to you, but the only way we finish it is for you to take off what's under that skirt because you want to make love to me. I want this to be your call."

"I can make the call right now, Digger."

"That's just sex drive, an itch that needs to be scratched. I want there to be more between us."

"I don't understand."

"You will." He leaned over her, his arm on the other side by her shoulder, his lips the only thing touching her. "Relax," he coaxed.

"Okay," she said, forcing a smile but looking more tense than ever. He had his work cut out for him, and if he ever came across that Mr. Mercy Fuck, he'd tear him apart.

Digger's tongue drew the outline of her mouth, and he planted a kiss at one corner, the other, then along her jaw-line to her right ear. He licked the soft lobe, then suckled it gently into his mouth. His fingers raked her hair from her face, then massaged her nape.

Her shoulders sagged a bit, and he kissed her throat, feeling her pulse beat hard and strong against his lips. His finger drew lazy circles across her chest, small at first, then ever widening, each time dipping a little farther beneath her spandex top and stroking the soft flesh there. Her breathing accelerated as his fingers slowed, then lingered at her cleavage. "You are so soft, so sweet, your skin's like silk."

"Why are you teasing me?"

"I'm not taking from you, Georgette. I want to give to you. I want you to be aware of how wonderful you are."

Her hand suddenly cupped his erection, and his eyes shot wide open. She said, "I really appreciate the offer and all your considerate plans and noble intentions but not now. You got something else I appreciate a lot more." Her hand on his dick pressed a bit harder, and with her other hand she shoved his shoulder, sending him reeling flat on his back, staring at his own ceiling, the lightning showing him how badly it needed painting.

Georgette released his dick and leaned over him. She ground out, "I've had no sex for quite a while—do you understand—a long while. Most of that was because I wasn't all that desirable, the last part because the men I came in contact with looked as if they wanted to eat me alive. But you didn't act that way. You're better, a gentleman. If you want to give me something, do it now, and I don't mean neck massages and some kisses. I want sex, with you, right here and now on this floor."

Then she kissed him, plunging her tongue deep into his mouth, driving home the point of exactly what she wanted in case there was some part of *I want sex right now* he didn't understand.

Panting, she sat up, swung her head to flip her hair from her face and straddled his waist, one knee on each side, her skimpy skirt nearly showing her wears that he so wanted to see. She ripped off his denim jacket that she wore and sent it flying across the room. She pulled the tube top over her head, revealing the most gorgeous breasts he'd ever seen in his life. Full, round, perky, lush . . . very lush, dusky tips. "Sweet mother have mercy!"

"Forget mercy, and for God's sake, Digger, be sure to forget your mother!"

She cradled one breast in each of her palms and gazed down as if taking stock. "At first I was kind of self-conscious with these puppies. My new body took a little getting used to." She flounced her breasts, nearly giving him an orgasm on the spot. "A seven-grand boob job and you want to kiss my neck? We can do a whole lot better than that."

She stood over him, one foot on each side where her

knees had been. She unzipped her skirt, tugged it upward, having difficulty getting it over her boobs, then slid it over her head. She tossed it wherever the jacket went, leaving her in the skimpiest pair of panties he'd ever seen. About the consistency of . . . dental floss.

He finally managed, "I wanted to make love to you and—"

"And now you don't?"

"I wanted to be gentle, dammit, and caring because of that other jerk and—"

"Digger, you're not him, and I can tell from all the looks I get from guys I'm no longer a mercy fuck. In fact, most guys take me for a member of the frequent-flyer club, but I'm not that either. I never got up my courage before tonight to take a man up on his offer of sex, but for you . . . with you . . . Well, you're special. You said for me to trust you, and I do with all my heart. I fixed your motor, didn't I?" She grinned. "How about you fix mine."

"I got to say I don't think I've ever had an invitation like that before." He scooted from between her legs and stood up. He scooped her up into his arms with a little yelp and kissed her. "And I accept."

He dropped her gently onto the couch, then shrugged off his T-shirt and dropped it to the floor. He leaned over her, and she held up her hand.

"Don't stop with your shirt, big boy. You'll just have to get up again, and I want action right now. And don't forget protection."

He straightened and looped his thumbs into the waistband of his jeans. "Are you always this damn bossy in the bedroom, girl?" He kicked off his shoes.

She paused as if considering something, then sucked the tip of her index finger between her lips and gave him a coy smile. "Guess I've been a naughty girl, huh. Maybe . . . you should spank me."

He froze. He couldn't move. He couldn't breathe. She curled her legs up, grabbed his hand and pulled him down onto the couch beside her. She kissed him, then lay across his lap facedown, her incredible rump right in front of him. "Ever spank a five-thousand-dollar tushy before?"

His dick swelled, pressing hard against his zipper and for sure into her soft patch of curls. "Hell, I've never spanked anything before."

"But you'd like to, least right now. I can so tell." She wiggled her twin mounds of delectable tight flesh while also massaging his dick with her front. "You gave that motor a nice sound pat. Try it now."

He rested his left hand on one soft, silky cheek. "Oh, God, I'm going to hell." He swallowed. "I can't."

She pinched his side.

"Ouch!" He smacked her bottom. It was like a reflex, and he felt ashamed until Georgette giggled and kicked her legs, and he watched a hint of pink form in the shape of his hand. "Okay, that's it, no more. I—"

She pulled the leg hair at his ankle, and he swatted her again, then three more times as she giggled more, sounding like a schoolgirl and kicking her legs. "Oh, Digger, you are too much fun."

She flipped over and threw her arms around him. "We'll have to do that again. I hear they have these velvet handcuffs." She looked at him, her eyes dancing with devilment. "I so like being a bad girl with you, Digger."

He leaned back and closed his eyes. "I swatted a woman. I'm damned."

"But the woman had fun and so did you. It's a little fantasy to spice up our lives of fixing motors and storms and paying the bills."

She kissed him, her tongue coaxing his into action. "That was a love tap, and I want more." She kissed him again. "And I intend to be bad enough to deserve it." She curled her index finger into his hair and Frenched him in the ear. Then she reached into his back pocket and slid out his wallet, fished around and pulled out a condom. She held it up. "Now I can take care of you."

She sat beside him and unbuttoned and unzipped his jeans. She slid her hand into the slit of his blue skivvies and freed his throbbing dick. "My, my, what have we here?"

"Pain."

She grazed her thumb over the swollen head, and he gritted his teeth. "Georgette, what happened to wanting sex fast and furious?"

"Forget fast, but I'm really getting into the furious part."

"Fast would be good now." He pulled the blue package from her fingers, tore it open with his teeth and covered himself. He pushed her back onto the couch, stood and stripped off his clothes.

She wanted Digger so bad she could almost feel his very ample attributes between her legs. Every fiber pulsed at the thought. She'd never felt like this before. Truth be told, more often than not men scared the hell out of her . . . except for Digger. "You sure have a great three-piece set there, hunky man." She removed her panties and held out her arms. "I think it's time you showed me how it works."

"I can't believe you've always been this bold."

"Only in my dreams, my fantasies, and now with you. Come on, giddyap."

He put his arm on the back of the couch so as to lean over her. He slowly ran his index finger between her breasts, looking his fill. He continued over the indent of her navel and onto the patch of dark, soft curls between her legs. She bit her bottom lip as he slid one finger into the slippery folds, and she sucked in a deep breath.

"You're so wet, so ready, all for me. I want this to feel good and—"

"Digger," she said in a hoarse voice. "If I feel any better, it'll be over with, and all I've gotten is your finger." She pulled his arm supporting his weight, and he landed flat, face-to-face on top of her, his chest to hers, his hips to hers, his wonderfully hard erection at the apex of her legs, waiting and wanting action. She could feel the heat of his dick right through the condom.

"Making love to you is some adventure and damn if I don't love every minute of it." He kissed her, and she wrapped her legs around his back the way she'd seen it done in books. It seemed to work pretty good because Digger kissed her as he slowly pushed into her.

"Relax, honey," he whispered against her lips as he eased in farther. Her skin sizzled, every nerve alive. She spread her legs, taking him deeper. "You're so much a . . . man." She arched against him, and he entered her completely. "Oh, Digger!" she breathed on a sigh. "You feel so damn good."

Then before she could stop it her body clenched in climax, and he held her tight, thrusting into her again, then again. Her heat convulsed around his erection, and her fingers dug into his back as she let herself go completely, consumed by Digger and being one with him as he reached his own climax.

Sweat dripped down his temples in spite of the cool air from the storm drifting through the room, every hard muscle in his body relaxing now. He rested his head beside hers as she said, "How'd you learn to do that?"

"It's you, honey, all you." His tongue traced the gentle folds of her delicate ear. "You're incredible."

"I never knew sex could be so fantastic."

"Ditto, ditto and more ditto." He kissed the spot be-

hind her ear, making her shudder. "You're perfect, Georgette. You were made for loving."

She circled her fingers through his hair. "It's the makeover, Digger, that turns you on. My new, improved body
that's all nice and firm and perfect. The best body money
can buy."

He levered himself up on his elbows and gazed down at
her. Hair tousled, eyes bright. He rested his index finger at
the tip of her chin. "It's not your body. As perfect as it is,
that's not what makes you a perfect partner. It's here." He
kissed her forehead, nearly making her cry from the ten-
derness and sincerity. Then he touched her chest. "And
you feel here what I feel. We're together, not just taking.
This was more than a physical climax, Georgette. And I
swear that's true and not some corny line."

"You're a romantic and a poet. You are some guy."

"I'm a man who appreciates you, the real Georgette."
He toppled them both back onto the floor, putting her on
top, exposing her heated body to the night air. She laughed
as she fell across him. "Now what do we do?"

He winked. "Hungry?"

"Starved." She studied him for a long moment the only
sound the raging storm. "You're an incredible lover, Digger
O'Dell. I had no idea it would be like this between us. I'm
so glad I met you. And just wait till I tell you about some
of the other fantasies I've had."

Chapter 11

As thunder rumbled and rain beat against the windows, Keefe stared at his father across the candlelit hallway of Hastings House. "What are you doing here?"

"And I suppose I should be asking you the same dern question." Rory shifted from one foot to the other. "What are you doing here?"

"Callie and I were coming back from Memphis and went off the road. What's your excuse?"

Rory harrumphed. "Grant ran you off, no doubt. He sure gets his trousers in a twist when we get Southerners visiting like Callie and the other gal who's staying here, and then there's the rain that seems to make him antsy as all get-out. Bet Grant's looking for his troops and—"

"Dad?"

He raked his hair. "Hell, boy, I came up here to check on Thelma. With Conrad off in New Orleans and this storm hammering down to beat the band I figured she could use a little looking after."

"Where's Bonnie?"

"She's with me, of course. What'd you think I'd do with her, sell her to the gypsies? She's sleeping in one of the rooms upstairs. Thelma's putting her down now. She said you were hanging around, but I thought you'd turned in or I would have come up and said howdy to you." He gave Keefe a hard look. "So, why the hell aren't you asleep . . . or something. You got Callie with you; what in blazes are you doing roaming the halls with that sweet girl upstairs?"

"Callie rescued a cat and she escaped. I'm doing cat duty. Have you seen her? Little dirt-ball kind of thing faster than greased lightning?"

Keefe caught Thelma coming toward him holding Dusty. "Is this the critter you're looking for?"

Keefe held the cat in one hand, then hugged it to his side, not so much from endearment, but for escape prevention. With holding a candle in his other hand it was the best he could do. Anyway, what was Thelma doing in the kitchen? Wasn't she supposed to be putting Bonnie down? Probably getting a bottle.

Rory said, "Well, now you got your cat and you can hightail on out of here. We all need to be getting some sleep. It—it's damn late."

"Like anybody's going to sleep in this storm."

Rory peered at him across the darkness. "Just give it a try, okay?" With a wave of his hand he shooed Keefe toward the stairs, Dusty snarling and hissing as if the devil had him by the tail. Rory called, "That cat sure needs a bath. I suggest you tend to it right now."

Keefe climbed the stairs, feeling two sets of eyes glued to his back like when he was a kid and did something wrong and was sent to his room. He turned and his dad did another shoo wave in return. Keefe made for the next floor, losing sight of Rory and Thelma.

Lightning and thunder gave Hastings House a real Poe quality. If a damn raven flew over his head, he wouldn't have been surprised. Keefe went down the hall and peeked inside Callie's room, no one home. He made for the bathroom across the hall, but that door was wide open, and she wasn't there either. He lingered for a moment, soaking up the aroma of Callie. Which probably wouldn't linger too long as Thelma had made good on her promise of a litter box, cat food and water. There was also an ice pack for his eye. Thelma was a busy woman. How'd she find time to take care of Bonnie and do all this?

He put Dusty on the floor and went to close the door to keep her in when the Houdini of the feline world snuck out the last tiny crack. Keefe saw her gallop down the hall and skid through another open door at the very end. "Fuck. I do not need this." Would this night ever end?

He dragged his tired body after the cat. The open door led to another flight of steps. These were plain wood, unfinished, attic quality. He felt as if trapped in some stupid B-grade movie full of plot holes. Why would a defenseless woman probably wrapped in a towel and a dirty cat who had to be hungry go up some creepy stairs to a place they didn't know, with the lights out no less?

Dusty was still in bath-avoidance mode, so that was her excuse for running away but what was Callie's? Basic reporter nosiness? Then he considered her in that towel, and he suddenly couldn't put two thoughts together. "Double fuck."

He followed the stairs, holding the candle high to cast light around. "Callie? Dusty? Freddy Kruger."

The stairs creaked. Heck, the whole blooming house did, and the storm didn't help. He got to the top, the rain extra loud with him right under the roof. Things were piled high here and there. In front of him were a chair and chaise lounge covered with a sheet, two trunks, an old sled . . . If it had *Rosebud* on it or if he heard a beating heart under the floorboards, he was so out of here. He'd had his fill of weirdness for one night. Dusty sat perched on a stack of encyclopedias.

Keefe lunged, missed Dusty, tripped on God knew what, then grabbed for something to regain his balance and not drop the blasted candle. Callie suddenly appeared and snagged his shoulder, both losing their balance and dropping onto the chaise, sitting side by side like crows on a fence. "Thanks."

"It's a little congested up here; you got to watch where you walk." She held the candle down by their feet. "You tripped over an extension cord. Wonder where that goes?"

"Probably charging up Frankenstein in the next room. What are you doing up here? I didn't even see you." She had on the towel outfit just like he thought she would. It covered her breast to thigh, leaving a lot of lovely bare, sweet-smelling skin.

"I was behind a bookcase. I heard footsteps."

"It's raining; there's bound to be noises. What did you think it was, Grant?" When she didn't answer he did a double take. "You're serious?"

"Well, something ran us off the road. What if it was him or some other ghostly thing? This house is old and has been through a lot. There's all kinds of furniture, old clothes, books, paintings, even a rumpled bed by the far window. Those guys on *Antiques Road Show* would weep if they saw all this neat stuff. There's got to be a ghost or two hanging out around up here. Maybe I could write a book."

"Beat the heck out of editor for *Soap Scoops,* I'll give you that."

She put her candle where Dusty had roosted and leaned against the rolled back of the chaise and stared out the dormer window to the storm. "Writing's a good way to starve," she said, almost as if talking to herself, and as if it was something she'd thought about a million times before.

He took in her soft blond curls framing her lovely face now free of rain-smeared makeup, and suddenly he didn't give a flying fig what she wrote. "Nice outfit."

"There's one just like it in the bathroom waiting for you. We'll be twins."

"I'll never look that good in a towel."

She gave him a slow, steady look, her eyes now sparking with something more than candlelight. "Depends who's doing the looking." The next flash of lightning didn't generate as much electricity as what passed between them. He kissed her forehead because he simply couldn't stand being this close to her without kissing her somewhere.

She stiffened. "The last time you kissed me you were trying to prove a point. I think I'd rather you kiss someone else. Where'd Dusty go?"

"I lied. I kissed you on the porch because I like doing it a hell of a lot, and the only way I could trust myself to keep away from you was if you were ticked off and stayed away from me. If you thought I was a louse, that's what you would do."

"Well, that was totally juvenile."

"I remember something about you imagining me as Lex when we did the deed in the gym? Not exactly the most mature approach to sex."

She blushed. He could see it even in the dim light. She fiddled with the edge of the towel. "Yeah, that was pretty lame, too. Okay, so now what? I want you, you want me, we even like each other except for the minor inconveniences of lying to each other, running into Memphis, dressing like a hooker and getting into a bar fight. That's a heck of a list for knowing each other only a week."

"Probably a record."

"You're afraid if things don't go well, I'll dis you in the press and damage your career, and for me, being another member of the I-just-got-laid-by-Keefe O'Fallon fan club doesn't work, though I suppose I already am a member. I just don't choose to reup my membership."

"There's no such club." He touched her cheek. "Sometimes you have to go with a leap of faith, Callie."

Her eyes were bright, trusting, beautiful. "And you're willing to go with that? Just jump into the middle of a relationship with all that is going on?"

"Long-term plans may not work for us, but you're here now. We have a few weeks, and to tell you the truth, that's longer than any relationship I've had in some time. While I'm busy running from the press, my date's usually posing and handing out her business cards. We're not using each other and I like being with you. I'm done playing games to keep you out of my life. I say we go for it and work with what we've got."

She took the candle from his hand, set it on the trunk and stood, her eyes never leaving his as she undid the towel, letting it slowly unfold around her body and fall to the floor in a soft swish at her feet. "Well, this is what I've got, and I'm willing to share . . . with you."

"I'm sorry I hurt you with that proving-a-point lie. And I'm not just saying that to get into your pants."

"I know, my pants are already off. Now, what about yours?"

"I kind of like it this way, me in clothes, you not. I get to focus completely on every delectable inch of you, no me to get in the way."

He stood and took her mouth as his arms swept around her silky body. He wanted to possess her. One person could never do that to another, but his urge to lay claim to Callie Cahill was overwhelming.

Her fingers tangled into his hair, her mouth opening wider, giving him more of herself. He ran his hands up, then down, her back, not able to get enough of feeling her warm naked flesh against his palms. His hands slid lower across the small indent of her spine by her waist, then lower still, gently cupping the soft rounds of her tight bot-

THE WAY U LOOK TONIGHT 173

tom. A ragged moan sounded in the back of her throat, and he pressed her pelvis against his arousal to show her just what she did to him.

She broke the kiss and said on a whisper, "I want you naked."

She undid his jeans, then slipped her hands into his briefs, gently taking hold of his erection between her palms. Every part of him suddenly went hot and hard, and he gazed down at her. "What happened to naked? You stopped."

"I got distracted." She released his dick, then eased his briefs and jeans downward over his hips, exposing him. She looked her fill, and he felt himself get harder still. She didn't even have to touch him to get him to respond to her. He kicked off his shoes, then peeled off his damp jeans and briefs.

"I think I like both naked." He pulled out his wallet and got a condom. She pushed him back, and his legs caught on the edge of the chaise, causing him to sit.

She chuckled softly. "How convenient." She straddled him, one knee on each side, her fine derriere perched on his bare thighs. She gazed down. "Goodness me, something's come between us, Keefe, imagine that." She took the condom and tore off the top of the package. With excruciating patience she began to cover him.

"Damn, woman." His eyes held hers as his body throbbed with anticipation. "People take less time to paper a room."

She gave him a siren's smile and massaged his penis. Then she kissed him and knelt, the hot folds of her sex suddenly touching the tip of his erection.

"Oh, babe." He rallied all his self-control, and right now there wasn't much. She lowered herself a bit, the tip of his penis pushing into her tightness.

He swallowed the desire to possess her eating at his insides and he gripped her waist to steady himself as well as her. She leaned forward and kissed him, her tongue seducing his as she lowered herself more, the gradual penetration exquisite torture and this experience and Callie Cahill something he'd never forget.

Callie's breasts skimmed against Keefe's chest, the tight curls of sandy hair against her sensitive nipples turning her on more than she thought possible. She lowered herself onto him a bit more. Then she pulled back up and lowered herself again, stroking his erection, nearly driving herself crazy in the process.

"Where did you learn how to do this," he hissed in a ragged voice.

"I'm winging it." She came down another inch, and his fingers molded her hips, then glided across her belly. "What are you doing?"

"Winging it." His thumbs rested at the apex of her legs; then he parted the soft wet folds beneath her tight curls, grazing her swollen clit. For a second she couldn't breathe. Her eyes refused to focus as heat coursed through her. "Keefe," she finally managed. "If you do that again . . . more . . . I . . ."

His thumbs slid deeper, paying no attention to her warning, and he kissed her while massaging her tender flesh. She took him deeper inside her body, and his strokes quickened against her, the pressure stronger. He captured her left nipple with his warm, wet mouth, his lips suckling.

Her body tightened, and she lowered herself completely, taking his shaft in one last plunge. Passion rolled over her in waves, and she felt his torso stiffen, perspiration dampening his skin. He sucked at her other nipple, his thumbs tormenting her as she raised herself again, sliding his erection out then in, increasing the rhythm as he stroked her faster, more deliberate, till her muscles tightened around his penis and she climaxed just as Keefe did, holding her, making them one.

She collapsed against him, her head resting on his shoulder, his breathing as uneven as hers. The rain drummed against the roof. The candles flickered as Keefe's large hands rubbed her back for a long while, neither of them wanting to let go of the moment. "How can something so wonderful complicate the living hell out of our lives?"

"It's who we are that's doing the complicating. The sex is pretty straightforward stuff. You, me, fitting parts. Can't miss."

She rolled to the side, and he took his briefs, wrapping the condom inside. "I wonder where Dusty is?"

"I wonder where we are?"

He cupped her chin in his palm. "We're where we want to be at this moment. Forget about the future. You and I are planners . . . Our careers, taking care of family, you name it, we plan for it. For once let's see where this takes us. I say we wing it. Seemed to work pretty good tonight."

She stood, snagged her towel and wrapped it around her. He got up and brushed his lips to hers as something creaked, and Callie gasped. "There it is again."

"It's the storm, babe, just the storm. We better find Dusty before he pees on some Civil War treasure and Thelma skins us alive." He grabbed the other candle, then looked down at her. You're not like anyone I've ever met before, you know that. You're who you are, no pretenses."

She looped her finger into the waistband of his jeans. He needed a diversion. Time to figure out what just happened. He said, "Let's go find a cat."

He followed her down the stairs past the bathroom. "I hear chewing noises."

Dusty stood by the bowl of food, chowing down. Callie said, "How do you feel about giving a cat a bath?"

"About the same way I feel about poking myself in the eye with a sharp stick. Ryan, Quaid and I found this stray once, and the only way Dad would let us keep Ninja was if he was clean."

"Ninja?"

Keefe pointed to the thin scar at the corner of his eye. "He deserved the name." Keefe put his candle on a shelf by the door and added Callie's next to it. "Okay, here's the plan. I'll hold the little critter around her shoulders, one douse in the shower, you shampoo, we rinse, dry with a towel, run like hell. This cannot take longer than one minute. I think five seconds is the world's record for holding a cat in a shower."

Keefe pushed back the shower curtain suspended from the ceiling, encasing the claw-foot porcelain tub. He turned on the water, testing the gentle spray. "Ready?"

"You're going to help me? Even with your eye swollen nearly shut?"

"This cat led me to you tonight. I can at least clean her up." Callie studied the shower. Hauling Keefe in there held a lot more appeal than a cantankerous cat. She grabbed the shampoo bottle and hitched her towel tighter. "Nice kitty, kitty." She gave Keefe a quick nod. He grabbed and put Dusty under the water. She snarled, hissed, growled and wiggled. "Hurry," Keefe said.

Callie lathered. Dusty squirmed more. Keefe added, "She's slipping."

Suds flew into the air, covering his face and Callie's hair. Bubbles slithered off her nose and stung his eyes. "Rinse."

Callie grabbed Dusty's back paws, and they held her in the shower as Callie counted, "One Mississippi, two Mississippi, three Mississippi, four Mississippi."

The cat thrashed about, and Keefe said, "I can't hold her. She's too slippery." Dusty sprang from his hands and dove for the corner. Back arched, tail straight up, dripping water, murder in her eyes.

Keefe swiped suds from his face. "Think we'll forgo the drying."

He took an old towel and dropped it on the floor. "Maybe

she'll roll on it. It's warm in here. She'll dry fine. I think she's a calico. She gives a whole new meaning to mad as a wet cat."

Callie put her fingers to her mouth to keep from laughing outright. "And you look like you went through a car wash without a car." She reached out, took a handful of Keefe's shirt and pulled him toward her. "Let me help you rinse off. But I have to warn you, it'll take longer than five seconds."

"Is that a promise?" He snagged her up into his arms. His teeth clamped onto the towel and pulled it the rest of the way free, the material slipping down, folding across his arms. He stood her in the tub, the warm shower raining around her. "You, candlelight, the water falling makes some picture."

"But I'm lonely." She reached for the shampoo. "Want me to wash your . . . hair?" He grinned as he stripped off his clothes again and joined her. He snapped the bottle from her hands.

"Hey," she said. "I had plans for that."

He kissed her, the shower water seeping into their mouths, his erection rubbing between her legs. He lathered up a dollop of shampoo, and she watched intently. "That was my idea."

"Now it's mine, with a little twist." And he slid his hand between her thighs.

"You devil," she said on a quick intake of air, feeling dizzy with renewed desire.

"I'm just getting started, honey." He parted her slippery folds of heat, her legs widening, letting him enter her, her whimpers echoing off the tile. He whispered, "I love pleasing you." He kissed her deeper, his fingers stroking, rinsing, then probing. She was so hot and wet for him.

Her fingers fondled his arousal, then slowly closed around him, and he nearly lost his balance. His index finger thrust deeper, then withdrew; her strokes became faster and more deliberate, imitating his rhythm till her body quivered, then clenched in orgasm. "Oh, God, Keefe," she murmured against his mouth.

Heat tore through him as he reached his own climax. Giving Callie so much pleasure and her doing the same to him was astonishing. She sagged against him as he fondled her back and neck. He kissed her hair. "You're addictive, you know that. I have you, and then all I can think about is having you again and again and again."

"I'm one giant potato chip."

"You're air. I can't get enough of you. Except the water's getting cold, and we have to get out of here."

She peered up at him, her legs intertwined with his, her arms around his back holding him tight. "This is some leap of faith, Keefe O'Fallon. Where is it going to lead?"

"Right now, to bed, just you and me and this storm all night. Tomorrow can damn well take care of itself."

Morning light streamed across the bed, and four paws pranced up her spine, followed by a meow. Okay, where was she? Every muscle in her body hurt; then she remembered why. She'd never spent the night making love before. She hadn't thought she had it in her . . . but she did. Holy cow!

Dusty jumped to the floor, and Callie pushed herself up and looked at the indent in the pillow next to her. Where was Keefe now? She stood, then slipped on the robe and heard Thelma calling from down the hallway, "Callie? Are you decent?"

Thelma entered with a tray of goodies in hand along with some clothes draped over her arm. She set the tray on the bed along with shorts and a T-shirt. "Keefe brought them back for you. So how are you doing this morning? Keefe said there was a ruckus in Memphis last night and I should let you sleep. Are you okay now?"

"The ruckus was me being naive and Keefe saving the day." Callie eyed the food. "But I'm better now."

She parked down beside the tray, and Thelma did the same. She handed Callie a glass of juice and took one for herself. "I'm sure what you got into wasn't that bad, and seems to me men enjoy saving the day once in a while. Fact is, a bunch of them are doing the manly thing as we speak and getting Keefe's Jeep out of the ditch with as much horsepower and as big an audience from town as absolutely possible. Everyone's out now taking inventory of the storm damage. We'll be hearing tales about this storm over at Slim's for the next six months."

"Anyone hurt?" Callie bit into a scone. "Dear heaven, these are great," she said around a mouthful.

"Why, thank you for that, and everyone in town is fine and dandy. The good part of this is it brings folks out and gets them all together and—"

"Yoo-hoo," came Georgette's voice from down the hall. "Anyone up here?"

Footsteps sounded on the wood floor, and Georgette came in and did a little wave. "Keefe said Callie was up here, and I had to see if she was okay. What a night and some storm to top it off, huh? Are those Thelma's scones? Digger made me sausage, biscuits and gravy, but I've always got room for Thelma's scones." She sat on the edge of the bed and helped herself to the pastry. "Sweet mother these are good!"

Thelma chuckled. "You've been hanging around Digger too much. Starting to talk like him. Heard you went and saved the *Liberty Lee*. Talk of the town this morning."

Georgette shrugged and brushed crumbs from her lips. "I hit the motor. Not exactly rocket science."

"Well, Digger's sure making it out to be the save of the century."

Georgette put down her scone as if she'd suddenly lost

her appetite. "Not that it's going to do him any good. Digger's butt-ugly broke. He said he's got money coming in, but it's not going to be enough to fix up the *Lee* according to coast guard specs to make it seaworthy enough for passengers. He was working on the boat last night, and I sort of went over his books that were on his desk." She blushed. "I see a ledger, I got to know what's in it. Anyway, he's got to find a way to make money right now; then maybe the banks will lend him more for improvements."

Callie said, "So Keefe can lend him money."

"That just gets Digger deeper in debt. He needs viable income to show on paper, and he needs it now so the banks will back him."

Callie poured coffee. "Have you told him?"

"I . . . I can't." She sat up straight, looking a little prissy. "It's not like there's anything between Digger and me, not really, nothing permanent, that is. But we are friends, and I can't break his heart like that. I know what it's like to have your dreams and no one believe in them but you. I can't tell him about the *Lee.* I've got to think of something. We've got to think of something."

The floor above creaked. "I keep hearing that," Callie said, pointing to the ceiling. "I even heard it last night and went up and looked around but couldn't see much in the dark, and with the electricity out that didn't help either."

Thelma poured coffee and handed it to Georgette. "Must be the house settling."

Callie eyed another scone. "After a hundred and seventy years you'd think it's done settled."

Thelma poured coffee for Callie. "You'd be surprised. Did you see anything up in the attic?"

"Well, you sure have a collection. I'd like to look around sometime, if you don't mind?"

Thelma spilled the coffee on the tray. "Well, look at me, all butterfingers this morning. Just give me some time to straighten things up and you can dig around all you want. I have stuff so jammed full up in that attic from turning this into a bed and breakfast, I'm afraid you might break your neck if you crawled around up there." She stood. "Guess I better be getting back to work."

Georgette clutched her purse, checked the contents, then joined Thelma. "Think I'll head on down the drive and see if Keefe has gotten his Jeep pulled out of the ditch. I heard all kinds of commotion a little earlier. I wonder how Sally and Demar made out last night."

Thelma laughed as she headed for the door with the tray. "And I'm betting that's exactly what Demar and Sally did and then some."

Thelma and Georgette left, and Callie finished off her coffee while gazing out the back window into the woods beyond the lawn. She had to get herself going. For sure Rory needed her to watch Bonnie so he could tend to any damage on the docks or his tows. And that was fine, but what wasn't fine was Keefe and her and last night. She ran her hand over the indent in the pillow.

What now? A leap of faith? But what if that leap landed her right on her butt when this was all over with. She'd fall for him, then have to get over it? Like he said, they had now, and that's what she had to go with. Besides, there certainly wasn't any turning back after last night. It wasn't a death-do-us-part commitment, but it wasn't a one-time quickie either. They meant something to each other, but what and for how long? That was the question.

Chapter 12

Callie handed Bonnie a cleaned chicken bone to gnaw and tried to ignore the disapproving looks from Eleanor Stick sitting at the back table at Slim's. The actors at Callie's table passed around what was left of platters of barbecue, and Sally asked, "Who needs one last beer?"

Keefe's celebratory early afternoon dinner at Slim's to thank the cast for working so hard was in full swing. She should be having a good time, too, and she was, sort of . . . except she was hungry and not for barbecue.

Three days since the storm, three days since she and Keefe rendezvoused in the attic and then in the shower. But now that they were back at Keefe's house with Rory right across the hall, sneaking around in the middle of the night was the best they could do. Blatantly sleeping with the baby-sitter seemed uncomfortably tacky. And when they parted it would be so much easier if half the town wasn't in on it.

Barry and Helen raised their hands to claim more beer, and Keefe laughed. "That's root beer for you two." Keefe stood and clinked his fork against a beer bottle to get everyone's attention. "I want to thank you all for coming before we start practice tonight."

Joe chuckled. "Since you're picking up the tab, it's our pleasure."

Ty added, "Feed us and we'll follow you anywhere."

Keefe said, "Well, you've all worked hard since we got this idea going. You've memorized lines and come to practice early, built sets and worked hard to get things right, and most of all you put up with me."

Roberta sighed, then laughed. "Ain't that the truth."

"Here, here," Betty said and took a sip of beer. Callie laughed along with the rest of the crew. As much as they all teased that's all it was. They liked Keefe, trusted him to make the play right, caught his enthusiasm to do the best job possible.

Keefe continued, "The play is coming along, and I think we're going to be ready."

"When pigs fly, Keefe O'Fallon." Mrs. Stanley huffed as she burst into Slim's and stomped over to the table. She peered around at all of them, then zeroed in on Keefe. "You have some nerve changing my play. Who do you think you are? I'm the teacher around here." She poked herself in the chest with her pudgy forefinger. "It's my name on that contract with the town and school board for putting on the summer plays." Her eyes narrowed. "I know what you're up to, trying to get me fired because I never liked you. Think you're so much better than me, well, you're not. Around here I'm King Tut."

"Wait a minute." Keefe held up his hand. "Me taking over the play was your idea."

"You're putting on *Arsenic and Old Lace.* Trying to show me up. Well, I got news for you; that's not going to happen because there's not going to be any play." She flipped out a piece of paper. "Says right here in my contract that I have complete artistic discretion, and that means it's up to me to approve the play put on or not, and I'm not approving this play." She stood tall and jutted her chin. "It's not the real *Arsenic and Old Lace.*"

Keefe waved his hand over the actors. "We don't have the time to put on the full play; it's long and has a lot of lines. The radio adaptation works fine, and even with that we have to go at least three more weeks to make it work. Why are you going off like this?"

She lowered her voice, "Because I'm not going to be showed up by the likes of you. And that's what this is all about, isn't it? Make me look bad because I didn't think you could act. Well, I got news for you; I still don't think you can act, and I won't be outdone by you. You'll not be putting your play on in my gym. I have final say, and I say no way. I'm putting padlocks on the doors myself, and you can all kiss your stupid little play good-bye."

Stanley stormed off, and Keefe stared after her. "I don't believe this. How'd she find out? She was out of town. And, I can't believe she's carrying a grudge all these years."

Betty hissed, "The bitch."

Roberta said, "I'm thinking this was a little plan of Stanley's all along. She thought you'd look bad with that dresses play, and now that you'll look good she's not going to let that happen."

Betty hissed, "The big bitch."

Joe leaned back in his chair. "So now what the heck are we going to use for an excuse to get together? The memorizing our lines cover was working out real good, and now . . ." He glanced at Betty.

Frank muttered, "Think we can start up another Bible study group?"

"Not after the last time," Blanche chimed in. "Dang."

Digger and Georgette entered and came their way. Digger said, "We just passed Stanley outside looking really pleased with herself. What's she doing back in town?"

"Screwing things up like always," Keefe answered.

Digger said, "Well, you all look like you spent your last nickel, and I sure know what that's like."

Callie handed Bonnie off to Keefe, stood and grabbed Georgette's hand. "Tell Digger about the *Lee.*"

Her eyes shot open wide. "Here? Now?" She licked her lips, studied Digger and wrung her hands together. "I . . . I can't do that. It's mean-spirited."

"Tell me what?" Digger asked. "What's wrong with the *Lee?* Even more than I think there's wrong? Good gravy. The thing's like a big old wishing well as it is. I keep tossing in money and waiting for things to get better."

Callie nudged Georgette. "Come on, do it. You owe him the truth."

Georgette eyed the crowd and muttered to Callie, "In front of everyone?"

"Just do it. Trust me."

Georgette huffed. "All right. Fine. But this is not my idea." She faced Digger. "You're not going to have enough money to save the *Lee.* You may have enough to fix her up somewhat, but you need venture capital, and the banks aren't going to help you unless you have income and—"

"See, that's it," Callie said. "Money coming in. Digger has a boat; Keefe needs a theater. So, we put the two together and we get a . . . tada . . . showboat, just like on the Mississippi over a hundred years ago. Open theater on the first floor. There's already a stage area. We simply expand it, add lights, a curtain, we're in business. I knew being in the entertainment business would finally pay off. No need to have the engines and paddle wheel repaired right away because the *Lee* stays where it is. Everyone will come and pay money; there's enough folks in nearby towns. Digger gets income, the show goes on, everyone's happy. Brilliant, huh?"

Georgette dropped her purse to the floor and hugged Callie. "You are brilliant."

"Not quite," countered Digger. "The boat needs a ton of work besides the engines and paddle wheel if you want to put on the play this summer. There's only me and Keefe and sometimes Callie, and I hire extra hands for the big stuff, but that's not enough to get the job done in a month."

Keefe put Bonnie to his shoulder and patted her little bottom to soothe her. He was getting more comfortable with her every day. "You know, if we didn't have to pay for all the repairs, we could pay the actors a little something. And if we put on more than one show, and next year if the paddle wheel got fixed and the engines working, the *Lee* could make her way to some of the towns in the area, putting on more shows and making more money for the *Lee* and the actors. Could be quite a business. Kind of exciting and a little travel thrown in." He looked at the actors. "What do you think?"

Nick stroked his chin. "Money? As in extra income?" He eyed Nellie. "Well, I'll be. Now, there's a new wrinkle, the kind I like to see for a change."

Joe smiled hugely at Betty, Frank kissed Blanche on the cheek and Roberta hugged Ty, his coffee skin taking on a pink hue.

Joe stood and swiped barbecue from his fingers. "I think you've said the magic words, Keefe . . . extra money. That could change things for all of us at this table and put some zip in our lives." He took Betty's hand and kissed the back. "Let's see, I worked at the hardware store for forty years. I know how to do damn near everything repairwise, been helping folks on that very thing for as long as I can remember."

Nellie stood. "I ran the *Landing Times,* so I know advertising inside and out. We'll bill this as Showboat Shenanigans."

Sally came over. "You know, Dad's been toying with the idea of adding outside dining to overlook the river. With the new housing and town renovations going on to bring folks in, Conrad stepping up work at the dry dock and hiring more workers and now the showboat, we need more space here. If he gets Demar on it, we can have it up in a month. Since the Braves are headed for the playoffs this year, Dad's been teaching Demar how to barbecue so Dad can catch more baseball games on TV. I think he and Demar are bonding over barbecue sauce, ribs and Coors Light."

Helen said, "The moon on the Mississippi is so romantic." She gave Barry a shy smile. "Barry and I can help string lights on the deck, and you should get some of those chiminea things to keep the bugs away."

Frank held up his hand. "I still do a mean guitar. Be glad to play for a free dinner now and then. Dinner and music before the shows is a good advertising idea. One of those package deals you read about." He winked at Blanche. "If somebody agrees to sing, it would be better yet."

Blanche blushed, and Ty slapped Digger on the back. "Well now, I think we can save that there boat of yours."

Digger shook his head, looking completely dumbfounded. "Why are you all doing this for me?"

"Hell, man," Nick said. "We're doing it for us. A little extra cash in our pockets is just what we need to change things around here. Besides, I'm not all that fond of retirement. I'm itching to get back into something, and this is perfect. We can work on the plays during the winter and put them on in the summer. I think we should do *Yankee Doodle Dandy* on the Fourth of July next year. Bet I can still do a little Buck and Wing."

Nick leaned over the table and said in a quiet voice, "We got the set for *Arsenic and Old Lace* already built in the gym, and with Stanley putting padlocks on the doors we might have to do something shady to get what's ours back." He laughed quietly. "I'm an ex-sheriff, never thought I'd be planning a break-in." He patted Nellie's hand. "Times sure are a changing."

Keefe picked up a drumstick and held it high. "I think we have a deal. All in favor . . . burp." Everyone laughed, and he added, "Our rehearsal tonight will be at the majestic showboat *Liberty Lee*. Afternoons for working on the *Lee,* evenings for working on the play."

Digger kissed Georgette. "If you hadn't figured out that I needed extra financing, this all never would have gotten going. You saved my boat again."

"I think this is a joint project." She glanced around, taking everyone in. "Accounting is so much bean counting, and this time I get to see the results."

Digger hooked his arm through Georgette's. "Just follow us, folks."

The actors paraded out of Slim's, Callie pushing the stroller and bringing up the rear. And as they headed on to the *Lee* she veered off and made for the O'Fallons' house, picking up Max in his red bandanna as her escort. Bonnie needed a bath and real food and bed. Callie wanted Rory to go over the alarm system again. The fiasco in Memphis had left her jumpy. Whoever M. Perry was, he probably knew who she was and for sure knew Keefe. Everyone knew Keefe, which meant M. Perry knew the O'Fallons were on to him. That was her fault. Keefe and the baseball hat probably wouldn't have fared any better, but the bottom line was she was responsible for what had happened.

While she and Max got Bonnie settled she thought about the guy with the black mustache and limp. Where had she seen him before? Why did she get the goose bumps when she thought of him now? She read Bonnie two stories and sang the song about the little spider that her mother used to sing to her and LuLu when they were small. Too bad Callie wouldn't be around to teach Bonnie the hand motions that went with the song.

She held Bonnie a little tighter, a little closer. She hated to let her go, but Ryan and Effie would be coming back from San Diego soon and Quaid from Alaska. They wouldn't need her, and Keefe was picking up Big-Brother 101 just fine. Besides, she had an article to write and, with luck, a new position as editor at *Soap Scoops* to deal with.

Bonnie fell asleep, and Callie put her in the pink everything baby bed. She took the baby monitor and Max with Dusty tagging along checked the back doors to make sure they were locked, then went onto the front porch to catch the sunset. Max sprawled across the cool wood floor, Dusty on the swing. Callie turned on the radio that was still there from the night they had taught Digger to dance. Peter, Paul and Mary sang about flying on a jet plane, and Callie opened her PC to check her e-mail and see if M. Perry had anything to say. As the machine charged up, she caught sight of Keefe coming across the yard from the docks below the cliff.

His hair was lighter, she realized. Being out in the sun just ten days had brought out the natural color better than any salon ever could. His walk was self-assured, like someone who'd come this way many times before and owned his surroundings. He might look all polished from being in New York and have a certain sophistication about him from being on TV and in front of the camera, but he fit this place, too. The rugged edge of Lex Zandor wasn't all acting.

Keefe was a man in charge, a man you could depend on to make things right, a man who didn't run when things went south, a man who trusted in his ability more than the cash in his bank account to get the job done. She'd never realized all that till she got to know him on the Landing, and that was not going to make leaving any easier.

"Hey," he said as he took the four wood steps in two hops. He leaned over the back of the wicker chair where she sat and peered at the screen. "Anything from M. Perry?"

Keefe's presence surrounded her like sunshine, making her feel good, happy to be exactly where she was. "Zip. Think I should e-mail him? Something innocent like 'I got held up in the storm and never made it to Kerby's. Sorry I missed you, let's reschedule.' "

"If he saw the three of you gals in those red boas, it's hopeless, Callie. But then again you've got nothing to lose by trying."

"And I could find out if he was there at all."

"Anyone look suspicious to you?" Keefe sat across from her on the settee.

"You know, there was a guy in a mustache running away when all the commotion started. But he had a limp, and being part of a bar fight when you have a bum leg isn't the best."

"Sounds more like someone trying to get out of harm's way than anything else. So now what?"

She still had that nagging feeling she'd seen mustache man before. But she saw him for only a few seconds while under attack from four brutes; that was enough to give anyone a nagging feeling. She typed off the message to M. Perry, then set the PC on the table. "So, where are the others? I didn't see them come up the hill with you."

"Working on the *Lee*. They're motivated like hell to make this work. The extra income should make marriage a real possibility for them all. I wouldn't be surprised to see the *Lee* host a few nuptials along with the shows this fall. And Digger wanted me to tell you the deal with him falling for Georgette to get her off my case is over. He wants Georgette on his own terms, not because of some deal he's made with us."

"But he really needs the money, especially now."

"He wants Georgette more."

She smiled at the thought. "We're matchmakers and didn't even know it. The *Lee*'s a showboat and a love boat. There's a lot of history here, and she needs to be refurbished accurately as much as possible. I bet there are some old photos stored somewhere on board. We should find them and do this restoration right."

He hooked his leg over the arm of the settee. "Okay, what's the future editor of *Soap Scoops* doing with all this interest in showboats and local history?"

"I majored in historical restoration, but you don't pay the bills and put your sister through private schools doing that. Editor of a fast-growing magazine is the way to go. LuLu will make a great attorney. She's so smart, always has been. A shame our parents didn't live to see her at this state of her life. Dad was an attorney, and LuLu following in his footsteps is just what he would have wanted. We've been headed in this direction for so long, and now we're almost there. I got her internships in law offices when she did her undergrad work, and now the dream comes true. What could be better?"

"I'm sure your parents would have been proud."

And Keefe knew all about having parents proud of you. "Thank God, Dad supported me in acting. Even in the hard times he let me do my thing. I'm sure he wanted to say, 'Look, you numbskull, take over the family business and drive the tows. Be done with this acting crap,' but he never said that. He just told me if acting was what I really wanted to do, to hang in there and make it happen."

Callie pointed to the road coming up from the docks. "That's Georgette."

"And she's walking fast. Georgette doesn't do anything fast except ride on Digger's Harley." Keefe stood. "I'll go see what's the matter."

"I'll stay right here. I've locked all the doors and down-stairs windows."

Keefe paused. "Something's worrying you, isn't it?"

"We're no closer to finding Mimi, and whoever is look-ing for her is kicking the search up a notch with those posters. I thought M. Perry might be a PI, but now I think Mimi was into something really big, and the people she's got the goods on aren't trusting anyone who could poten-tially turn on them and get them into more trouble. M. Perry is either part of the evildoers themselves or someone unsavory who's been hired and operates outside the law."

"That investigative mind of yours is on full alert."

"There's a lot going on. I'll stay right on this porch. Rory is due back in a few hours. He's helping Thelma with a plumbing problem since Conrad is still in New Orleans. He's been spending a lot of time helping her out."

"They're really close, best of friends. When Mom died Thelma stepped in. She's family." Keefe trotted down the steps and met Georgette on the road, her face pulled into a worried frown, slightly bedraggled—Georgette was never bedraggled, least since Keefe knew her. She pushed damp hair from her face as Keefe stopped her and asked, "Hey, hold up. Where's the fire?"

"I . . . I'm not feeling good. Thought I'd get a Coke and some aspirin at Slim's before it gets worse."

He put a reassuring hand on her hot shoulder. "Do you want to come into the house? I'm sure we have something for a headache."

"No, no. I just need a fountain Coke. Settles my stom-ach." Georgette swiped a bead of perspiration from her upper lip. "I get these all the time. I've got to go."

"I'll come with you." He took her hand. "It's okay, Georgette."

She looked even more frantic. "You don't have to come. I'll be fine."

He tugged her along. "You don't look fine. We'll get your Coke and sit for a spell, and you'll calm down and feel better." They crossed the road and walked along till the familiar neon beer lights glowed from the windows of the bar. Keefe opened the door. The crowd was just starting to build, young Jimmy Jude at the old upright playing "Howlin' For My Baby." They flagged down Sally at the bar and she came over and looked from one to the other. "You two out together? That's bound to get tongues wagging around here."

"We're out looking for a Coke and aspirin for Georgette's headache."

Sally smiled and patted Georgette's hand. "We'll fix you right up. You'll be good as new in no time."

Georgette asked, "Uh, I didn't happen to leave my purse here, did I?"

Sally shook her head. "No one's turned it in, and the Landing's real good about that sort of thing. I'll go get what you need."

Georgette said to Keefe, "I must have left my purse at Digger's. Do you mind—"

"Paying for your aspirin and Coke would be my pleasure. I think you're looking worse."

Sally gave her the pills and soda, and Georgette downed them. Keefe said, "Let me take you home. All this smoke and music isn't doing you any good."

Sally reached behind the bar and snagged keys from a hook. "Dad's truck is out back. Should have a full tank of gas. Watch out for Grant, though since it's not raining, you should be okay."

Georgette frowned. "Grant."

"Ghost."

Georgette's eyes rolled. "And I thought I had a headache before."

Keefe took the keys from Sally and headed Georgette toward the door till he heard behind him, "Hey, O'Fallon."

Keefe turned and got sucker punched right in the jaw, sending him reeling backward into a table, drinks flying. The guy came at him again, and Keefe faked a left swing but landed a solid blow with his right into the guy's gut, making him double over, then added a swing to the jaw. He was damn tired of guys swinging at him.

"That's enough!" Sally yelled, brandishing a baseball bat and charging around the bar. She slammed the bat on the table. "This here's a respectable place."

In two seconds Demar was at her side, apron covered in barbecue sauce and looking meaner than a bull with a jackhammer up his butt. He snatched the bat and shoved Sally behind him.

Keefe held up his hands in surrender. "Hey, man, I didn't start this."

"Like hell you didn't, O'Fallon," said the guy who'd hit him. "You're turning my son into a damn pansy just like yourself. You're nothing but a coward, and now you're hiding behind a girl." He coughed and tried to right himself as he rubbed his jaw.

Demar glared. "Seems to me the pansy here sure kicked your ass and doesn't need to hide."

Keefe added, "Who's your son? Who the hell are you?"

"Like you don't remember me. Butch Longford ring a bell? I used to beat the hell out of you till—"

"Till Quaid came along and I learned how to fight. Who the hell's your son?"

"Barry. Bad enough his mama insisted on Barry, now he's doing some fairy princess thing on a stage and acting like some fruitcake when he should be playing baseball. And if it wasn't for you giving him that part, he'd be the best pitcher this town has ever seen." Butch made a dive

for Keefe, and Demar held him back. "Knock it off, Longford."

"Then tell him to leave my boy alone."

Keefe said, "Barry's a good actor, loves the theater, and
if you give him half a chance and you come to the play,
you'll agree. Look, I'm sure you love your son and want
what's best for him."

"I want you to go back to New York."

"You want Barry to be you and all the things you aren't.
How much a coward is that? I'll make you a deal. Let
Barry do the play, you come see him perform, and if you
can look me in the eye and tell me he's not a damn good
actor, I'll build the high school a new baseball field with
my own money."

Keefe knew he had Butch. The whole town was here as
witness, and if he didn't agree to the offer, he'd look like a
total narrow-minded fool. If Barry was good and Butch
said he wasn't, he'd look like an ignorant imbecile.

Demar growled. "That's fair enough. Now you two
shake."

Butch took Keefe's hand. "I hate your guts, O'Fallon."

"And I don't give a damn." He turned and ushered
Georgette toward the door.

Outside Slim came around the corner from the alley
porch out back. He handed Keefe a towel with ice along
with a great smile showing perfect white across his dark
face. "Lordy, it was nice to see you flatten that asshole
after all these years," Slim said in his deep voice that
seemed to resonate around in his barreled chest before it
came out. He chuckled, the sound deeper still. "I can't
wait to tell your daddy about it, do his old heart good,
too, though he has other things for making that happen
right now."

Slim's eyes widened as if he'd said something he shouldn't
have. "Bonnie I'm talking about," he added in a rush. "That

baby is sure a peach and could brighten anyone's life, especially your daddy's. I better be getting back to my ribs and chicken. If they burn, there could be a mutiny." He winked at Keefe. "Damn fine job, boy. Damn fine. Sure as hell made my day."

Slim ambled toward the back porch where the usual slow circle of gray smoke disappeared into the darkness, making the whole Landing smell of great food.

Georgette took Keefe's arm and smiled. "I have to agree with Slim; that was a pretty awesome punch, especially for a pretty-boy TV star."

Keefe laughed and steered Georgette toward the truck. "When I auditioned for the role of Lex Zandor they wanted someone who could dance and throw a punch and make them both look good." He helped her, then climbed in the other side. "The things you do for show business."

"Almost as crazy as stealing a set of stairs. Who would have thought people would actually do that?"

Keefe drove for Hastings House. "Please tell me you're kidding."

"They're doing the deed as we speak. Joe said it took them all a week of working like dogs to get those stairs done, they were perfect and they sure as heck weren't going to do all that work over just because Stanley got herself into a snit about the play."

Keefe pulled into the drive of Hastings House. "What if they get caught? Did they think of that? It'll be real hard to put on a play behind bars. If Stanley catches them, she'll press charges."

"I don't like that woman at all. I had a teacher like that once. Said I was stupid. I gained twenty pounds that year and never slowed down."

"We all had a teacher like her once, and that's a damn shame."

Keefe kissed her cheek. "Hope you feel better soon. Lie

down with a cold towel, I hear that helps. If you feel worse, tell Thelma." He waved to Georgette as she entered the house, then headed back to town. He had to stop the cast from getting those stairs. He didn't need them in the pokey; that would screw up the plans for Digger and the *Lee*.

Keefe parked the truck a block away from the school, thankful for only a sliver of moonlight and streetlights that were quaint as hell but not all that bright. Whistling, he headed for the school, hands in pockets, doing his best performance of Opie in Mayberry. He caught a flash of light across the gym windows at the top and heard something thud and clank inside. Damn, they were already there. The term Showboat Shenanigans took on a whole new meaning, and across the street Stanley was headed his way.

Fuck!

She pursed her lips as she drew up in front of him her back to the gym. "And why are you out at this time of night, Keefe O'Fallon? Thinking about apologizing to me? And I just might accept it if you give up being director and let me take over."

"I'm taking a walk just like you." Behind Stanley the door to the gym opened, and a set of stairs paraded out, eight pairs of legs supporting it. The spectacle turned the corner, probably to a waiting truck in the back.

He continued, "And since the weather report makes no mention of hell freezing over you can bet I'm not letting you direct my play." Oh, crap. Was that Callie holding open the door?

"It's your funeral, and I'm not taking a walk just for the heck of it," jeered Stanley. "I'm here to check on my gym. This afternoon I told the school board you were putting on an inferior performance, a play that really wasn't a play, and they backed me all the way. We don't need an embarrassment in this town."

Think of something to say. Stall! "Well, it's not going to work."

Her eyes narrowed. "What's not going to work?"

"Stopping the performance. It didn't stop Shakespeare when they shut down the Rose; he merely took *Romeo and Juliet* to the Curtain. If it worked for old Bill, it can darn well work for me."

She put her hands to her hips and jutted both her chins. "There is no other theater in town, Mr. Smartypants, and why is your jaw bruised? You're still nothing but a no-good ruffian causing trouble around here."

Oh, hell, was that a . . . balcony coming out now, eight pairs of legs walking under it? And once again Callie as doorman . . . rather doorwoman. Everyone else was hauling sets, and Digger was in charge of the getaway truck. But right now Keefe had to say something to Stanley to keep her occupied. "We do have another stage, the *Liberty Lee.*"

"That rust bucket?" she scoffed on a sour laugh, making Keefe angry enough to spit nails. He'd had enough grief from arrogant assholes who thought they knew everything.

"Let me tell you something. The *Lee* is going to be great, the play is going to be great and I'm going to do whatever I can to get you out of teaching theater and putting on plays in this community. You're ruining potentially good actors by not giving them a chance, especially young men because you like sweet little girls to play in sweet little plays. And you being the superintendent's sister is going to protect your job for just so long."

The balcony turned for the back of the school, and the door slipped from Callie's fingers, making a bang. The only reason Stanley didn't notice was because her face was so red and puffed in outrage it probably sealed her ears shut. "How dare you," she finally spluttered as Callie dashed to the back of the school, making him weak with relief. Stanley continued, "One of these days you're going to get yours, and I'm not the only one who wants that to happen."

"Whatever," he said to Stanley as Callie caught his eye from around the corner of the building, smiled sweetly, gave a knowing wave, then took off. Thank God for that. An engine caught behind the school, and Stanley's ears perked like a bloodhound's. "What's that? Someone breaking into my gym."

"It's not yours, it belongs to the town and that sound is a car. Kids necking behind the school no doubt." Digger probably had the stairs and balcony balanced on the back of his pickup and was slowly taking them to the *Lee* by way of the back roads. Then they'd paint the set, and Stanley would have no proof that it was the same one that had gone missing from the gym. But right now he just needed to keep Stanley riled a few more minutes so everyone could make a clean getaway. "You should take early retirement, do us all a favor and get out of here." That should make her implode.

"Maybe you should drop dead."

He heard the truck engine fading. That was good. "You know, I'm sorry we didn't have this conversation earlier. I feel better now, don't you?"

"Bite me."

Keefe arched his brows in mock surprise. "My, my, such language."

Stanley gave him the bird and stormed off across the street, not even checking the gym. It had worked. Showboat Shenanigans had succeeded in getting the sets; now they had to succeed in using them. A lot depended on the play going well—Barry's future as an actor, saving the *Lee and Keefe O'Fallon's* debut as a director. He hadn't thought about that before, but he liked directing a lot more than he thought he would. But a small gig on the showboat wasn't exactly the big-time, and it sure didn't pay the bills.

He'd had enough drama for one night, a cold beer and sitting on the front porch sounded perfect. And he wanted to talk to Callie. Whatever had possessed her to be a burglar? Knowing Callie, it hadn't taken much.

He returned the truck keys to Slim so as not to interrupt Sally and Demar sneaking kisses in the kitchen. There was more cooking at Slim's than ribs and chicken, and he felt jealous. He crossed the road and headed home. Demar and Sally had found some middle ground between a cop and keeping secrets and learning to trust each other. For him and Callie there was no middle anything. She wasn't about to give up her editor job to move to New York and watch him be a soap star.

Lights glowed from Quaid's room on the second floor. Callie was home, and he smiled at the thought of seeing her, talking to her, spending time with her. The porch light was on, and he took the stairs two at a time and opened the front door, least he tried to. Locked. Well, hell, Callie was taking this security thing seriously, and that was good except he'd forgotten his key. A locked house on the Landing was hard to get used to. Okay, he locked his place in New York, and he had a security system, but this was different. This was home. He rang the bell and whammed the pineapple door knocker he'd given his dad one Christmas when Keefe first moved to New York.

He tried the doorknob again as it was yanked open from the other side, pulling him straight into Callie wrapped in a towel. He snagged her in his arms to keep both of them from stumbling, did anyway and flattened her against the wall, his arms caging her on either side. "We got to quit meeting like this." He grinned. "Then again, I think I really like meeting like this."

"You need a key. With all the racket you were making I thought something terrible happened. I grabbed the towel and ran."

"Dad?"

"Came for Bonnie and spending the night at Hastings House in case the plumbing repair isn't repaired."

"A flooded house would not be good."

Her hair hung straight and wet, drops trickling down her neck and face, off the tip of her nose, across her chest and disappearing into the towel. Her breasts rose and fell, the soft mounds of delicious flesh visible above the blue terry cloth. Her eyes went from emerald to jade, the only sound the grandfather clock and their breaths coming as one.

She licked her bottom lip. "So," she said, her voice barely a whisper, her body leaning into him. "What's the big emergency?"

"This." He wound his fingers into the top of the towel, pulled it loose and let it drop to the floor. "I'm getting pretty good at undoing towels."

"I'm getting pretty good at dressing in them when only you're around."

A half smile fell across his lips, and he gazed at her loveliness for a long moment. "This get-up is on purpose?"

"You pressing me to the wall isn't?"

"Oh, Callie girl, what are we going to do?"

"Guess." She gave him a sweet smile, a glint of devil lurking in her big green eyes. Then she tangled her fingers in his hair and seared his mouth with a kiss, the heat from her body seeping right through his clothes. He swept her into his arms and turned for the stairs.

"There," she said in an uncontrolled breath against his mouth. "I can't wait." She eyed the newel post, the swirled top the size of a small stool. He set her there, her legs embracing his middle as he stood on the second stair, took a condom from his wallet and branded her with his own kiss. He dropped his jeans, she gripped his shoulders, her legs wide and welcoming, and he held her tight and thrust into her sweet flesh so ready and wet for him.

Her body convulsed in climax, meeting him thrust for thrust, consumed with making love to him. His own climax more intense than he'd ever experienced, his connection to Callie filling him with a total sense of completeness.

She rested against him, her body still quivering . . . or maybe that was his. Neither of them moved, the grandfather clock ticking off the seconds of euphoria, then minutes, neither of them wanting to break the moment, the spell.

She kissed his neck, sending more aftershocks through him. "You are the master of the bedroom," she said in a smoky voice. "And the hallway and the attic. Making love to you is a fantasy come true."

Chapter 13

Georgette walked out of the bank and put the money in her new purse. She couldn't believe she'd actually lost her purse. How could she do such a thing with that phone of Bob's in there? What if someone found it? Turned it on? That's why she couldn't make a big deal out of looking for it and had faked the headache. If it showed up on its own, fine. If the robber took the cash and ditched the purse, so much the better.

She'd cancelled her credit cards right away so no one could use them. Her driver's license was in her other purse, so she didn't have to replace that. Since neither her purse nor someone wondering why she'd recorded Keefe and the others had surfaced in the last two days she was probably in the clear, her purse gone wherever stolen purses go.

Thank heavens for wire transfer of funds. First thing was to repay Digger. She'd borrowed money from him so she could eat, saying her bank had messed up her ATM card. He'd lent her the cash without blinking an eye, and she knew for a fact he didn't have any to lend. He was a fine man, not the man for her, of course, but very fine all the same . . . and she'd used him shamelessly to get to Keefe.

She didn't feel good about that, but he'd probably never

know, so what was the harm. She headed for Slim's to get an iced tea to chase off the blistering afternoon heat and saw Rachel coming her way, looking totally bewildered. What could it be this time, the printers sent matchbooks with her name printed in gold instead of silver? Oh, the tragedy of it all. And why was she at the Landing with only two weeks till the wedding? Georgette stopped under the shade of the huge elm by the hardware store.

"Oh, Georgette, I'm so glad I found you."

"The town's not that big, Rachel, and don't look so frantic. I said I'll be at the wedding, and I will. You didn't have to come down here. I won't gripe about wearing yellow chiffon or the tiara or the—"

"There isn't any wedding," she wailed, tears streaming down her perfect face. "Rex has been fucking around on me with everything in Savannah that wears a skirt, and we both know that's not exclusive to the female population."

She sobbed and threw her arms around Georgette. "I don't know what to do. Mother wants me to forgive and forget and go on with the wedding. It's going to be the social event of the year. I've already received my entire silver service in gifts and my china." She looked at Georgette through her tears. "I have such a lovely china pattern, Chantilly. I love Chantilly, have since I was a little girl. I never thought I'd actually get it."

"For Pete's sake, Rachel, you can't get married because you have great china and silver."

"Rex's father promised a house on Hilton Head Island and a Porsche if I came back. He even threw in a credit card at Saks; you know how I love Saks. Rex's political career is finished if this comes out."

"What's out is Rex. I have to say I never saw that one coming." She patted Rachel's back. "You can't sell out for a house, a car and status."

"And Saks. People have sold out for a lot less, you

know. I'm not all that into sex, and maybe if I could convince Rex not to be, this will blow over. His father threatened to have him neutered; that might help."

"I think he was kidding . . . or maybe not, knowing the
Prescotts and their desire to get into the political scene."
Georgette hugged Rachel, something they hadn't done in
years.

"Can I stay here with you for a while and hide out? I'll
call Mother and tell her I'm okay, but I have to figure out
what to do, and no one will think to look for me here. I
mean, us together is rare."

"It wasn't always, you know. Remember fishing the
Savannah River off the front porch?"

"Oh, my God, I actually held a worm, didn't I?" She
made a face, then it softened. "I caught a striped bass
once. We let it go and threw it back."

"Yeah, I remember that, too." Better times, closer times.
Georgette took Rachel's hand. "Let's get some iced tea,
and then I'll take you over to Hastings House. It's a nice
bed and breakfast, though I have to tell you I think the
place is truly haunted all to hell and back. There's so much
ruckus going on at night."

They entered Slim's and found a table easily enough in
the middle of the afternoon. A good-looking guy she'd
seen around plucked out a soul tune on a guitar, and Sally
came over to their table. Georgette said, "This is my sister,
Rachel, and we'd like two iced teas, please."

Rachel sighed, "Make mine a Long Island iced tea with
refills. It's been that kind of day."

Sally patted Rachel's shoulder. "We all have that kind of
day from time to time, honey."

Sally left, and Digger came over. He looked tired to the
bone, but when their eyes met he brightened up and smiled
at her. The man had the best smile ever. "Digger, this is my
sister, Rachel. She's here for a visit."

Sally brought the teas and handed Digger a beer. Rachel slurped down half the liquid in one long gulp as Digger and Georgette looked on in total wonder. Seven shots of booze was a lot of booze. Rachel swiped her mouth with the back of her hand, belched, eyes not focusing, and said to Digger, "My fiancé is a transvestite, or bisexual or something and I'm trying to decide if I should marry the rat or not. I'm not all that into sex, so that's not a deal breaker but . . ."

To his immense credit Digger didn't look shocked or appalled. He looked sincere and took Rachel's hand. Leave it to Digger to know the right thing to do. "You're a beautiful, classy, uniquely wonderful lady like your sister, and you don't have to settle for anything that's not perfect for you or anyone who doesn't treat you with respect. This man is not for you, and you're lucky to find out now before he hurts you any more. If you and Georgette would like to come to dinner on the *Lee* tonight, I'd be honored to have you as my guests."

"Thanks." Rachel belched again. "I'll remember that." She polished off the rest of the Long Island, and Georgette seriously doubted she'd remember anything since half her brain cells were now inebriated.

Sally put another Long Island in front of Rachel and a bag beside Digger and said to him, "Here's the food you ordered for the acting company. Tell Joe I gave him two extra pickles like always." She patted Digger on the back. "Acting company sounds pretty good, doesn't it? The Landing sure is getting snooty these days."

Digger stood. "I best be getting back to work. Pleasure meeting you, Rachel. Better times are ahead, I'm sure." He touched Georgette's cheek, his blue eyes a little smoky, a soft smile on his lips and a slight blush in his cheeks. "I hope to see you tonight. And you're looking lovely today as always. You . . . You make my day."

Then he left, and Georgette realized she wished he'd stayed, not just because he complimented her, but because she liked being with him. Rachel killed off the second half of her tea, looking a little woozy . . . Make that a lot woozy. She slurred, "I'd give my eyeteeth to have a man look at me like that."

"Like what?"

Rachel giggled. "Digger is so completely in love with you that he can't see straight."

"It's you who can't see straight because of the quantity of alcohol you're consuming."

Rachel pried her eyelids open enough to see out. "Digger is crazy for you, the kind of crazy that puts cars and houses and shopping sprees to shame. You can't buy love like that. Believe me, I know that now. Complete love happens, like . . . magic."

She let out a deep sigh and propped her chin in her palm. "It's how I always wanted Rex to look at me, and he never did and truth be told, I probably never looked at him like that either. I was marrying status; he was marrying respectability and a political future. Did you know that Daddy being a self-made man guaranteed Rex the blue-collar vote?" She patted the glass in front of her. "I think I have reached a state of clarity."

"You've reached the state of zonked."

She started in on the second Long Island. "I was nothing but a political contribution. All you are is loved. I like your way better."

"Digger has nothing but a broken-down boat. He's a loser, Rachel."

Her eyes narrowed. "If you think that, then you're the one who's the loser, Georgette, even worse than me. When you had your great makeover you should have made over what was inside while you were doing the stuff on the outside. The money ruined us, you know that? All of us.

Mother was too busy with the Savannah social scene, I followed her and you never knew where you fit in." She poked Georgette's chest. "You got to be true to yourself, not anyone else, or your life is nothing but a big old sham. I wanted to please Mother by marrying Rex. I wanted to ride on Rex's coattails and be the Washington princess because he'd certainly be the prince. Then I found out he was more of a queen."

She finished the second drink, stood, righted her shoulders and smiled. "Now I'm going to play that piano over there and forget about men and my disastrous life thus far."

"You hate playing the piano. You took lessons only because Mother bribed you with a new spring wardrobe each year and playing got your name in the society section of the newspaper when you gave your recital in Ms. Hillar's piano room."

Rachel hiccupped. "Actually, I love playing the piano, but pretending like I didn't is how I got the clothes." She massaged her forehead. "I think I'm tired of playing games. I think I've had my fill. I think I want to find someone like Digger. And if you have one ounce of sense in your head, you'll realize I'm right."

Rachel weaved her way to the old upright and sat down on the little round stool so well worn by others who'd sat there before. The guy on the guitar stopped playing and gave her the once-over and smiled as Rachel played something Beethoven. He strummed his guitar, then kicked up the tempo. Rachel looked at him and did the same as if meeting his challenge. Then she did some fancy improvising that stunned Georgette as guitar man followed and added to it. Beethoven goes jazz. Georgette didn't know her sister had it in her. Surprise, surprise.

But what really surprised Georgette even more was that

Rachel was right on with her comment about Digger and about Georgette. Digger did love her, and she'd used him without a second thought, and that was the worst part of all. She felt sick. What was she doing? How could she do something like that? She wasn't always so horrid, was she?

Rachel stood, shoved back the stool with her foot and launched into hypermode piano playing, matching the guitar player note for note. She danced as she played, her behind gyrating to the music, the guitarist doing the same in perfect sync.

Rachel always knew what she was about—superficial or otherwise—and what she wanted. Georgette's approach was a poor-me, ugly-duckling attitude because she didn't know what she wanted and blamed everyone else for not getting it. Then she'd drowned her sorrows and lack of self-respect in a Snickers and half gallon of chocolate chip ice cream. But the fact that she was willing to use Digger to write some stupid article to get her parents to notice her constituted a new low in her life.

She felt numb, and it wasn't from alcohol. Rachel's words were like getting smacked upside the head. Rachel seeing Rex for what he was and coping gave Georgette the courage to face who she was. No wonder she wasn't the favorite daughter; right now she didn't like herself much.

Thank God she'd lost her purse. She would have written that article for Bob. She would have told everyone about Keefe coming home to take care of Bonnie and hoping to find the missing Mimi. That could have gotten people looking for Mimi, driving her more into hiding than ever, and could have exposed Bonnie to danger by bringing around reporters and curiosity seekers. For sure it would have exposed Keefe's private life and Rory's. They deserved better from her; they were her friends.

Rachel's breakup with Rex was the best thing that ever

happened to Georgette Cooper and from the looks of Rachel-unplugged, the best thing that ever happened to her. *Thank you, Rex.*

Georgette went to the bar and ordered a Long Island iced tea for herself, came back and Bob was sitting at her table. She slowed her steps and took in his shaggy mustache and beady eyes. A chill ran up her spine, and she sat, then leaned across the table, glad the music muffled her words from anyone passing by. "Look, before you start, I'm not doing the article. I quit."

He sneered. "I don't think so."

She felt icy fingers grip her insides. How could she get mixed up with such a sleaze? "I lost your phone. I have no idea where it is. But I won't do the article no matter what, and no amount of publicity or money will make me change my mind."

His eyes went from nondescript gray to black dots. "Stupid bitch. How do I know you didn't sell the information to someone else?"

"Keefe and his friends are my friends. What are you going to do to me?"

"Forget I ever saw you, and I suggest you do the same." His face pulled into an ugly frown. "And I really mean that." Bob got up and sauntered toward the door. She'd never been so happy to see a man leave in her life. At least that was over with. She prayed she'd never find her purse and that whoever had it spent the money and had fun.

"Hey," said Rachel as she came back to the table. "I'm taking a rain check on Digger's for dinner. Clyde on guitar asked me to join him."

"Rachel," Georgette stage whispered. "You can't just go off with a man you don't know."

"Heck, look what happened when I went off with a man I did know. That didn't work out too good, did it?" She patted Georgette's head. "But don't you worry, Clyde builds stuff, said he was going to help Slim put in that out-door eating area, some decks and maybe an arbor. Sounds cute. Seems everyone in town knows this guy. Kind of a handyman. Just one of the good-old-boys around here. Who was that guy you were talking to?"

"No one important." Georgette prayed that was true. She stood. "Have a good time tonight. Try not to do any-thing on the rebound, huh."

Rachel went back to the piano and started in on some tune, and Clyde joined in. Georgette suddenly wanted to find Digger, be reassured everything was okay and make up to him for using him and being a snob.

How could he still like her when she acted like that? If she ran to the market, she could get some fresh fish. It wasn't like catching it herself, but if she asked the person at the market, they could refresh her cooking memory. And hadn't her mama fixed hush puppies with fish? That might be good, too.

She wanted to please Digger, let him know he was im-portant to her. If he liked her before, she planned on mak-ing him like her a lot more. She glanced around. She could live in this town, maybe set up an accounting, investing of-fice. She was happier here than she'd ever been in Savan-nah. Tonight she'd be nice to Digger . . . except in the bedroom. She had other plans for there. Naughty plans. She wondered if they sold that whipped cream in a can that came out in swirls.

Digger hammered another board in place, then stood back and admired the stage as Keefe said, "That's not a bad job, not bad at all. The height isn't as good as I'd like, but if we have the staircase reach onto the main floor and have Teddy Roosevelt—"

"That's Uncle Brewster, and Nick's doing the part, right?"

"Right. He can yell *charge,* running through the audience then onto the stairs. That would work and give us enough room for the balcony."

Digger said, "With the play being all in one room the use of audience space adds to the interest. Nick brought over some props. They're upstairs lying on top of that big cedar chest we need for the body. He found an old-time radio that we need for the news flash, a fedora for Mortimer, that's Barry, and a vintage police uniform with all the trappings that should work well."

Keefe turned to Digger and laughed. "You know this play as well as I do. Would you mind doing lights and sound effects? The actors won't have to do double duty with acting and behind-the-scene stuff if you manage it."

Digger grinned. "Thought you'd never ask." He nodded at the stage. "Thanks for doing this, Keefe."

"Hell, man, thanks for letting us use your boat. We'll get Georgette to start selling tickets and come up with a promotion budget."

"Did I just hear my name mentioned," Georgette said as she sashayed around the corner. Digger felt the air run right out of his lungs as he took her in. Not the usual sophisticated clothes this time but better. Skimpy white denim shorts tied with a pink sash and a matching bow in her hair. A flowered halter top that showed off her lovely breasts and tempting cleavage. Only a bit of makeup—none of the usual heavy stuff—and pale pink lips, not the dark red. He felt dizzy, intoxicated, and he hadn't even had one beer since he went to Slim's to pick up food for the crew. Heck, he hadn't even drank that beer he was so absorbed with Georgette. "H-hi," he finally managed.

She held up a brown bag. "I'm going to cook dinner. Fried catfish, okra, hush puppies, apple cobbler and a jug of something called white lightning from Leroy, butcher at that market. He said it was your favorite."

"Leroy only sells lightning to his best friends."

Georgette winked. "I charmed him."

And from the way she looked—and acted—Digger was sure Leroy had been charmed right out of his socks. Digger was.

Keefe put his hammer in the open toolbox. "I'm going to let you two eat."

Georgette said, "Why don't you and Callie join us for dinner?"

"I'm heading over to Slim's to test Demar's ribs. He's no Slim yet, but he's getting there. I'm doing the taste test." He patted his stomach. "Tough job but someone's got to do it." Keefe walked off, and Georgette stood beside Digger and Frenched him in the ear. "Howdy," she breathed in a sultry voice, setting every part of his body on high alert.

"I'm hot and dirty."

"Bet your lips aren't dirty. Let me taste and see." She ran her tongue over them. "See, no dirt." She plunged her tongue into his mouth, meeting his, mating with his. "See," she said again, her lips on his, the bag of groceries keeping them apart. "No dirt anywhere."

"I need a shower, Georgette, then . . . Then we can do whatever you want."

"I'll tell you what I want, big boy. I want fried catfish and all the trimmings and then . . ." She slid her tongue into his mouth again. "I want you for dessert. I have whipped cream and cherries. I have big plans for the cherries. How does hide and seek sound?"

"Holy hell."

She kissed him, then turned for the stairs. His dick was as hard as the upright holding the *Lee* together. How was he supposed to shower? He couldn't get his pants off without doing himself permanent damage. He tried to slow his heart, his breathing, soften up his dick by thinking of all the work he had to do on the *Lee*. He hobbled up the stairs past the kitchen area with the door open and Georgette singing some tune about whatever Georgette wants, Georgette gets and little Georgette wants you. She winked as he went by, and he walked right into the chest with all the props on top, the sudden pain not diminishing his desires one bit.

She said, "Want me to kiss you and make it all better?"

"No." He held up his hands in surrender, taking steps away from her. "That will not make me better. No more kissing till I can do it right."

She pulled the top from the jug of white lightning, held the cork up and licked it, her tongue going slowly from bottom to top. "You mean, do me right?"

"Ah, hell, Georgette." If he didn't get out of here right now, he'd take her right on the kitchen floor and not give one hoot how dirty he was.

He showered in record time, trying to ignore his aroused state, concentrating on the aroma of fried catfish and hush puppies. He didn't succeed. As much as he looked forward to the food he looked forward to having Georgette a hell of a lot more. He pulled on jeans that he could barely zip and shrugged into a T-shirt. Barefoot and horny, he came into the kitchen area. She had a tray loaded with food and handed it to him. "Can you take these things outside? I set places." She brought the white lightning and glasses and followed him. "Have a nice shower?"

"No."

"That's because I wasn't there to help you out." He nearly dropped the whole damn tray thinking of Georgette in the shower with him. Wobbling, he set the tray down, then parked in a chair. Georgette sat beside him, and he loaded the catfish on his plate along with everything else and said, "It's a beautiful evening." He took a bite of the fish. "This is great. I really appreciate you cooking for me."

She winked. "Wait till you see what else I do for you."

He choked. "Georgette, if you keep this up—"

"I'm betting *it* stays up all by itself, Digger. Can I take a little peek?"

"That's it." He tossed his napkin on the table, stood, yanked back Georgette's chair and scooped her into his arms. "Where are we going, Digger?" she giggled.

"Bed. Now. You're driving me crazy."

She wrapped her arms around him, kissing him on the neck. "I'm so glad."

He went down the hall, kicked open the door to his room, thankful he hadn't fixed the latch, and dropped her onto the middle of his bed. He yanked off his shirt.

"Don't stop there."

His hands stilled on the waistband of his jeans. "I won't if you won't."

"Silly boy, I haven't even started." She stood in the middle of his bed then kicked off her sandals, and they plopped onto the floor. "Got a quarter?"

"Why?"

"Amuse me."

"I intend to do a hell of a lot more than that." But he got a quarter from his dresser and tossed it to her.

"Heads or tails? We'll flip to see who takes off what next." She tossed the quarter into the air, caught it and flipped it over on her arm, keeping her palm on top so they couldn't see the coin. "Call it."

"Heads."

She pulled back her hand. "Tails. Guess that means I lose my top." She undid the knot at the back of her neck, letting the material fall forward, revealing her incredible breasts.

He gulped air as she undid the one snap at her back that held the top in place, and it fell onto the bed . . . exactly what he wanted to do.

She flipped the coin again. "I call it this time. Tails." She pulled her hand away showing heads. She crooked her finger at him. "Jeans please."

He yanked them off, leaving him in blue briefs. She said, "I can't wait to see what's underneath. Oh, it's moving; it must want out. What do you think?"

Think? He couldn't. She flipped again, and he caught the quarter midair, tackled her around the waist, and they collapsed onto the bed. She laughed as she landed on top of him. "Cheaters never prosper," she taunted.

"Wanna bet. I think I'm prospering real good here."

Her eyes danced with excitement. "I want you to tie me up, Digger, and make wild passionate love to me."

His eyes bulged. "I can't do that, honey. It just isn't in me."

"We did a little spanky and that was fun, right?"

He felt himself blush head to toe remembering his hand on her lovely rear. "Yeah." he sighed. "It was really great but . . . bondage?"

"No, no, no. Not that, this is more like teasing. Here, let me show you what I want you to do to me." She removed her shorts and sat on his chest, a knee on either side, the heat from her sex searing his abs through the skimpy excuse she had for panties . . . and such fine panties they were. She took his hand and brought it to the old ironwork that was his headboard. "Hold on there and give me your other hand so you know exactly what I want you to do to me."

Right now he'd give her anything she wanted. She guided his hand into position. She gazed down at him. "There, that's not bad, is it?"

"Well, no but—"

"Ohmygod, there's someone coming." She pointed out the window.

"Where?" He looked but didn't see anyone, and instead

of an answer from Georgette he felt something tighten around his wrists with a decisive click. His eyes fused to Georgette's, and he pulled his hands, but they wouldn't come free. "What the hell are you doing? I'm handcuffed to my own bed."

"Well, you just admitted it wasn't bad."

"Georgette!"

"And it's for a good cause."

"Georgette!"

"I want you to have fun." She ran her fingers through her hair, scattering it in all directions, making her look hot and wild and wanting. "I found the handcuffs on the chest coming up the stairs, and I couldn't resist."

"Resist what."

She leaned over, bracing her arms on either side of his head, her lovely nipples skimming his chest. He watched them bead into firm nubs from rubbing against his coarse hair. And he'd thought he was turned on before. Watching her body become aroused was the biggest turn-on of all.

"I couldn't resist making you mine." She brushed her mouth over his. "All mine, all your best parts, for me to explore at my leisure tonight." She kissed him.

He wanted to say something, but right at the moment with Georgette's tongue in his mouth he couldn't talk. She broke the kiss, and he said, "I'm yours, I swear. You don't have to convince me. I'm not running away."

She stood over him, giving him a great view of the red spot of silk covering her. She jumped to the floor and gazed at him, then plucked the waistband of his briefs. "Well, we sure don't need these old things." She slid his briefs over his hips, his erection free for her inspection. She touched him, and he gritted his teeth and sucked in a quick breath.

"I can only stand so much of that."

"You're right. No hands. But you have so many delicious parts, and I want to brand them all as mine and no one else's. I bet there's something in the kitchen that I can use for that. Don't go away."

"I've been tied up by a comedian."

She winked. "Closer to an artist. Just you wait." She went off, and he relaxed a little. He had a magic marker in the kitchen, and letting Georgette draw on him would be fun. He could handle that. She came back, her hands behind her back. "Guess what I found?"

"The markers."

"A can of whipped cream. Now, where do you suppose that came from? I love whipped cream. One of my favorite foods."

"Georgette, this is a really bad idea. How much control do you think I have? I'm not Superman."

She peered at his erection. "Looks pretty super to me. But there are other parts." She turned the can upside down, shaking it. "You have great abs, you know that. I'm going to mark them as my very own." She pressed the side of the nozzle, and a neat *GC* in whipped cream decorated his stomach.

He closed his eyes, fighting for restraint. "I can't do this."

"And you have a very fine chest." She added *GC* to his pecs. "And your lips. Oh, you have the most wonderful lips." His lips were decorated with whipped cream. He licked and suddenly asked, "How are you going to get rid of all this whipped cream?"

She added a dollop to her index finger and slid it provocatively into her mouth, looking more sexy than any woman should. "Yumm."

He pulled on the cuffs. "I can't have you do that. I'll never last. This isn't fair."

She gazed back to his body and tsked. "And I saved the best part of you to claim for last." Her eyes again feasted on his erection.

"No."

"Oh, yes."

She turned the can over and circled his hard-on. "Didn't want the guest of honor to get a chill." She kissed the top of his dick, and he nearly fainted dead away. She drew an arrow on each thigh, pointing straight at his penis. She winked. "In case I forget where it is."

"You're going to kill me."

"That I can promise will not happen." And he felt her warm lips meet his abs and her sweet tongue lick him clean. "I got low-fat so I wouldn't put on the pounds."

She perched on the bed and licked the cream from his chest, then the corners of his mouth, kissing him, letting him suck the sweet taste from her tongue. Her nose touched his. "Now, for the real fun."

"I can't hold on forever, Georgette."

"I'm so counting on that." She straddled him, her back facing him. His body went rigid in anticipation of what was to come. She leaned over, giving him a perfect view of her sweet, nicely rounded derriere. Her tongue licked his thighs, then around his erection. Every cell of his being strained in anticipation, and when her tongue touched the tip of his dick again he nearly lost his mind. She licked his length, pausing each time at the tip.

"Georgette," he pleaded. "You have to let me loose right now."

"But I'm not finished."

"But I am. Condoms in the drawer . . . I think. God, I hope so." She slid her panties off; reached for the drawer, took out a foiled package and covered him. She turned back around again, this time kneeling over his throbbing penis. Her eyes stayed focused on his, hers dark and hungry, and she slowly lowered herself onto him till she completely took him in. His head pounded; his heart hammered. Sweat trickled down his neck. Bracing herself on his shoulders, she lifted her bottom, then lowered, the intense rhythm perfect, the look of passion on her face driving him wild till she took him one last time and they climaxed in a rush of pure heaven.

She sprawled across him, her rapid breaths matching his, then slowing bit by bit. He said, "Do you know what I intend to do to you the minute you release me?"

She turned her head and smiled at him. "I can't wait to find out, Digger."

Chapter 14

Keefe sat at the table at Slim's, waiting for his fourth plate of ribs in as many days. Never in all his life and love of ribs did he think he'd get tired of them, but he was. Plus his cholesterol reading must be through the roof, and he'd put on five pounds. Demar placed a platter of ribs in front of him, then sat across the table and waited as Keefe bit into the juicy meat.

"Well," Demar coaxed.

"It's great."

"But not perfect." Demar leaned back. "Okay, what's it going to take to make you say it's the best? Fifty bucks? A hundred? Name your price."

Sally came over and kissed his head. "You trying to bribe the judge, my man?"

"Would I do that?"

"Hell, yes." She kissed him again.

Keefe held up a rib section. "This is really good, but it needs more time in the smoker. Where's Slim?"

"On his way to Atlanta for a Braves game, got baseline seats. And you are damn picky," Demar groused and snagged the plate away from Keefe.

Keefe plucked a rib hanging off the end of the platter. "I'm trying to make you perfect."

Demar grinned and kissed Sally. "That's her job." He headed for the back porch and the grills, and Keefe asked Sally, "So, what's going on with you two?"

"Don't know. Demar's a policeman, and I'm not asking him to give that up for me. But Clyde Miller's back in town. He's going to oversee the new construction of the houses going up and help Dad put in the outside eating area."

"Didn't he just finish a two-year stint putting in that eighteen-mile bridge across the Louisiana swamps? Think he about lost his mind trying to make peace between the environmentalists, the politicians and keep the whole project on budget. Had a piece in *Time* magazine on him last month."

Sally nodded. "He's looking for some R and R and quality guitar time, and I better get back to work or I'm going to be looking for a new job."

Keefe bit into the rib he'd salvaged from the platter as a pretty young woman with dazzling green eyes came up to him. "Keefe O'Fallon? I was wondering—"

"I don't have autographing stuff with me, but if you come around later on, I'll leave a picture and T-shirt here for you and some—"

She laughed. It was a familiar laugh, one he'd heard before. "I'm looking for my sister, Callie Cahill, and the guy out back cooking the most wonderful barbecue on earth said you might know. I'm LuLu Cahill."

Keefe grinned, wiped his hands, stood and shook her hand. "First of all don't give that guy out back too much encouragement or his head will get so big there'll be no living with him, and Callie's at the house, I think. Or she could be out strolling the baby in some new pink outfit she bought."

LuLu chuckled. "I don't think she's the only one spoiling baby Bonnie. Callie's told me all about your family."

He liked LuLu Cahill a lot, probably because she reminded him of Callie. He said, "I haven't seen Callie for a while." Like last night when he'd snuck into her bed. "But I'll help you find her."

He held the door open for LuLu, and they stepped into the sunshine. "Are you taking a vacation before you start law school? I think your sister's as excited as you are about going to Duke."

"I doubt that."

"There she is," Keefe said, pointing toward the market down the street.

"And I bet that bunny outfit Bonnie has on is one you bought."

He grinned. "Guilty. How'd you know?"

"The hat is baseball cap style, not a bonnet. Something a guy would appreciate." LuLu laughed, and Callie caught sight of them, her eyes widening in recognition. She waved and pushed the stroller in their direction, meeting up in front of the bank, the blue awning offering some respite from the sun. She hugged LuLu. "You look wonderful. What are you doing here?"

LuLu grinned, but it looked more like a tension grin than a real one. Something was up in the land of Cahill. LuLu said, "I came to see you, of course."

"Missed me that much?"

"We need to talk."

Callie's face blanched. "Are you all right?"

"Actually, I'm fine. Better than I've been in a while." She took Callie's hand and pulled in a deep breath. "We should probably go somewhere private for this, but I might lose my nerve. I've been practicing this speech all the way from Atlanta, so here it goes. I've enrolled in art school. I'm going to Cal Arts in Valencia, California. I want to go into film, be a director. I don't want to be a lawyer. I'm getting loans and paying my own way, and I don't want you to pay for anything else. You've given me enough."

LuLu bit her lip and shrugged. "There, that's it, I said it. I'm driving out to California now."

Callie didn't move. Was she even breathing? Finally she managed, "You're driving out alone to California from Atlanta? What if you have car trouble, get stranded, get mugged, carjacked, the victim of road rage? Have you lost your mind? What are you doing besides ruining your life? You have to go to law school."

"I'm in a ninety-five Honda Accord, nothing much to carjack or rage over. And I'm twenty-two, Callie, and . . . and Jerome is going with me."

"Cat? Dog? Goldfish?"

"Guy. We've been living together for the last year. He's going to acting school."

"You're living with an . . . actor and not going to law school?"

"Hey?" Keefe chimed in, and Callie continued, "And you're sleeping with him?"

LuLu kissed Callie. "I've got to go. We need to make St. Louis tonight. You and I will visit. This is a really good thing. You don't have to work at *Soap Scoops* anymore. You can do antique restoration and write and whatever else you want to do like you planned on before you had to raise me." She stepped back and held her arms wide. "See, I'm raised. Mission accomplished."

"Have I ever complained? What happened to your dreams about being a lawyer like Dad? I don't believe this."

"That was your dream, part of trying to keep the family together. And we are together; you and I are family." She kissed her cheek. "I'll write. I'll call. I'll keep in touch. I love you. Don't hate me."

Callie grabbed LuLu's hand. "You can't do it. You're making a terrible mistake. This stupid idea is nothing more than a whim of Jessie's or Jerome's or whatever his name. His acting idea is influencing you to do the wild and carefree thing. Wild and carefree does not pay the bills, LuLu, and will get you nowhere except a waitressing job at the local chili house. You're going to be a lawyer, dammit."

LuLu pried Callie's fingers from her arm. "No, I'm not, and following your dreams is never stupid. I'm leaving now." LuLu swiped away her tears, turned and ran down the sidewalk, nearly colliding into Eleanor Stick, rounding the corner and crossing the street.

Callie fumed, "How could LuLu do this. Wreck everything we worked so hard for. That . . . that ungrateful little snot."

"Whoa." Keefe held up his hands. "You raised her; you don't own her. Go after her, tell her you're sorry and you support her in whatever she wants to do."

"Like hell. I can't do that. I hate this."

"Well, you better get over it or you'll lose your sister. You're making this about your life, Callie, not hers. Think about what you're doing."

Callie peered up at him. "She's sleeping with an actor, for God's sake."

"So are you."

"She's giving up law school to direct? What kind of life is that?"

"My kind of life."

"Exactly. No stability whatsoever. Who can live like that?"

He stilled, letting her words sink in. "Obviously not you." He shoved his hands in his pockets. "Guess we know how you feel about what I do."

"Well, we sure know how you feel about what I do. You've never kept that a secret either. Shoe pinches when it's on the other foot, doesn't it?"

"I've got play rehearsal. You see, I'm the director."

"Well, bully for you. I'm sure that can pay the bills when they come due."

"Come see me when you cool off."

"I am cool and rational and know what's best for my sister."

"Yeah, well, she just left here in tears, and you gave her no good reason to contact you again. You tell me how rational that is." He walked toward the showboat, anger boiling in his gut. How could someone he cared about so much be this stubborn? LuLu was right. If you didn't have dreams and follow them, you had nothing at all.

Callie rocked Bonnie on the porch. She hadn't spoken to LuLu since she left two days ago, and she hadn't spoken to Keefe either. She'd never understand his cavalier approach to life, and he'd never understand responsibility and doing what needed to be done. She fed Bonnie the last of her bottle and sat her up for a burp. Gently she patted her back, the first stars of night appearing over the Mississippi.

Rory's Suburban pulled into the drive, and he got out and made his way around the stroller she'd left by the driveway and then up the steps. He swept Bonnie into his arms. "There's my little princess." He kissed her, and she smiled at him as if he were the only person on earth. Callie remembered when LuLu looked at her like that, but no more. One of these days LuLu would realize her older sister was right.

Rory said, "Think I'll take sweet pea here for a walk to Hastings House."

"Weren't you there this morning?"

"Leaky pipes. Thelma is having a devil of a time with the plumbing."

"Maybe she needs a professional plumber to help her out with this."

"Too expensive. Besides, that's the way those old houses are. If it's not one thing, it's another, and I want to help Thelma as much as I can. Even though Conrad's back he's so busy with the dry dock and getting the business together he's never around to help out."

"Thelma's lucky to have you around."

Rory studied her. "Now you and Keefe can meet up over at Slim's. Hear they got a gal on piano and Clyde on guitar and they're bringing down the house."

Callie looked back to the river. "I'm pretty tired tonight, and Keefe's got play practice."

"Eight-thirty's too late for practice and too early for bed. So, what's really going on between you?"

"Big difference of opinion. Keefe's a card-carrying member of the follow your dreams club, and responsibility is my middle name. We don't exactly see eye to eye."

"Christ in a sidecar, girl. Is that what's keeping you apart? No two people ever see eye to eye all the time. My Mimi's out there somewhere, and we have no idea how this is ever going to end. The state is building a case against these swindlers, and she has the goods on them. But if they find her first, it won't be pretty."

"Why doesn't she just turn herself in for protective custody or whatever that is?"

"She went to the Attorney General's Office when she found the second set of books for that company she worked for. They were overcharging the state in hours while working on their own projects and using substandard building material on levees and docks. The next day she nearly got run over by a bus because someone pushed her from behind into the street, and that night someone broke into her house. She crawled out the back window, got in her car and didn't stop driving till she slid into that ditch by Hastings House. Meaning she doesn't know who to trust and someone in the state office is involved."

"How did you find all this out? I thought Mimi ran before she told you anything."

"Ah, Demar. He's putting this together. Until the police uncover that person who sold Mimi out in the state office and get the honchos at that company she's in danger."

"Does Demar have any idea who it is or where these guys are?"

"Lot of people come and go in government jobs. Hard to tell. But that's not the issue now. You and going to bed too dang early is." He tucked Bonnie into the crook of his arm. "Skedaddle now. Bonnie and I will see you in the morning. If there's another pipe springing a leak, we just might spend the night."

"I think you spend more time visiting at Hastings House than here."

"That's just your imagination." Whistling, he trotted down the stairs, strapped Bonnie into the stroller and headed off. Being with Bonnie made him happy, and he didn't seem as upset as when Callie first got here. Maybe because deep in his heart he knew he and Mimi would find a way out of this and make things work.

But that wasn't helping her situation and Keefe's. Maybe if they talked. What the heck about? How they didn't agree? Not a great solution but better than staying here and looking off into space and missing him. And she did, darn it. She missed him a lot and not just in her bed each night or in the hallway or in the gym or the attic. As great as sex was with Keefe she missed the man.

She set the alarm and headed for the docks. Keefe was probably still there. She remembered something about attaching a balcony to the upper level of the stage and how it was going to take some doing to get it to hold. He was in the middle of a project, and this may not be the best time to hunt him down, but if she didn't keep walking right now, she'd lose her nerve and may not get it back again.

Overhead dock lights illuminated the way, the *Lee* aglow at the very end. On play nights they could light the area with those patio torches, giving it a welcoming feel, maybe get someone dressed as a gambling man and playing the banjo. This wasn't even her play and she was making plans, probably because it was easier than thinking about what to say to Keefe. She wanted to clear things between them. She had no idea where this relationship that wasn't a relationship was going, but for sure it was going nowhere if they weren't speaking.

She climbed on board and found the stage and only Digger hard at work. "Hey," she said. "How's it going?"

"Slow. Haven't seen you in a while or heard about you from Keefe. What's going on with you two?"

"Is he here?"

"Up at Slim's grabbing dinner for us all. We're starved and too busy to cook. Even got Georgette painting the railing upstairs, though just between you and me and the *Lee* I think she's got more paint on herself than the boat." He grinned.

"But just think how much fun we'll have getting it off of me," Georgette said in a sexy Southern lilt as she came down the stairs, went to Digger and kissed him on the cheek, leaving a smear of white. She flashed Callie a big smile. "Hope I didn't embarrass you with that crack."

"Nope, just made me jealous." And before Digger or Georgette could reply she added, "Here come Demar and Sally, wonder what brings them this way at night."

Digger scooped his arm around Georgette. "Maybe

Keefe sent them down to help. Getting this balcony up is really kicking our butts." But when Demar and Sally stepped on board neither of them looked too happy to be there.

Digger said, "What's up?"

Sally glanced at Demar as if she didn't know what to do. He said, "We just got back from Memphis and found this on the newsstands." He held up a copy of *Soap Scoops* with Keefe's picture on the front along with Bonnie's. *I Want to Protect My Sister* splashed across the front.

Callie snapped the magazine from Demar's fingers, feeling sick to her stomach as she read. "How'd they get this? Who did this?"

Sally reached into a paper bag and pulled out Georgette's missing purse. "I found it behind the bar today. I pulled it out, and it flipped onto the floor, and I heard this." She held up the phone, and Keefe's voice played.

Sally continued, "First I thought it was Keefe calling on the phone. Then I recognized my own voice coming from the speaker and the conversation from that night on the porch when we first contacted M. Perry."

Georgette went white as the paint on her face, and Digger dropped his arm and said to her, "You recorded our conversations? Why would you do that?"

Demar added, "The information on the recorder is what's in the article."

Georgette looked as if she was going to faint. "I know this looks bad, but I didn't do it. I mean, I recorded the information and was going to do an article for this magazine, but I changed my mind because I really like you all and Keefe. I swear it's the truth. My purse went missing. Whoever took it used the information and sold it to *Soap Scoops*. That's got to be what happened."

She looked at Sally. "Remember that night I had my headache and asked if I left my purse at the bar?"

"When I said that I didn't have it you said you left it here on the boat."

"That was a fib to cover up the fact that it was really missing. I didn't want an all-out search that could go on and on. I knew it would look bad if you heard the recording, and I didn't want that. I was hoping it would turn up on its own. I never wrote the article."

Digger said, "Or you did write it and made this all up to cover your ass."

"I'm not making anything up, I swear. The purse got stolen before I erased the tape. I even met with this Bob Smith guy who wanted me to do the article and told him I wasn't doing it and to count me out. I told him I lost the purse."

Digger scoffed, "Bob Smith? Can't you do better than that, and why would you want to do an article like this anyway? Why would you even think about doing such a thing?"

Callie could see Georgette's hands shake and felt sorry for her. They'd been through a lot together these last two weeks. "I . . . I wanted the notoriety, for my parents to realize they had another daughter . . . me. When I didn't win Keefe's contest and get my name and pictures all over the place this Bob Smith person showed up. He heard me talking to Rachel at Slim's and said this was my chance to shine." Georgette frowned. "And I bought it. I wasn't thinking that the problem was with me and not Rachel. I was after revenge, getting even, but . . ." She looked at Digger. "But you helped me get over that and be happy being the person I am."

Digger asked. "How are we supposed to believe someone who recorded our personal conversations behind our backs? I was stupid enough to fall for you, Georgette, really fall for you even without being paid for it."

"Paid? What do you mean paid?" Georgette's eyes covered half her face, and a pulse beat at her temple. Sally and Demar stepped back, and Demar said, "I think we're out of here. We can barely keep our own love life on an even keel; we sure don't want to get in the middle of anyone else's."

Digger added, "I don't intend to be stupid twice."

Georgette glared. "Tell me, is this being stupid before or after you getting paid to fall for me? Why didn't you tell me about this?"

"Why didn't you tell me about the recording? And I repaid the money to Keefe because I wanted you fair and square and to have nothing stand between us."

Taking a hint from Demar and Sally, Callie hurried down the dock, calling to Digger and Georgette, "Just for the record I don't think Georgette's guilty. I need to tell Keefe what's going on."

On the way up the hill Callie tried to think of the best way to break the news of this article to Keefe. He'd have a stroke, and the evidence was stacked against Georgette as the author. But Callie meant it when she said she really couldn't see Georgette turning the information over to *Soap Scoops*. Maybe at first when she got to the Landing she could have done something so insensitive, but Georgette had changed since then. Besides, Bonnie liked her, and Bonnie had great instincts. And, to make matters worse, this was a new low for the *Scoops*. They hadn't employed the sensational press approach till now, all of which meant she could kiss her editor job good-bye.

Callie entered Slim's, and the whole place went dead quiet. Only a recording of some jazzy soul music from the jukebox sounded and even that stopped. Keefe stared at her from across the room, a copy of *Soap Scoops* in his left hand. He looked angrier than she'd ever seen him on or off TV. She came in saying, "I honestly don't think—"

"Honest?" he seethed. "What do you know about being honest?"

Callie looked behind her, thinking Keefe was talking to someone else. But he wasn't. "Excuse me?"

"How could you write this article?"

"Whoa." Callie stopped in her tracks. "Me? You think I did that? That I would talk about Bonnie and Mimi in an article that would get everyone out hunting for Mimi and drive her farther away? And talk about Bonnie so that people would come here and gawk at her? Have you lost your mind? I tried to find Mimi in Memphis. Remember boas, hookers, bar fight? Stop me when recognition sets in. Why would you think I did this?"

"You want to be editor of this rag; looks like you'll get your wish."

"I gave you my word I'd never do this."

"That was before I sided with your sister against you, and that pissed you off." He smacked the paper. "That's why you did this, to get even."

"Like hell."

"You forget that I've been through this reporter routine before. All's well till you don't get your way or you get ticked off or the wind blows from the east or whatever else ruffles your feathers, and you get out your poison pen and finish off someone's life. You'd think I'd learn the first time to stay the hell away from a damn reporter."

She planted her hands on her hips. "Look, you sanctimonious imbecile. I did not write that article. I gave you my word I wouldn't do something like this, only print a story about you, just you. The fact that you think my sister going to film school is a better idea than law school only proves beyond a shadow of a doubt that your brain is malfunctioning. And, Digger already accused Georgette of writing the article, so I suggest you both get together as to which one of us you want to tar and feather and run out of town."

"You can leave tomorrow. I can get that Tot Tenders agency in Memphis to send a sitter by noon, and you can get the hell out of my house."

She tossed her head. "Fine."

"Fine."

Callie stuffed her copy of *Soap Scoops* in her pocket, stomped her way to the door and slammed it behind her.

Chapter 15

Callie punched in the alarm system code, opened the door, picked up Dusty and continued to stomp her way up the stairs to Quaid's room, Wonder Dog in her wake. She flipped on the light and put the cat on the bed as Max sat by her foot. She yanked her luggage from the closet to a chair and started tossing in clothes, the animal audience looking at her as if she'd lost her mind.

A pink headband that matched one of Bonnie's sundresses slipped out of one of the pockets. Callie picked it up, running her thumb over the tiny lace flowers. Some of Callie's anger subsided, and she took her digital camera from the dresser and played back all the shots she'd taken of Bonnie. On Rory's lap, eating peaches in her cereal for the first time, in the baby bathtub, on Rory's shoulder. "I'll get some of these framed and send them to Rory, thanking him for his hospitality."

Dusty sat beside her, rubbing against her arm. Max probed his big head on her knee. "This is such a mess. Keefe's mad at me. LuLu's mad and I'm out of a job. I should have stayed in Atlanta and saved myself all this grief."

Callie pulled the copy of *Soap Scoops* from her pocket and studied the photo of Bonnie. "First of all, how could anyone in their right mind think I'd do this to Bonnie . . . or take a picture of her with the bank as a background? And the picture looks grainy, like it was taken at a distance then blown up. This is really poor quality, really bad work. I never do work like this."

Callie looked closer. "Bonnie's wearing the dress with the pink bunnies that Keefe bought for her." She set the paper by the camera. "So, when did I have her dressed in that? And I've never even seen Georgette with a camera, so that rules her out for taking this picture."

Callie flipped through her pictures of Bonnie again, none of the bank or Bonnie in that particular dress. What was going on? Were the newspaper article and Mimi somehow related? Callie finished packing, then took a shower hoping to clear her head, but none of this made sense. Why would someone write this article at all? She had a motive, and so did Georgette, but neither of them did the deed. So who? And why?

Callie slipped into pajamas and tied on a robe. The clock in the hall chimed midnight, but no Keefe. Probably spending the night at Sally's or Digger's or Hastings House. Any place far away from her. Well, that was just . . . fine!

She could leave now and be home in four hours, but she wanted to say good-bye to Rory and see Bonnie one more time. She went downstairs, pausing at the bottom, hand on the newel post, remembering Keefe and the best sex of her life, except it was more than that. She was falling for him. Heck, she done fell and look where it got her.

Before tonight she'd trusted him because he'd trusted her about writing the article, she'd admired him because of his devotion to his family and friends and the theater, she'd respected him because he stood up for what he believed in and who he believed in.

Too bad those feelings weren't returned! The only time they understood each other was in the sack or some version thereof. A relationship built on sex wasn't much of a relationship.

She got orange juice from the fridge, fed Max and Dusty treats and went into the living room, searching for something to read to get her mind off everything. Did such a book exist? Lightning flashed outside the big windows. The wind kicked up sending the trees into a frenzy, another storm on the loose. She lit a Tiffany lamp on the sideboard and studied a picture of Bonnie and another picture of Rory with a lovely woman in his arms. Mimi probably. How sad that they weren't all together tonight upstairs snuggled in bed.

A family album sat beside the pictures, and Callie opened it. O'Fallon's Landing 1860—wooden docks, painted sign, big white stern-wheeler on the Mississippi in the distance. A faded poker chip was tied with a frayed ribbon and looped through a cut in the page. What was that all about? Incredible. She loved this stuff, seeing what came before and how people got to where they were now.

"That's great-great-grandparents Joshua and Kathryn O'Fallon," Keefe said from his prone position on the couch, hands clasped behind his head, shoes off, surprising the heck out of her. She hadn't even seen him there.

He continued, "Joshua won Kathryn in a poker game. That was the last chip he had when he made the bet. She was the love of his life, and her daddy wouldn't let her marry Joshua. He bet that chip and his Landing, and Kathryn's daddy was so sure he could best Joshua at anything that he went along with it. Joshua won. That's their two sons, Thayer and Owen. They say I look like Owen."

Callie glanced back at the page. "He is a handsome devil, and God knows you've got the devil part down pat, and just for your information I'm not leaving O'Fallon's

Landing till I prove I'm not the one who wrote the article."

She had no idea where that suddenly came from. Maybe inspiration from Joshua having the guts to risk all to get what he wanted. Or Kathryn's daddy being a total dick and needing to be set straight. "I'm staying on if I have to live in my car and eat cheese doodles. I'm not running away because you think I betrayed you, which I didn't. Do you remember when Bonnie had on that little pink bunny outfit you bought for her?"

"Who gives a damn?"

"I do, you arrogant bastard. Do you remember or not?"

"She had it on the day LuLu came to town. She commented on it having a baseball cap instead of a bonnet, a guy thing. What difference does that make?"

"It's the outfit Bonnie has on in the photo in *Soap Scoops.*"

"So you took her picture then, so what?"

"You were with me in front of that bank. Did you see me take pictures?" Callie closed the album. "You don't know me at all. You don't know one darn thing about me."

He sat up, his eyes dark and a little dangerous through the dim light. More lightning lit the outside as the first drops of rain plopped against the porch roof. "I know you have a place behind your left ear that makes you tremble in my arms, I know your breasts get warm and full when I suckle them and that you like for me to cup your bottom when I make love to you."

"If you really knew me, you'd know I would never take such a mundane, boring picture of Bonnie in front of the bank. I work for a magazine, I take photos all the time and I have more panache than that. And if you had half the pluck of Joshua O'Fallon or your dad, you'd believe in me no matter what the odds." She studied him. "We don't

make love, Keefe. We screw, and there is a world of difference."

She turned and headed back to her room, oj in one
hand, album in the other and leaving Mr. Keefe O'Fallon
behind her with every intention of keeping him there.

Keefe knew it was morning even though little sunlight
came through the windows. He dragged his sorry butt off
the living room couch and stood as a hard rain beat against
the French doors that opened onto the front porch. It was
one of those all-day rains, the kind that soaked the earth
and made puddles and turned the world gray.

His back ached. He was getting too old to spend nights
on the couch, but the thought of sleeping upstairs with
Callie there was out of the question. Blast her for publishing the article and blast her double for making him care
about her. And he did care, dammit. He didn't realize how
much till he saw the article and felt so completely betrayed.

She needed to be editor, he got that, but to do it this
way, at the expense of his family, hurt one hell of a lot. He
slogged his way into the kitchen and got coffee going, even
put in an extra measure for a bigger shot of caffeine to
combat the situation and rainy day.

He felt Callie's presence behind him before she said, "I'll
be out of here as soon as the new sitter shows up."

"I can manage."

"Don't want Rory to think I just up and left him and
Bonnie for no good reason."

"Oh, I think having their life splashed over the front
page of *Soap Scoops* is reason enough."

She got a cup from the cabinet and poured herself some
coffee. "That's your opinion."

Rory's silhouette posed at the back door. "Open up,
dang it. It's us. Raining cats and dogs out here." Keefe let

his dad and Max inside. Max shook, sending a spray everywhere, and more water dripped from Rory's hat and slicker that looked as if he'd gained twenty pounds. Then he popped open the snaps, and a grinning Bonnie stuck her head out.

Callie laughed, Bonnie giggled, even grumpy Keefe couldn't keep a smile from his face. Rory said, "Had to keep sweet pea here dry, and putting her in this carrier thing worked just great. It was . . . Thelma's idea."

Keefe got a towel for his dad and dried Max with another. Rory hung his slicker by the back door and unclipped Bonnie, then handed her off to Callie. "She'll need some more breakfast, didn't feed her all that much at Thelma's, and she needs a bath. Digger called, and the *Annabelle*'s headed upriver and lost a barge, blast it all anyway. Digger's going out after it on one of the tows, but I got to . . ." His voice trailed off, and he looked from one to the other. "What the hell's going on between you two now? We could freeze ice in here with the looks you're giving each other."

Callie strapped Bonnie into her pumpkin seat and set it on the kitchen table. Keefe took a copy of *Soap Scoops* and handed it to his father. Rory looked at it and shook his head. "Well, if this don't beat all. We'll get every soap fan within a hundred miles coming on down to check you out and see Bonnie. Damn inconvenient, that."

Callie poured cereal for Bonnie, and Keefe said, "And it will keep Mimi from making contact, afraid someone will recognize her."

Rory stroked his chin. "Yeah, that, too. But what does this have to do with you two?"

"Callie's a reporter for this rag, Dad. When she came she traded her baby-sitting skills for an interview with me with the understanding the interview be only about me and not Bonnie and you. We didn't tell anyone because if the word got out, everyone would be after her to put them in the story."

"Well, what about me?" Rory poked his chest. "You could have told me."

"Wasn't any need to. The story was supposed to be about me and only me. Then this article appeared."

"Which I didn't write," Callie said while tying a bib around Bonnie.

Rory shrugged. "So?"

"So she spilled the story anyway."

"Hogwash. If Callie gave her word she wouldn't write the story, she didn't. If I didn't think she had more gumption than that, I never would have left sweet pea with her. Besides, I knew who she was all along. Had that PI fellow find out. Can't just turn my baby over to any stranger; you got to be dang careful about those things."

Callie stopped dead. "Why didn't you say something?"

Rory rolled his broad shoulders. "Well now, you two didn't say anything, so I figured you had your reasons. Besides, I can't go telling you everything, now, can I? No fun in that. And Bonnie thinks you're the berries, and that PI fellow said you had a good reputation which in your business must be as rare as a hen's teeth. What's going on with me and Mimi and Bonnie isn't top secret, and there are people all over this town who could write this if they had a mind to."

"But—" Keefe started, but Rory finished, "Seems to me somebody got the story and turned it in to do just what's happening now, cause a brouhaha in this here family. Someone who doesn't like us all that much, and to tell the truth, there aren't all that many. I try helping folks more than hurting them, but people get their dander up over almost anything, so who knows."

"Callie has a motive, Dad. If she got the story, she had a good chance to be editor of the magazine. You're blind to the obvious, there is no other explanation."

Rory headed for the stairs, Max at his side. "And if you choose to believe that, you've got less brains than this here pup." Max whined, and Rory apologized, feet and paws retreating up the stairs.

The front doorbell rang. Keefe swore and headed down the hall calling, "Try not to cause any more mayhem in my family till I get back, Cahill."

"Eat dirt and die, O'Fallon." She fed Bonnie a spoonful of cereal and gave her some juice from a sippie cup. "Another milestone in the life of Bonnie O'Fallon."

Keefe came back into the kitchen, a young woman in a trench coat and heels behind him. "This is the baby-sitter from Tot Tenders."

Callie's heart dropped to her toes. This was it. Time to say good-bye. Even if she wasn't leaving town, she wouldn't be feeding Bonnie cereal and giving her a bath and watching all those cute firsts . . . peaches, sippie cup, first step. "Thought she wasn't supposed to be here till noon."

The woman said, "I just finished another job and was in the area, so they sent me over."

"Do you live around here?" Callie asked.

"Uh, Nashville area." She opened her purse and flashed some identification card, then stuck it back in her purse. She took off her coat and laid it across a chair and looked at Callie. "I can feed the baby."

Callie thought she was going to be sick. But Bonnie was not hers to get sick over. If looks could kill, Keefe O'Fallon would be dead as a tombstone right now. "Fine," Callie said as she stood. She passed the spoon to the woman, who was not exactly dressed to feed a baby. A suit? Good grief.

Keefe said to Callie, "I'll get your luggage."

"I can manage on my own just fine." She squared her shoulders and pushed past Keefe and up the stairs, feeling his gaze boring into her. She got her luggage and snagged her computer and ran into Keefe in the hallway. He said, "I understand why you did it, I really do, and I forgive you."

"There's nothing to forgive, you big jerk. To think I fell for you, tried to think of how we could be together in New York, give what we have a chance . . . I must have been out of my freaking mind. I'll come back for Dusty."

"Forget New York, stay here," Rory said as he came into the hall, and Keefe said to him, "There's a new babysitter downstairs to watch Bonnie, from a good agency in Memphis, highly recommended."

Rory looked from Callie to Keefe, rain pelting the windows and roof, thunder rolling down the river valley. "Well, I don't give a flying fruitcake how highly recommended she is. Callie's taking care of my Bonnie, and that's the bottom line. I don't rightly know how this story got in that magazine, but I'll find out."

Rory yanked her suitcase from her hand and all but tossed it back into the room. "Now, I got me a business to run." He turned to Keefe. "And you can help Digger with that barge, make yourself useful as well as ornamental and causing problems around here. I'm going downstairs and fire that sitter and get to work, and you two figure out how you're going to make this all happen so you don't go killing each other and driving me nuts." He turned in a huff. "Dang kids!"

Rory trotted down the steps and made for the kitchen.

Callie shrugged. "Well, now what do we—"

Rory appeared at the bottom of the stairs. "Okay, where is this blasted baby-sitter, anyway?"

Keefe said, "In the kitchen feeding . . ."

Rory suddenly looked pale. "Ah, fuck."

Keefe raced down the stairs, pushing past Rory, Callie following. She looked in the living room and dining room. She came back into the hallway as Keefe said to Rory, "You take the road past town. I'll take the river road. She couldn't have gotten far. Callie, you stay here. We're looking for a gray SUV."

Callie ran out the side door, rain beating down, plastering hair and clothes to her body. She jumped in the Jeep, Keefe right behind, Rory already squealing tires, backing his Suburban out onto the road. Keefe raced toward the river road, windshield wipers on supercharge. She cinched her seat belt hard to keep from sliding around as Keefe took the turn, then down a hill, Hastings House looming through the stormy gloom . . . and an SUV off in the gully, door wide open, engine running, headlights blazing.

Keefe skidded the Jeep to a stop, and together they ran to the SUV. Bonnie sat in the back in a car seat, playing with her plastic rattle, blowing baby bubbles. Keefe sagged against the car. "Ohthankgod!"

Callie yanked open the back door and touched the baby's cheek, feeling light-headed with relief. Keefe said, "You take care of Bonnie; I'm going after the baby-sitter. Call Demar," he yelled through the rain as he took off down the road. "And someone needs to find Dad before he has a heart attack."

Keefe didn't wait for Callie to answer, knowing she'd take care of Bonnie and the rest. She was like that, his equal, doing the job without a bunch of whining and crabbing. But right now he had to find that damn sitter. If he didn't do another thing with the rest of his fucking life, he was finding her and getting to the bottom of all this fucking crap.

He tore down the road, but when he turned the bend and could see a distance there was no sign of the sitter. He stopped, catching his breath. She could have gone toward

Hastings House or into the woods. The Mississippi was off to the other side, and no one would run toward a river in a storm. He ran up the drive for Hastings House as Callie bolted out the front door. "You take the grounds to the front; I'll do the woods in the back. Thelma has Bonnie, and no one's getting that baby through her. Georgette called Digger. Demar's getting your dad. Bases covered."

Callie ran for the back of the house toward the woods, and Keefe followed. "I'd say she's in here. Best place to hide is the woods."

Callie nodded, and they took off across the grass to a narrow path disappearing into the trees. Water streamed between the leaves, but at least it wasn't a full cascade. They swiped their faces, mud slowing their progress as the woods sloped down a hillside. Ferns, undergrowth, made getting off the path difficult. He caught Callie as she tripped on a root; she grabbed for him when his foot snagged a rock. Light diminished. Callie stopped short. "Horses galloping? Where's that coming from?"

"It's raining, and two Southerners are running around in his woods. This is not a happy time for Ulysses. If you hear halt, just keep going."

"I'm not in the mood for ghosts."

"Are you ever in the mood for ghosts?"

"They make great stories."

Keefe followed Callie to the creek, the gently flowing brook now an angry torrent of rushing dirty water and debris.

"Help me," came a voice from downstream. The sitter held on to a tree trunk for dear life, thigh deep in water, hair streaming down, caked in mud. "I can't get out, current's too fast and the creek side's too steep."

"We'll get you." Keefe stepped off the path, and the woman wailed, "Oh, God, don't leave me. It's getting deeper, and I can't hold on much longer and . . . and this place is haunted. Dear God, is it haunted. You got to get me out of here. I'll tell you everything."

Keefe held Callie's hand tight. "Grab on to me, and whatever we do, we don't fall in that creek."

She nodded, the water getting worse by the second. They made their way along the bank through the brush and rocks till they got to the woman. Callie said, "Now what? The bank is really sharp."

Keefe took the waistband of Callie's jeans, clenching tight. "I'm going to hold on to you and this tree. You're going to reach in and pull out the baby-sitter. Let her go, and she's done for, got it? But for God's sake don't fall in yourself."

"You are such a little ray of sunshine."

"Well, if that doesn't work for you, maybe this will." He yanked her close and kissed her hard. "I'm sorry I doubted you. I'm an ass. Does that help brighten your day?"

"Maybe."

He smiled, feeling infinitely better. "Beats the heck out of telling me to go to hell."

"Crossed my mind."

The woman yelled, "Will you two get on with it. I'm drowning here."

Keefe hooked his arm around a tree and grabbed the top of Callie's jeans at her back. The water, brown and muddy, roared. She reached both hands down to the woman. "Take my wrists," she yelled. "Not as slippery as my hands."

The sitter grabbed hold as did Callie, and Keefe pulled her toward him, the baby-sitter scrambling out of the water and up the embankment. She flopped down on the ground, sobbing. "Thank you, I thought I was a goner."

Keefe grabbed her under her arm and pulled her up.

"Let's get to the house. And don't try anything. You kidnapped my sister, and I'm in a really bad mood."

The woman nodded and stumbled toward the path. Then they all made their way back through the woods and across the lawn to the back door. Keefe pounded, and Digger opened it. "Our kidnapper?"

"I had to do it," the woman sobbed and trembled as she stepped inside.

Thelma brought blankets, and they each took one and wrapped up, kicking their muddy shoes to the side. She said, "Let's go into the kitchen. I have tea, and it's warm in there. The house maid has Bonnie and is changing her diaper."

Keefe felt his adrenaline kick in again. "Who is this maid? Where is she and—"

Thelma patted his cheek. "Bonnie's fine, dear. Trust me. She's okay. Rory's with them." Thelma led the way into the kitchen, and the baby-sitter all but collapsed into a Windsor chair. "Thank God you found me when you did. I would have drowned, or that g-h-o-s-t would have gotten me. He . . . He ran me off the road, and I knew you would all find me, and I tried to hide and . . ." She broke into tears. "I had to take your baby or they were going to frame me for embezzlement."

Demar said from the doorway, "Who's they?"

"I used to work at River Environs. There were three presidents, and I think they were all defrauding the state. Jolie Baines was in accounting and came across a double set of books. They want her baby to get to her. I got a call from someone who said if I didn't deliver the baby to them, they'd say I was the one keeping the double set of books. They told me to pose as a baby-sitter from Tot Tenders and take the baby. When I got to Memphis I was to call a number, and he'd tell me what to do. But then this . . . something ran me off the road and followed me into the woods. I even heard horses. Do you believe . . . horses in the woods."

Demar asked, "Where's the number?"

"In my purse in the car."

Demar peered down at the woman. "You and I are going into Memphis and make that call, and you better pray we make a contact and get the guy, or you're going to prison for kidnapping for a very long time."

The woman stood. "I'll help any way I can." She turned to Keefe. "I'm sorry. I was so scared. I still am. These are bad people. They weren't kidding about framing me." She looked around. "Ever see that movie *Ghostbusters?* If I were you all, I'd find one for real or wear garlic around my neck or something. This place gives me the creeps."

She followed Demar from the room, and Thelma brought out scones. Digger sat. Georgette stood off to the side. Rory came in with Bonnie in his arms. He kissed the baby. "So now tell me what the hell happened. I'm guessing you got that sitter person since you're all sitting here pretty as you please drinking tea."

Keefe ran his hands over his face. He couldn't eat; he could barely breathe. His heart ached from what almost happened. He'd handed his baby sister over to a complete stranger because he was a fucking idiot and more worried about being right than concerned for her welfare. He should be condemned to hell for all eternity. How would he ever make this up to his father? If Rory disowned him, he had it coming.

Rory wrapped a blanket around Bonnie. "So how'd this woman get into our house?"

Keefe said, "Last night at Slim's I said I was hiring Tot Tenders to replace Callie. Meaning whoever is behind this was at Slim's. Even knew the timetable because I said by noon."

Callie said, "And this woman shows up early."

Georgette asked, "Do you think this has anything to do with the article in *Soap Scoops?*"

Keefe shook his head. "I think whoever did that was after me. There was no way of knowing I would get rid of Callie and hire a person from this Tot Tenders when I saw the article. That was the break the guy was waiting for to get to Bonnie. When the happy hooker scheme at Kerby's didn't work to get to Mimi, he had to find something else. Then the article and my reaction played into his hands."

Rory asked, "What's the happy hooker scheme?"

Keefe said, "The womenfolk posed as hookers to meet up with someone to get information on Mimi. It didn't work. Red boas were involved."

"And you didn't ask me," Thelma pouted.

"Sorry I missed that one?" Rory added as Callie looked at Keefe and said, "That's where I saw the guy with the mustache, remember?"

Georgette gasped. "The guy who asked me to do the article and find out as much as possible about the O'Fallons had a mustache and a limp. That's Bob."

Callie nodded. "Now we're getting somewhere. Bet if we asked around at Slim's someone saw him there last night, too. We should contact Demar and tell him this might be the guy he's after. Bet he's the informant at the Attorney General's Office. A gopher for those three presidents at River Environs."

Georgette said, "So if he didn't submit the article, who in the world did? I want to find out and beat them to a pulp for ruining my life."

Digger stood and draped his arm around her. "Now, sugar, it's okay. I believe you now."

"Now?" Georgette stepped away from him. "Now when it's convenient you believe me, Digger O'Dell." Her eyes went to thin slits. "It's going to take a heck of a lot more than calling me sugar for me to forgive you." She poked him in the chest. "You didn't trust me." She poked him again, driving him backward. "You didn't give me the benefit of a doubt. You just assumed I did you wrong."

"Well, I . . ."

"Well, screw you and the horse you rode in on. You blew it, big boy." She jutted her breasts and twitched her hips. "You can kiss these and my very fine multi-thousand-dollar ass good-bye. And don't even try and follow me with your apology and sweet talk."

She strutted from the room, and Callie applauded along with Thelma and Rory.

Digger stood tall. "Hey, I had my reasons, and they were good ones."

Callie pointed after Georgette. "Were they as good as that? But if we're going to get to the bottom of this, what we have to do right now is consider the one person in town who has it in for Keefe."

Rory rocked Bonnie in his arms. "It shouldn't be that hard." He studied Keefe. "So tell me, son, who the hell have you pissed off this time?"

Chapter 16

Georgette folded her favorite red halter top and put it with the others in her suitcase. She'd come here because one man dumped on her and was leaving because another man did the same thing. There was a message here . . . forget men.

But the one good thing that came out of all this was that Georgette Cooper knew who she was and she could live with that. In fact, she just might start a support group for people who did makeovers and how to deal with the new you. Chances were if you didn't like what was on the outside, you probably weren't too happy with what was going on inside either. Changing was a package deal.

There was a knock on the door, and she opened it to . . . "Callie?"

She scurried in, still wrapped in her blanket, and eyed the luggage. "Don't leave, least not yet. Everyone thinks I'm taking a bathroom break, but you and I need to talk. We need to figure out who's responsible for this article. They messed up your life and mine, and they're not getting away with it and making money from our misery."

Georgette said, "In my humble opinion it's the men in our lives who are to blame. They could have believed us, but did they? No! I'm so mad at Digger I could wring his very handsome neck that attaches his very handsome face to his terrific torso."

Callie grinned. "I know exactly what you mean, but we need answers for our own peace of mind." She sat on the floor. "Don't want to get Thelma's wing chair wet. I'm still soggy."

Georgette sat down beside her. "I don't know what else we can do. I called the magazine, and they said they wouldn't reveal their source."

"Even with me working at the magazine I couldn't find out. She could have used a phony name; that happens a lot, too. Let's see what we have. You lost your purse at Slim's; it turned up at Slim's which smacks of someone taking it and bringing it back. Which is someone in town who frequents Slim's."

"That's the whole town."

"I had a conversation with my sister and talked about my working for *Soap Scoops,* and on that day Bonnie had on the outfit that was in the article. So it's not just Keefe they wanted to hurt, but me, too."

"How do I figure into all this?"

"You supplied the how this happened. The why is revenge or greed or both. The what is the magazine."

"So, we're looking for the who?" Georgette bit her bottom lip. "We know the same people pretty much like you and Keefe and Rory."

Callie's eyes widened. "Eleanor Stick! She can't get a job after Keefe told everyone she's a terrible baby-sitter."

"I've seen her at Slim's."

"And you took her place baby-sitting Bonnie."

"And she was on the street when my sister came to town. She almost ran into her. She found your purse at Slim's and then she had all the information she needed to get even."

Georgette jumped to her feet. "We have proof, we have motive and all those other things they talk about in mysteries." She assumed a sassy look. "We're damn good, Callie Cahill. We should tell Keefe and Digger. We should confront this bitch and—"

"No Keefe or Digger. Just you and me, woman to woman with the Stick."

"My car's around back, and you need to get into dry clothes." Georgette pulled out jeans and an aqua T-shirt and a matching parka.

Callie looked at them. "I'm taking you shopping with me. You have great taste."

Georgette beamed. She'd never felt so good, even when she got all done over. "Thank you, and thank you for including me in this and being my friend."

Callie took Georgette's hand. "No matter how this plays out we'll always be friends." She changed, and when she came out of the bathroom, Georgette said, "Let's do it."

Callie stuck her head out the door, catching a glimpse of the maid as she ducked around the corner, least she guessed it was the maid. Who else would be darting around corners? "The coast is clear."

They crept down the stairs and out the front door, voices still in the kitchen. Georgette started the car and went slowly down the drive, the gray SUV still on the road. Georgette said, "The rain's slacking off; by noon it will be a sauna out here. Where should we look for Eleanor?"

"My vote is Slim's. She's got to be feeling very confident about the place. Her showing up for lunch has definite promise."

Georgette pulled into the parking lot. They got out and dashed into the bar. The early lunch crowd trickled in but no Eleanor. Georgette started for one of the back tables, and Callie took her arm and guided her toward the ones in front. "We did nothing wrong, and we are not hiding."

Sally came over with two iced teas and sat down. "Wow, you've had some morning." She leaned across the table and whispered, "Did you catch that guy the baby-sitter is working for? Demar called on his way to Memphis, but I've kept my mouth shut, which is taking a lot of will-power, I might add. Whoever he is he must have been right here at the bar soaking up my beer, Dad's barbecue and the town gossip, waiting for his chance to set a trap for Bonnie."

Callie sipped her sweet tea. "And the article in the magazine was it."

Sally said, "I know neither of you is responsible for it. We all tried to help Mimi and Bonnie. No matter how bad it looks I know you are both innocent."

Georgette smiled. "But we know who did write the ar—"

"Oh, Georgette," Rachel squealed as she rushed up behind Georgette and hugged her around the neck. "I've been looking all over for you."

She went to the other side of the table and held out her left hand for all to see, a new gold wedding band. "I'm married!" She squealed again, then blushed and giggled. "Clyde and I went into Nashville and just . . . did it. I know it's sudden, but I love him, I do. He does construction, working on bridges, and now he got a job working with a crew to build houses here in town. He's so nice to me." She lowered her voice and whispered, "And the sex. Oh, my God, the sex."

She giggled again and blushed, her pretty face even more lovely. "I'm thinking about opening my own interior decorating shop to help make ends meet. We'll do fine. I'm so happy."

Sally stared from the ring to Georgette. "Clyde Miller? You married Clyde Miller?"

Rachel bit her bottom lip. "Yes, and I love him to death. I am so ready for the simple life. We're going to live here, in a little house he'll build for us. It's like a fairy tale. We can have a little white picket fence and roses."

Sally said, "Uh, just a minute, girl. Those bridges Clyde works on . . . He builds them as in his firm designs and constructs them. He's known all over the world, one of the best in the field. Written up in *Time* magazine. I think he's building a bridge in Saudi Arabia at the end of the year."

Rachel stared, not breathing, then managing. "No, not my Clyde. You got the wrong Clyde."

Sally nodded. "Sweet thing, how many Clyde Millers are there in this town? Your little hometown boy is the local boy wonder."

Rachel plopped down. "I . . . I had no idea. He dresses in raggedy jeans, Gap T-shirts. One has a hole by the neck; it's his favorite. He plays the guitar—really well, I might add. I cut his hair because it was too long."

Georgette went over to her sister and hugged her. "You will be so happy, Rachel. You were made for this. You love Clyde for who he is not what he is, and the rest will fall into place."

"He could have told me."

"He probably did, but you just saw a simple man and you loved him. What could be better than that?"

"Saudi Arabia? Do I even know where that is? Do they drive camels or something?"

Georgette laughed. "They do the car thing, lots of oil. They can afford Clyde."

Rachel stood. "I had no idea." She hugged her sister. "I didn't plan on this. Think I can still have my roses?" She smiled at Georgette. "But none of it really matters, does it, as long as I have Clyde. I wish you the same thing, Georgette. I really do. I wish you love and fun and some craziness you didn't count on. But this is a lot of craziness." She bit at her bottom lip. "What do I do?"

"Go find Clyde?"

She giggled. "You know, I think I'm still opening that decorating shop. Someone's got to spruce up these new homes Clyde is building, and if he's off globe-trotting, the kids and I will be here keeping the home fires burning." Her grin grew. "Ta-ta."

Georgette sat down as Rachel scurried away. "Kids? Home fires? This is not the Rachel I knew back in Savannah. All her life she wanted to marry a rich and famous man, and it happened when she didn't plan for it at all." She laughed. "I've never seen Rachel this happy."

"And soon you will be, too," Callie said as she nudged her. "Here comes operation big mouth."

Sally looked perplexed, and Georgette grabbed her purse and said, "Come with us. This will be interesting."

Sally followed, mumbling, "This is the day for interesting."

Eleanor sat down at one of the back tables, and immediately Georgette, Callie, and Sally joined her. She sneered. "What the heck do you three want?"

Georgette set her purse on the table. "I say you owe us a free lunch with all that money you made from the article you sold to *Soap Scoops.*"

Eleanor huffed. "I have no idea what you're talking . . . Oh, what the heck. You're right. I did it and proud of it." She fluffed her tight bun. "I wrote the article and sent it to that magazine." She looked at Callie. "The one you write for. I got that little tidbit when I heard you talking to your sister, or more like yelling at your sister. You do have a temper, missy."

Georgette said, "And when you found out about the magazine, you already had the phone."

Eleanor grinned, and it looked kind of scary, like that Chuckie doll in the movies. "That's exactly right, a chance to get revenge on Cahill here for taking my place at the O'Fallons' and get even with that holier-than-thou Keefe. Until he opened his big mouth I could make a living at baby-sitting, and then I got nothing; the well dried up."

She glared at Callie. "So, tell me, how does it feel to have your life turned upside down with no chance of ever getting it back? Keefe will never trust you, and that's plumb awful for him because he's nuts about you and you're nuts about him and now nothing will ever come of any of it all because of me."

Her Chuckie grin grew. "No one would believe the baby-sitter could pull something like this off, and it's your word against mine anyway. Not so great with the shoe on the other foot, is it, my dears? Fact is, I'm going after Cahill's job at *Soap Scoops*. I've got what it takes."

"Ruthless?" Sally offered.

"I prefer tenacious, but ruthless works just fine. It's a tough world out there, chickies." She waved her hand. "Now go away and lick your wounds and leave me to eat in peace."

Georgette exchanged glances with Callie and Sally, and Georgette said, "Well, I guess you won this one."

"You bet your sweet patootie, I did."

The girls wandered over to the bar. Callie and Georgette sat at stools. Sally went behind. She snagged three beers, twisted the tops and passed them out. They clanked the long necks together and gulped. Sally propped her chin in her hand and said to Callie, "What are you going to do about Eleanor and her going after your job?"

Callie took another gulp. "Write her a letter of recommendation. I am done with that rag. When they ran that story I knew it was over. I'd like to stay here, work at the *Landing Times* and do freelance magazine articles about the area. Maybe write a book, *The Mississippi Mud,* talk about the river towns, how they grew, legends; the legends are the best part. But with my reputation ruined by this *Soap Scoops* article no one will talk to me. They won't trust me to do their story right." She shrugged and looked at Sally. "Need another waitress?"

Sally grinned and took her hand. "You bet. But something else will turn up for you, I know it."

She turned to Georgette. "I'm sorry you got caught up in this, I really am. You were an innocent bystander and got sucked in. You and Digger seemed to really hit it off, and in time you two will work it out and—"

"Hold your horses, girl," Georgette said. "There's nothing to be sorry for. I have a present for you . . . and me, too, for that matter, because I'm thinking of staying here. Rachel will need someone to water her roses while she's off globe-trotting, and I can do taxes and financial consulting on the Landing. I think I want to live on the river again."

She winked. "Eleanor knew I made the recordings; she just never knew how. Are you ready, chickies?" Georgette took her purse, pulled out the phone Bob had given her, hit rewind, then play, cranked up the volume and held it up for all to hear.

The room filled with the voice of Eleanor Stick telling how she wrote the article for *Soap Scoops.* Everyone stopped eating, no clinking dishes or glasses. They listened as the conversation continued, their gazes going from the three at the bar to Eleanor at the table in the back. She finally stood, held her head high, gave everyone the bird and sauntered out accompanied by a round of applause.

Georgette stopped the tape, and the girls clinked long necks again. Callie said, "I don't believe you did that. How brilliant. To Georgette."

"I'll drink to that," Digger said as he entered the saloon and stood at the end of the bar, hands on hips, low-riding jeans looking more handsome than ever.

Georgette dropped the phone back in her purse, and Digger said, "Talk to me, Georgette."

She tsked. "I thought I heard someone call my name." She looked the other way. "I must be imagining things; no one's here." She yawned, and Digger turned her stool around till she faced him. "I'm calling your name, and I want to talk to you."

She shrugged. "So talk. It's a free country. I can't stop you."

He glanced around. "Okay, if this is where it has to be, I can live with it. You're going to hear me out. I'm sorry I didn't trust you. I'm sorry I didn't believe you. I don't know who's responsible for that article, but I know it's not you. Life's not worth living without you in it. When you left Hastings House I thought you'd gone for good, and that about killed me."

"But here you are not dead and pestering me to no end."

He snapped the beer from her hand, slammed it on the counter and picked her up into his arms. "Sass. I come here with an apology, and I get sass."

"And what do you think you deserve?"

"A chance to make it up to you, to show you how sorry I am, and I don't care what evidence there is that you wrote the article. I don't believe one damn word of it. I know you, and that article isn't you at all."

Callie handed Georgette her purse. "You might need this." Georgette handed it back. "Na, I think I'm going to have a lot more fun this way." She looped her arms around Digger's neck. "And where are you taking me, Digger O'Dell?"

"Memphis." He kissed her hard. "To the Heartbreak Hotel because my heart's breakin' without you, girl. And we're staying in the Burning Love Suite. If I can't convince you there, with all that red velvet and lace and big Jacuzzi, how crazy I am about you, I don't deserve you."

The saloon erupted in wolf whistles and clapping and suggestive words of encouragement as Digger carried Georgette out into a hint of sunshine. She said, "Aren't you supposed to be working on the *Lee?*"

"She'll just have to wait a spell. I have another woman who needs working on." He put Georgette on the back of his motorcycle, then hitched his leg over the front.

"But I don't have any clothes to sleep in, Digger." He turned, and she gave him her best innocent little girl look and batted her eyes. "And my-oh-my, I don't have any money either, not a penny. I guess I'm at your mercy, Digger. What are you going to do about that?"

He laughed deep in his throat as he revved the Harley. He stole a quick kiss, then headed down the road toward Memphis.

Chapter 17

Callie came down the stairs after putting Bonnie in for a nap. She started to clean up the living room, picking up toys and blankets as Rory came in. Callie said, "Little dumpling is snoozing. You just missed her."

"It's the other dumpling I'm looking for, the big one, who tends to shoot off his mouth."

"If you're referring to Keefe, I haven't seen him since this morning at Hastings House. I guess the play is taking up a lot of his time."

"Probably feeling damn ashamed since he pulled that stunt on you at Slim's. How in blue blazes could he think you'd do that article? Makes no sense."

"Actually it makes a lot of sense. I think he was mad at himself for being an actor and putting his family in danger. You all mean the earth to him, and if it weren't for him, that article would never have been written. Coming after me was pretty logical. He was angry at himself, the magazine and all connected with it. And, he said he was sorry."

"He did?"

"We were sliding down a creek bed to rescue that babysitter."

Rory grinned. "Well now, there's only one thing that makes a woman accept a half-ass apology like that and come to a man's defense when he's been a complete jack-ass. You love him, jackass and all."

She stiffened. "I don't think so."

Rory stroked his chin. "Well, you're wrong, but that will take care of itself. So, have you turned in your resignation to that *Soap Scoops* yet?"

"How'd you know about that? I just wrote the letter an hour ago. Didn't even put it in the mail yet. I told them to hire Eleanor Stick. She has that bulldog approach to getting a juicy story, something I never did all that well. She should be good at it."

Rory sat in the blue wing-back chair and fiddled with Bonnie's pink rabbit. So tell me, what are you good at, Callie Cahill?"

"Right now I've got unemployed aced. But tomorrow I'm headed over to Hastings House to persuade Thelma to let me dig around in her attic. The place is a museum."

Callie went to the sideboard and tapped the O'Fallon family album. "I'm going to write about something other than TV personalities, like the Mississippi River and the towns and families. Include pictures from long ago like the ones in here—and new pictures of families and towns the way they are now."

She held up a picture of Bonnie, Rory and . . . She stopped and studied that picture hard. Slowly, her eyes met Rory's across the living room. The only sound the ticking of the grandfather clock and a breeze in the oaks outside. His eyes darkened a shade, and she swallowed, then smiled. "You know, some of these pictures are best kept in a drawer where they're safe and out of harm's way."

Callie put the picture in the back of the drawer in the sideboard. "I think before I go over to Hastings House tomorrow morning I'll give Thelma a call and ask her if it's a good time for me to visit."

Rory nodded. His eyes misty. "She can get kind of busy from time to time over there."

"Plumbing's a problem, too."

"Can be." Rory nodded again. "Thought I'd check it out now. See if everything's okay." He stood and paused for a moment. "Just for the record, I like you a lot, Callie, and nothing would make me happier than to see you and Shakespeare get together and live right here on the Landing. I got some property upriver that would suit a writer, an actor and some grandbabies just fine. Think you can make that happen for an old man?"

"Since there isn't any old man around here, and you're playing on my sympathies, I don't know." She kissed him on the cheek and sighed. "I'll give it my best shot, and I have no idea what that means."

Rory grinned and slapped his thigh. "Well, hot-damn. The old man trick gets 'em every time."

Callie laughed, "You're incorrigible."

"Hell yes, and proud of it."

Rory strolled out of the room whistling. Family was everything . . . unless they were jerks and didn't support you when you needed it most.

She hated that Keefe hadn't supported her, but she'd done the same thing to LuLu, so she was in no position to throw stones. Guilt sat like a rock in Callie's chest. Okay, she had to make things right with her sister. Going to film school was not what Callie wanted at all for LuLu, but the bottom line was that didn't matter. What did matter was she loved her sister more than anything.

Keefe watched the actors troop across the deserted dock, the *Lee* riding gently on Mississippi River swells, a mockingbird singing a night song in the distance. Demar walked down the dock toward him, stopping to talk to Roberta and Ty and the others.

He stepped onto the stern-wheeler and pulled two beers from a sack. Opened one and handed it to Keefe, then took the other for himself. They took a gulp, a puff of river breeze stirring the evening air. Keefe asked, "What happened to the baby-sitter and her contact? Last I heard from Sally you'd made the phone call and were waiting."

Demar grinned. "Got him, mustache, limp and all, just like the girls said. And he used to work in the Attorney General's Office in Nashville. He hasn't confessed to anything, but I bet he's the one who told the honchos at River Environs that Mimi had that second set of books, and that's why they tried to get her."

"But we still don't have the three presidents of the company. I bet they're long gone by now."

"Not necessarily. They have huge financial holdings here and can't touch them as long as they're suspects. They're going to try and get rid of Mimi and her evidence, and then they're free as birds." He nodded at the stage. "You really get into the directing thing. Everyone's talking about how good the play is. Ever think about doing it full time?"

"I already have a job that pays one hell of a lot better, and if I don't get back to it pretty soon, the writers will have me polished off in a gang war or something, and I'll be back to ground zero."

"Is that so bad?"

Keefe eyed Demar. "Okay, what are you getting at? Not like you to beat around the bush."

"You're good here, Keefe. I've seen you directing; it's your thing. Ryan's coming back, the same with Quaid, your dad's the best and he has Bonnie. Being with family and real friends is something money can't buy. What you have on the Landing is unique."

"And I'm thinking this unique has a lot to do with a feisty brown-eyed babe up the hill."

"Slim treats me like a son already. I'm staying. This town is the best gig out there, take it from someone who's been bouncing around his whole damn life. Guess you heard about Eleanor Stick and her performance that was recorded live at Slim's Restaurant."

Keefe ran his hand over his face. "I did."

Demar gave him a wide-eyed look. "So why in the hell are you here and not groveling at Callie Cahill's feet and getting it on with her?"

"Because I don't know what to do. After humiliating her in front of half the town last night an *I'm sorry, baby* and a bouquet of roses doesn't really cut it."

"You were trying to protect Bonnie and your dad—she gets that, everyone does—and if you sit here yakking at me and doing nothing, you lose her for sure."

"Okay, what do I tell her? Come with me to New York and watch me be a soap star? That's not going to win her over, and it sure as hell is no life for her."

"Guess the question is, is it the life for you?" Demar stood and gazed down at Keefe. "You got to figure out what you want and then how to get it. I bet you've been doing that all your life, and this is no different, except there's a woman involved. If nothing else, you owe her an apology. Think of it that way and see what happens. You need a plan."

"Hell, I need a damn script."

"Then get it."

Demar walked back down the dock, and Keefe never felt so damn alone. His life was so fucked up he didn't know how to fix it. A start was to talk to his dad and see if

Keefe O'Fallon was still in the will. He tried to smile at the joke but couldn't. What he wanted was to see if his father was talking to him, period.

Keefe trudged up the hill toward the house, Max coming to meet him, tail wagging, eyes shining bright. He still wore the red Wonder Dog bandanna Callie bought for him. Keefe remembered when she tied it around his neck and he pranced around the kitchen. They'd all applauded. Callie Cahill fit in his family better than he did. Callie got it. She understood just how important family was. That's why she wanted LuLu to be a lawyer, that's why she took such good care of Bonnie, that's why he loved her.

"Keefe?" his father said as he crossed the driveway. "Where have you been? You almost walked right into me. Must have some mighty big problem pressing on your brain."

"I think it's amazing that you even talk to me."

"Christ in a sidecar, boy, why wouldn't I talk to you?"

"Dad, I gave Bonnie to a complete stranger."

"You didn't do nothing of the sort. You did what you thought was best for your family. Just because it wasn't the right decision doesn't mean the intent was bad. Hell. None of us are perfect. You do your best at the time and you move on."

He stroked his chin. "Course, there is something you can do for me. I'm not getting any younger, you know, and it sure would do an old man's heart good to see you settled and happy." He hitched his chin toward the house. "Think you could give that a try for your old dad?"

Keefe felt a smile split his face, something that hadn't happened in a while. "Old dad, my ass. You got a baby. You got more energy than anyone I know, but the happy part sounds damn good. Just don't know quite how to make it happen."

"I'm guessing if you go talk to that little filly you brought with you two weeks ago, she might help you out. Sure worth a try."

"What the hell do I say?"

"Something nice, don't piss her off. Tell her she has nice shoes; women like that."

Keefe laughed. "Knowing Callie she's probably barefoot. Where are you headed?" He sobered. "Hastings House?"

His dad looked him in the eyes. "Thought I might mosey on up that way."

"Nice night for a walk, and I bet the plumbing's acting up again."

"Could be. Everyone knows how those old houses are."

"You and Thelma are best friends, family. You can trust family to come through for you no matter what."

His dad gave him a little nod. "That's the truth."

Keefe hugged his father. "I'm not leaving till we get Mimi back in this house with you, Dad. You can count on that. You can count on me."

His dad grinned as Keefe let him go. "I know I can, son."

Keefe watched Rory head on down the road, a spring in his step and whistling a tune about a towboat on the river.

Keefe took the front steps two at a time. He puffed out a breath of air. Stage fright, that's what this was. He was about to put on the performance of a lifetime. He started to knock, and Callie yanked open the door. "Where have you been?"

"Been? I . . . uh . . . had play practice, and then I talked to Dad and—"

"He's off to check on the plumbing at Hastings House." They both smiled, and she took his hand, making him suddenly light-headed. "Stanley quit her teaching job." Callie bit her bottom lip as if waiting for him to say something.

Okay, he had to get this right. "I'm sorry I didn't trust you about the article."

"You already said that."

"Well, it wasn't a very good apology."

"I'm not picky. What about Stanley?" Callie's eyes sparkled, and her hair shimmered in the light from the house. She was barefoot and wore denim shorts and a blue T-shirt, and he felt as if no one on earth loved him the way this woman did.

He drew her out onto the porch and closed the door behind her. He sat on the wicker settee and pulled her onto his lap. Then he kissed her. This was what he wanted, home, family, Callie. Most of all Callie.

"Maybe we should throw her a retirement party." His gaze met Callie's, and she grinned and wrapped her arms around his neck. "And why would we do that?"

"Because I could take her place."

Callie's eyes danced with happiness, and she kissed his lips, his eyes, his nose, every inch of his face. "Really?"

He kissed her back. "God, I love you. How can I screw things up so badly and wind up with Callie Cahill?"

"Because I love you, too. I want to be with you no matter what, and if you want to be a soap star or—"

"No way. My home is here, my heart is here, because you're here. I can teach drama in the winter, and in the summer I'll do the showboat. I'll go in partners with Digger, and we can get the *Lee* operational by next year and take her on the water."

"Is that what you want?"

"I want you no matter where that is. You being here and the way you look tonight is a dream come true."

Take a look at Lori Foster's
"Playing Doctor"
in the upcoming
WHEN GOOD THINGS
HAPPEN TO BAD BOYS.
Available now from Brava!

With an indulgent smile, Axel Dean watched the young lady exit the room of suffocating, overbearing people. Damn, she was sweet on the eyes. Tall, nearly as tall as him, with raven black hair and piercing blue eyes and an air of negligence that dared him, calling on his baser instincts, stripping away the façade of civility he tried to don in polite company.

Her straight hair skimmed her shoulders, darker than his own, blue-black without a single hint of red. It was so silky it looked fluid, moving when she moved, shimmering with highlights from the glow of candles. The white catering shirt and black slacks didn't do much for her figure, which he guessed to be slim and toned. She didn't have the lush curves he usually favored, but what she lacked in body she made up for in attitude.

And attitude, as he well knew, made a huge difference in bed.

As a waiter passed, Axel plunked his empty glass down onto the tray and headed for the sliding doors. He hated uptight formal affairs that being a doctor often obligated him to attend. That didn't mean he had to linger. That didn't mean he had to mingle.

Especially when more enlivening entertainment waited outside.

Making certain no one paid him any mind, he slipped through the doors and onto a wide balcony lit by twinkling lights that mirrored the stars in the evening sky. He waited, saying a silent prayer that no one followed him. Every time he attended a gathering, women hit on him. And that'd be fine and dandy by him, given that he adored women, but not within his professional circle.

He absolutely never, ever dated anyone in his field. Not even anyone related to someone in his field.

Despite the marital bliss of both his brother and his best friend, he had no intentions of settling down any time soon. That being the case, it wouldn't be wise to get involved with relatives, friends, or associates of the people he worked with. Walking away could cause a scene, and then the entire situation would get sticky and uncomfortable.

There were plenty of women who weren't interested in medicine, like secretaries, lawyers . . . or caterers.

He'd been prepared to be bored spitless tonight. Then he'd seen her hustling around the crowded room with robust energy. At first he'd assumed her to be a mere waitress for the catering company, but given how she performed each and every job, from putting out food to collecting empty dishes to directing the others, she might actually be the one in charge. Given her air of command and confidence, he figured her to be in her late twenties, maybe early thirties. Sexy. Mature. Flirtatious.

His heartbeat sped up, just imagining how the night might end.

When no one followed, Axel went down the curving wooden stairs to the garden paths behind Elwood's home. The pompous ass loved to flaunt his money, and why not? He had plenty to flaunt.

Spring had brought a profusion of blooming flowers to fill the air with heady scents. The chilly evening breeze didn't faze Axel as he searched the darkness for her. Then he saw a flare of light, realized it was a match, and made his way silently toward her.

She had her back to him, going on tiptoe to reach the top of an ornate torch anchored to the ground and surrounded by evergreens. Just as the wick caught, Axel said, "Hello."

She went perfectly still, poised on tiptoes, arms reaching up to the top of the torch. Slowly, in an oh-so-aware way, she relaxed and turned to face him.

Two lovers. And an unforgettable passion
that transcends time in
AGAIN
by Sharon Cullars.
Coming in May 2006 from Brava . . .

Inner resolve is a true possibility when temptation isn't within sight. Like the last piece of chocolate cheesecake with chocolate shavings; that last cigarette; that half-filled glass of Chianti . . . or the well-defined abs of a man who's had to take his shirt off because he spilled marinara sauce on it. Not deliberately. Accidents happen. At the sight of hard muscles, resolve flies right out of the window and throws a smirk over its wing.

Part of it was her fault. Tyne had offered him a shoulder rub, because during the meal he had seemed tense, and she'd suspected that his mind was still on the occurrences of the day. After dessert, he sat in one of the chairs in the living room while she stood over him. Even though he had put on a clean shirt, she could feel every tendon through the material, the image of his naked torso playing in her mind as her fingers kneaded the taut muscles.

As David started to relax, he leaned back to rest his head on her stomach. The lights were at half-dim. Neither of them was playing fair. Especially when a hand reached up to caress her cheek.

"Stop it," she whispered.

He seemed to realize he was breaking a promise, because the hand went down, and he said, "I'm sorry." But his head remained on her stomach, his eyes shut. From her vantage, she could see the shadow of hair on his chest. She remembered how soft it felt, feathery, like down. Instinctively, and against her conscious will, her hand moved to touch the bare flesh below his throat. She heard the intake of breath, felt the pulse at his throat speed up.

She told herself to stop, but there was the throbbing between her legs that was calling attention to itself. It made her realize she had lied. When she told him she wanted to take it slow, she had meant it. Then. But the declaration seemed a million moments ago, before her fingers touched him again, felt the heat of his flesh melding with her own.

He bent to kiss her wrist, and the touch of his lips was the catalyst she needed. The permission to betray herself again.

She pulled her hands away, and he looked up like a child whose treat had been cruelly snatched away. She smiled and circled him. Then slowly she lowered herself to her knees, reached over, unbelted and unbuttoned his pants. Slowly, pulled down the zipper.

"But I thought you wanted . . ." he started.

"That's what I thought I wanted." She released him from his constraints. "But right now, this is what I want." She took him into her mouth.

She heard an intake of breath, then a moan that seemed to reverberate through the rafters of the room. She felt the muscles of his thighs tighten beneath her hands, relax, tighten again. Her tongue circled the furrowed flesh, running rings around the natural grooves. She tasted him, realized that she liked him. Liked the tang of the moisture leaking from him. And the strangled animal groans her ministrations elicited.

There were pauses in her breathing, followed by strained exhalations. Then a sudden weight of a hand on the back

of her head, guiding her. She took his cue, began sucking
with a pressure that drew him further inside her mouth.
Yet there was more of him than she could hold.

He was moments from coming. She could feel the trem-
bling in his limbs. But suddenly he pushed her away, dis-
gorging his member from her mouth with the motion.

He shook his head. "No, not yet," he said breathlessly.
"Why don't you join me?" Before she could answer, he
stood up, pulling her up with him, and began unbuttoning
her blouse, almost tearing the seed pearls in the process.
The silk slid from her skin and fell to the ground in a lan-
guid pool of golden-brown. He hooked eager fingers
beneath her bra straps, wrenched them down. Within seconds, she was naked from the waist up, and the current in
the room, as well as the excitement of the moment teased
her nipples into hard pebbles. His fingers gently grazed
them, then he grazed each with his tongue. Her knees
buckled.

"How far do you want to go?" he breathed. "Because I
don't want you to do this just for me."

Her answer was to reach for the button of his shirt,
then stare into those green, almost hazel eyes. "I'm not
doing this for you. I'm being totally selfish. I want you . . .
your body . . ." She pushed the shirt over his shoulders,
yanked it down his arms.

"Hey, what about my mind?" he grinned.

She smiled. "Some other time."

They undressed each other quickly, and as they stood
naked, his eyes roamed the landscape of her body with un-
deniable appreciation. Then without ceremony, he pulled
her to the floor on top of him so abruptly that she let out
an "oomph." His hands gripped the plump cheeks of her
ass, began kneading the soft flesh. She felt his hardened
penis against her stomach and began moving against it,
causing him to inhale sharply. His hands soon stopped

their kneading and replaced the touch with soft, whispery caresses that caused her crotch to contract with spasms. One of his fingers played along her crevice as his lips grabbed hers and began licking them. His finger moved to the delicate wall dividing both entryways, moved past the moist canal, up to her clitoris, started teasing her orb just as his tongue began playing along hers. She grounded her pelvis against him, desperately claiming her own pleasure, listening to the symphony of quickly pumping blood, and intertwined breaths playing in her ears.

He guided her onto his shaft. Holding her hips, he moved her up, down, in an achingly slow and steady pace that was thrilling and killing, for right now she thought she could die with the pleasure of it, the way he filled her, sated her. She felt her eyes go back into her head (she had heard about the phenomenon from other bragging women, and had thought they were doing just that—bragging. But now she knew how it could happen.)

"Ooooh, fuck," she moaned.

"My thoughts exactly," he whispered back and with a deft motion, changed their positions until he was on top of her. Straddled on his elbows, he quickened his thrusting, causing a friction that drove her to a climax she couldn't stop. Her inner walls throbbed against the invading hardness, and she drew in shallow breaths as her lungs seemed to shatter with the rest of her body.

She put her arms around his waist and wrapped her legs around his firm thighs. His body had the first sheen of perspiration. She stroked along the dampness of his skin, then reciprocated the ass attention with gentle strokes along his cheeks.

"I want . . . I want . . . " he exerted but couldn't seem to finish the sentence. Instead, he placed his mouth over hers until she was able to pull his ragged breaths into her needy lungs. The wave that washed over her once had hardly

ebbed away before it began building again. Now his pace
was frantic, his hips pounding her body into the carpeting,
almost through the floor. Not one for passivity, she pounded
back just as hard and eagerly met each thrust. The wave
was gathering force, this one threatening a cyclonic power
that would rip her apart, render her in pieces. She didn't
care. His desperation was borne of sex, but also she knew,
of anger and frustration. He was expelling his demons inside her, and she was his willing exorcist . . .

*Blood was everywhere. On the walls, which were al-
ready stained with vile human secretions; on the wooden
floor, where the viscous fluid slowly seeped into the fibers
of the wood and pooled between the crevices of the
boards. Soon, the hue would be an indelible telltale witness
of what had happened, long after every other evidence had
been disposed of. Long after her voice stopped haunting
his dreams. Long after he was laid cold in his grave.*

*He bent to run a finger through one of the corkscrew
curls. Its end was soaked with blood. The knife felt warm
in his hands still. Actually, it was the warmth of her life
staining it.*

*He turned her over and peered into dulled brown eyes
that accused him in their lifelessness. Gone was the sparkle—
sometimes mischievous, sometimes amorous, sometimes
fearful—that used to meet him. Now, the deadness of her
eyes convicted him where he stood, even if a jury would
never do so. The guilt of this night, this black, merciless
night, would hound his waking hours, haunt his dreams,
submerge his peace, indict his soul. There would now always be blood on his hands. For that reason alone, he
would never allow himself another moment of happiness.
Not that he would ever find it again. What joy he would
have had, might have had, lay now at his feet in her perfect form. Strangely, in death, she had managed to escape*

its pall. Her skin was still luminescent, still smooth. If it weren't for the vacuous eyes, the blood soaking her throat, the collar of her green dress, the dark auburn of her hair . . . he might hold to the illusion that somewhere inside, she still lived.

He reached a shaky hand to touch her cheek. It was warm, soft, defying death even as it stiffened her body.

He bent further, let his lips graze hers one last time. Their warmth was a mockery. Her lips were never this still beneath his. They always answered his touch, willingly or not.

He saw a tear fall on her face, and for a second was confused. It rolled down her cheek and mixed with the puddle of blood. He realized then that he was crying. It scared him. He hadn't cried since he was a child. But now, another tear fell, and another.

Through his grief, he knew what he would have to do. She was gone. There was no way to bring her back. Her brother would be searching for her soon. She wasn't an ordinary Negress. She was the daughter of a prominent Negro publisher, now deceased, and the widow of a prominent Negro lawyer. She had a place in their society. So, yes, she would be missed. There would be a hue and cry for vengeance if it were ever discovered that she had been murdered.

Which was why he could not let her be found.

He knew what he had to do. It wasn't her anymore. It was just a body now. Yet, he couldn't resist calling her name one last time.

"Rachel."

Then he began to cry in earnest.

Tyne pushed through the sleep-cloud that fogged her mind. The dream-world still tugged at her, reached out cold fingers to pull her back. But her feet ran as fast as they could, ran toward the name hailing her, pleading with her to hurry. The name reverberated around . . . *Rachel* . . . *Rachel* . . . *Rachel* . . .

"Rachel . . . Rachel . . . "

The sound woke her. She slowly opened her eyes, lay there for a moment, not remembering. Gradually, disorientation gave way to familiarity. Shaking off sleep, she became aware of her surroundings. Recognized the curtains that hung at the moon-bathed window, saw the wingback chair that was a silhouette in front of it. Sometime during the night or early morning, he had retrieved her clothes and laid them neatly on the chair's back.

He was shifting in his sleep, murmuring. Then she heard the name again, just as she had heard it in her dream. "Rachel." He strangled on the syllables, his voice choked with emotion—with . . . grief, she realized. She sat up, turned. His back was to her, shuddering. He was crying . . . in his sleep. Was calling to a woman—a woman named Rachel. Someone he'd never mentioned before. And obviously a woman who meant a lot to him, and whose loss he freely felt in his unconscious state. So he'd lied about never having been in love. But why?

A pang of jealousy moved through her, pushed away affection, gratification. She didn't want to be solace for some lost love he was still pining for. Didn't want to be a second-hand replacement to someone else's warmth in his bed. She looked over at the clock. It was almost four anyway. She might as well get home to get ready for work.

She shifted off the mattress delicately, grabbed her clothes from the chair and started for the door. She would dress downstairs to make sure she didn't wake him. She turned at the door to look at him. The shuddering had stopped. There was only the peaceful up and down motion of deep breathing. She opened the door, shut it lightly and made her escape.

Here's a scintillating look at
Alison Kent's
DEEP BREATH.
Available now from Brava!

While Georgia had holed away in the suite's monstrous bathroom to shower, shave, shampoo, and pull on a clean pair of undies, her T-shirt and jeans, Harry had been busy. Busy doing more than getting dressed and ratcheting up the who-is-this-man-and-where-did-he-come-from stakes.

He wore serious grown-up clothes as beautifully as he wore casual, and as well as Michelangelo's David wore his marble skin.

She'd walked out of the steamy bathroom and only just stopped herself from demanding what the hell he was doing breaking into her room before she realized her mistake. He was that amazing. And her heart was still dealing with the unexpected lust.

The man was the most beautiful thing she'd seen in forever. Her first impression made from Finn's truck when looking down from her window had been right on the mark. But he was so much more than a girl's guide to getting off.

His smile—those lips and dimples, the dark shadow of his beard—was enough to melt even the most titanic ice queen. Not that she was one, or anything . . .

Sitting as she was now in the hotel's salon, having her hair and makeup done, she kept sneaking looks over to where he sat waiting and reading a back issue of *Cosmo*. Every once in awhile he'd frown, shake his head, turn the page. If she hadn't been ordered not to move by her stylist, she might never have stopped laughing.

When Harry told her he'd arranged not only this appointment but another with the hotel's boutique's personal shopper for jewelry, shoes and a dress, she'd asked him if he thought she was made of money.

He'd pulled out his wallet, handed her a five to pay back the tip, then reminded her she was the one donating to General Duggin's Scholarship Foundation tonight.

Making sure she arrived looking the part of a wealthy collector rather than pack rat was the least he could contribute to the cause—a cause he'd then started to dig into, asking her questions about her family and the importance of the documents Charlie had sent her to find.

Since she'd been stuck on the pack rat comment, frowning as she ransacked her duffel for the sandals she knew that were there, thinking how she really *had* let herself go since being consumed by this quest, she'd almost answered, had barely caught herself in time.

The story of her father's wrongful incarceration and her determination to prove his innocence had been on the tip of her tongue before she had bit down. If Harry knew the truth of why she wanted the dossier, he would quickly figure out she had no intention of delivering it to Charlie Castro.

Then, no doubt, they'd get into an argument about the value of her brother's life versus that of her father's name, and he'd want to know why the hell were they going through all of this if not to save her brother.

She really didn't want to go there with Harry. She was having too much trouble going there with herself. Finn would understand; she knew he would. As long as he was alive to do so when this was over . . .

At that thought, she groaned, the sound eliciting the stylist's concern. "What's wrong, sweetie? Too much color? Not enough? The highlights are temporary, remember? Three washings max, you'll be back to being a brunette."

"Oh, no. I was thinking of something else," Georgia assured the other woman, meeting her reflected gaze. "I hadn't even looked . . ."

But now she did. And she swore the reflection in the mirror couldn't possibly be hers. "Wow," was the only thing she could think to say, and so she said it again. "Wow."

"Yeah. I thought so, too." The stylist beamed at her handiwork—and rightly so. Georgia had never in her life looked like this. The highlights in her hair gave off a coppery sheen. Her layers, too long and grown out—she had been desperate for a new cut, had been trimmed, colored, and swept up into an intricate rooster tail of untamed strands.

And then her face . . . was that really her face? The salon's makeup expert had used a similar color scheme, spreading sheer terra-cotta on her cheeks, a blend of copper and bronze on her eyelids, finishing off with a gorgeous cinnamon-colored glaze on her lips.

And all of it matching the beautiful ginger-hued polish on the nails of all twenty fingers and toes. She could go for this girly girl stuff. Really.

Especially when she lifted her gaze to meet Harry's in the mirror. He stood behind the stylist, his shoulders wide in his designer suit coat, his hands jammed to his lean waist, his smile showing just a hint of teeth.

She had no idea when he'd moved from where he'd been sitting to her chair, but the look in his eyes, the fire in his eyes, and the low sweep of his lashes was enough to make her swoon.

It had been so long since a man had shown *that* kind of interest in her that she didn't know what to do, how to react, to respond. Except the truth was that it wasn't the men. It was her.

She had refused to let any man close enough to do more than notice her skill for ferreting out valuable antiques for years now, longer than she could remember.

But now, here came Harry into the middle of her personal catastrophe, a veritable stranger who had the body of a god and a killer smile and eyes that were telling her dangerously sexy things about wanting to get her naked. He was helping her in ways that went above and beyond.

And she still had the night to spend in his room. "Can we charge the makeup to the room? I'll pay you back."

"Sure." His eyes sparkled. His smile grew wicked. "And it's my treat."

The stylist swept the cape from around Georgia's shoulders and Harry offered his hand to help her from the chair. It was a Cinderella moment that she had no business enjoying, but she couldn't help it.

She hadn't done a single thing for herself in so long that it was impossible to brush aside this feeling of discovering someone she'd thought lost.

She was well aware of why she and Harry were together, the full extent of what was at stake. But it had been years, literally *years,* since she'd considered herself attractive—not to mention since she'd felt confident that someone of the opposite sex found her so.

Harry did. She didn't doubt it for a minute. Even if it did up the nerve-wracking factor of the long evening ahead in his company.

While Harry tipped the stylist and settled the bill, she took the bag of cosmetics from the cashier, absently noticing how the attention of every woman in the salon, whether overtly or subtly, was directed toward the checkout station and the fit of Harry's clothes.

She wanted to laugh; here she was, panicking over sleeping near him when he could crook a finger and have any woman here in his bed.

And then she didn't want to laugh at all.

She wanted to grab him by the arm and drag him out of there, leaving a battlefield of bloody cat scratches in her wake. Like he belonged to her or something, and how ridiculous was that? He was nothing but a man who happened to be in the wrong place at the wrong time, who was going out of his way to get her out of a jam.

Finn would have done the same for a woman in need. Her ex, hardly. They'd been married, and he wouldn't have done it for her. Unless there was something in it for him . . . hmm. Too bad she hadn't snapped to that before.

Harry scrawled his signature across the bottom of the ticket then handed the pen to the cashier. Georgia cocked her head and considered what he could possibly hope to gain from helping her out. He was going to a lot of expense . . . and sex was the first thing, the only thing, that came to mind.